GRANNY SNOWS A SNEAK

(A Fuchsia, Minnesota Mystery)

by

Julie Seedorf

For information, email **Cozy Cat Press**, cozycatpress@aol.com or visit our website at: www.cozycatpress.com

COZY CAT PRESS

ISBN: 978-1-939816-55-9

Printed in the United States of America

Cover design by Keri Knutson
http://www.alchemybookcovers.com

Edited by D.A. Sarac

1 2 3 4 5 6 7 8 9 10

Author's Note: Granny has become dear to my heart. In the beginning with the first book in the series, *Granny Hooks A Crook,* it may seem as if Granny is an old, memory flawed, fluffy old lady ready to be put out to pasture. Her character develops over time and in the books that follow. There are layers to Granny that no one would suspect and in the Fuchsia Minnesota series, we are peeling back the layers to see why Granny is who she is today.

We all have layers in our lives that are hidden. We may hide them because we are afraid. We may hide them because we want them to be forgotten. We may hide them because we have to get through the life we are living each day without revealing what is underneath the why's of what we do, what we do in the way we live our life. In many ways we are no different than Hermiony Vidalia Criony Fiddlestadt. The challenge for all of us is to let our little light shine, rejoicing in our true character and being who God intended us to be.

ACKNOWLEDGEMENTS

I thank Patricia Rockwell and Cozy Cat Press for believing in me. Annie Sarac, thank you for your honesty and your editing skills.

Thank you also to Boneyard Coffee and Tea in Champaign, Illinois, for allowing the use of their business name in my book. I also say thank you to my readers, Sally and Tami, for creating the winning name for the new Ella's Enchanted Forest in the book— Sally for the Pink Percolator, and Tami for the Coffee and Confections part of the name. Finally, I would like to give a big shout out to the rest of my readers who entered the contest.

DEDICATION

I dedicate this book to my Grandmother, Edith Young. Her likeness to my cover Granny is uncanny. Though she left this earth when I was six years old, I recently feel her presence in my writing with the strange coincidence of her clone on my cover. I remember her gentleness and her love. Thank you for the inspiration, Grandma.

CHAPTER ONE

Franklin put his right hand out and took Granny's left hand in his. He gazed into Granny's eyes as he moved closer. Granny leaned her head toward Franklin—waiting. Franklin leaned forward and ever so gently pulled Granny into his arms, just enough, so he could reach her lips. At that moment, Granny felt a rough tongue on her face.

She swatted the tongue away, trying to meld back into her dream of the kiss, after the moment when Franklin and she had said, "I do." The tongue was back. Granny opened one eye, slowly coming out of her dream, turned her head slightly, and looked straight into the face of Mrs. Bleaty, her pet goat.

After pushing Mrs. Bleaty away with a small tap on the nose, Granny wiped her face and tried to turn over on the bed, but her body wouldn't move. She felt a heavy load pressing the bottom part of her body, as if her legs were weighted down.

Granny again tried to move. Had she had a stroke during the night? Should she call 911? Granny opened both eyes and looked down to the end of her body. No, it was not a stroke; it was the shysters! Her pets Baskerville, Fish, Little White Poodle, Furball and Tank were plastered to her body and sleeping soundly.

Granny wondered why they were still here. Usually, the shysters and Baskerville hightailed it out of the house in the evening to make their nightly rounds of the town, ending up at Franklin Gatsby's house to get some sleep before they retraced their steps and made it back to Granny's, later in the afternoon.

Granny sat up on her elbows contemplating how to wake up the menagerie of snorers. "Wake up!" Baskerville opened one eye and looked at Granny in somewhat the same way that Granny opened her eyes in the morning. He then closed the one eye and went back to his snoring. Granny looked at Mrs. Bleaty, who was still trying to lick Granny's face. "Enough! My wrinkles are staying no matter how much you try and lick them off."

At that moment, the doorbell rang. Baskerville and the shysters jumped when they heard the ring. Granny had recently gotten a new doorbell that played music, and the doorbell was chiming the words to the song, *Go Granny, Go Granny, Go Granny, Go*. Granny pulled on a sedate robe and her flip-flops.

As Granny shuffled down the hallway, she concluded it was a strange morning, and it wasn't even 8:00 a.m. She had better call Franklin and let him know that the shysters hadn't left her house last night. That was a mystery she would have to figure out.

"All right, already," Granny shouted as the doorbell kept chiming. Her early morning visitor was very impatient.

She glanced at the shysters and Mrs. Bleaty all lined up by the door instead of heading outside to check out the visitor through Baskerville's pet door. *What is up with that?* Granny wondered.

She moved to the door and felt the cold hitting her feet, left exposed by her flip-flops. She hadn't even had time to check her toes to see if they were red or blue. She surmised they would be blue anyway since it was winter.

"All right, all right," Granny said again as she unlocked the door and opened it. The wind grabbed the door as she pulled it open and a big gust blew into the house, catching her tiny frame and knocking her backward. The only thing that kept her from falling over from the force of the door and the wind was Baskerville and Mrs. Bleaty, who anticipated what was going to happen and braced themselves against her.

A bundled up older gentleman, holding a snow shovel as a cane, hustled into the room. "'Bout time you opened that door, Granny." The man's speech was crackled and crotchety.

"What do you want, Silas?" Granny barked at the man.

"I have to go downtown. No one can drive in this blizzard."

Granny turned and lifted the shade on her living room window. The snowflakes were flying by and she couldn't see Mavis's house across the street. That must be why the shysters were still at home. Fuchsia was having a raging blizzard. That explained the color of her toes too.

"So why are you here?" Granny asked testily.

"I told you; I need to go downtown," the crotchety older man barked as he moved towards Granny's stairs to the basement.

Granny quickly put herself between the man and the basement stairs. "Explain yourself! Where are you going? Baskerville, Fish, Little White Poodle, Furball, Tank, attack!" Granny instructed as she pointed to the older man.

The older man reached into the pockets of his winter coat and brought out some bacon and sardines, and tossed them into the bowls on the floor. He crossed his arms and gave Granny a challenging look as the animals ignored Granny's command and slurped up the treats in the bowls.

Granny stomped her feet, planting them solidly on the floor. "Again I ask, what are you doing here?"

"Move it, Granny," the man said gruffly as he moved toward the steps. "I need to go downtown and my house doesn't have access to the underground streets of Fuchsia. Yours does. See you later." Silas Crickett moved forward, grabbed Granny in a bear hug, gave her a quick kiss on the cheek as he lifted her tiny petite frame out of the way and proceeded down the steps with Granny following behind, and out the fireplace door into the room that led to the underground streets of Fuchsia.

Granny slammed the fireplace door shut behind her neighbor Silas, and with a little wicked grin on her face, she walked into the room behind the fireplace that led to the streets. With a chuckle, she turned the lock. Walking back into her family room, she shut the fireplace door, reached into the inside regions of the fireplace and again turned the hidden lock on the fireplace door. *That should fix him from coming back this way*, Granny thought.

Granny got back upstairs just in time to hear her cell phone ringing the Dragnet theme, signaling that Franklin was calling. The menagerie of animals scattered as Granny flip-flopped back to her bedroom. "What?" she barked into her cellphone.

"Have you seen the shysters? When I woke up they weren't here." Franklin asked in a worried tone.

"Have you looked out your window? No one in their right mind would go out this morning, even our animals."

"Sounding a little smug this morning aren't you, Hermiony?"

"With you, Franklin, always," Granny chirped back.

Franklin and Granny were engaged, and were to be married the day after Christmas. Franklin had moved to

Fuchsia to get away from the big city. After being a New York City detective, retiring in a small town had seemed the perfect fit for him. Unfortunately, he hadn't counted on the fact that small towns have their share of crime too. He hadn't counted on meeting Granny, who seemed to always land herself in the middle of the trouble. He hadn't counted on her unusual spark, driving him to fall crazy in love with her.

"I need a new weapon, Franklin."

"Ah, Granny, I thought we agreed that now that your son, Thor, is the new lead detective and chief of police for the Fuchsia Police Department, he retired you from your undercover work with the merchants. Of course, maybe you don't remember."

"I do remember. But I need a weapon against my new neighbor who moved into Sally's house. He attacked me this morning." Granny sputtered.

Franklin, familiar with Granny's sometimes over exaggerated truths, sighed. "Ok, what happened?"

"I'll explain it to you as soon as you come and take me downtown," Granny cajoled.

"No, we are not going downtown in this blizzard. Are you forgetting your car is stored at my house since we haven't rebuilt your garage after the fire?"

Franklin was referring to the garage next to Granny's house that had been destroyed by an arson fire earlier in the year, along with her treasured cars. Franklin had given Granny a new, restored, '57 Chevy Red Corvette convertible to replace her old one on the day he had proposed to her.

Granny lifted the phone to her face and gave it a dirty look. She pressed the EyeTime button and Franklin's face appeared on her screen. Granny looked straight into Franklin's eyes through EyeTime and said, "And who are you?" With a cackle, Granny pressed disconnect and looked down at Mrs. Bleaty who had come into the bedroom and was now trying to eat Granny's cellphone.

"It's time for all of you to brave the storm," Granny said to Mrs. Bleaty as she grabbed her collar.

Granny pulled Mrs. Bleaty down the hall by the collar while instructing Little White Poodle, Tank, and Baskerville that it was time to go out. Fish and Furball could stay put since they had indoor litter boxes that they used when the weather was bad.

Once again, when Granny opened the door, the wind blew her backward, and the snow hit her in the face. She quickly shut the door and leaned her 100-pound body against it to get it shut. "Ok, I get it. I guess when ya gotta go, you'll go; but remember it has to be outside."

Granny, whose real name was Hermiony Vidalia Criony Fiddlestadt, sat down on the cold floor next to her warm furry creatures. She hugged Baskerville, a big hound dog, whom she had acquired after she had put his owner in the hoosegow. As she was hugging Baskerville, the rest of her furry friends attacked her with love, licking her face and purring loudly. Fish, a part Siamese cat, was a pet store dropout, and Little White Poodle, whose owner also got put in the hoosegow, were hers. Tank, a dog built like his name, and Furball, a cat that resembled her name because she was puffy and looked like a large ball, belonged to Franklin, but had adopted Granny. "All right, all right, I can't help it if you are all wimps." Granny laughed as she moved them off of her and stood up. What was she going to do today since there was a blizzard outside?

Granny took another peek outside through her living room curtains and proceeded back to her bedroom. Once there, she opened her closet door and pulled out some jeans and a bright red sweatshirt. Since she was no longer undercover, she could ditch her undercover

Granny clothes, such as the hose she wore on her legs and her polyester skirts. The jig was up, so it was time for a new wardrobe. The sweatshirt and jeans weren't exactly what she had in mind but she hadn't found the right look for her new social status. She was an engaged woman, after all, so she had to look spiffy now.

Granny pulled on her newest purple sparkly snow boots, grabbed her winter coat and purple earmuffs before bidding farewell to the shysters, and made sure their pet doors were not frozen shut before she left. At least the doors were not blocked by the blowing snow. It seemed to accumulate farther down the porch away from the door.

Making sure she had the key to her door to the underground streets so she could get back in, she made her way to the basement, out the fireplace door, and through the room and through the underground streets, locking the door behind her.

CHAPTER TWO

Granny dropped the key in her pocket since she had left her pocketbook home this time. Today she had no umbrella, nor her large knitting needle disguised as a cane. Her last solved crime had also ended her sneaky, undercover, decrepit Granny routine. Although she was old, no one actually knew her age—she wasn't as slow and disabled as she had led people to believe. Granny sighed a big sigh. Now that she was no longer working undercover for the Fuchsia merchants, she wondered what she was going to do with her life. It was certainly going to be boring if her kids or Franklin had anything to say about it.

As Granny walked the underground downtown, she noticed the changes that were taking place since the City Council had decided to open the previously unknown streets and make it easier to shop in Fuchsia in the winter. Properties of Fuchsia homes were inspected by the Fuchsia Property Inspector. Granny liked to call him *Specky* because he was always inspecting something. Specky had examined the basements of the property owners along the underground streets, and had found places in the walls that had never been opened up to give the homeowner access to the underground area. It was then left to the homeowners themselves to decide if they wanted to open their doors to the new avenues of underground Fuchsia. Amazingly, they all did, and as Granny walked by the doors, there were Christmas wreaths and bright rugs accenting all of the underground entrances to the homes—the same as you would see on a normal street above ground.

Granny still felt strange walking down a street without a prop—like her umbrella or knitting needle. Luckily, her children no longer wanted to put her in the wrinkle farm, even though she was still a little forgetful from time to time. They must have realized that her forgetfulness occurred because she was always on the move, her mind always focused on catching the next crook—although now that job seemed to be over, and the forgetfulness was just part of her undercover persona. Thor was probably right. It was time for her to behave herself, especially now that Thor was marrying Heather, and Heather's daughter Angel was going to be her granddaughter. Granny knew she had set a good example for her other grandchildren when they were growing up. Her daughter Penelope had never complained—until recently—about Granny's behavior. Granny had always done the right thing with her grandchildren, even if she hadn't let the real Hermiony Vidalia Criony Fiddlestadt *out* until she was sure her kids were grown up in the way they should go, and her grandchildren too. But now, she had Angel to think of.

Granny walked slowly, thinking about the changes in her life the last few months and the changes in the Fuchsia underground. As she neared the lift that Graves' Funeral Home used to transport caskets underground to the Fuchsia Cemetery, she stopped. Maybe her friend Delight and some Boneyard Coffee would cheer her up. Delight was now working in her new coffee and teapot-shaped building that she had renamed The Pink Percolator. Unfortunately, it didn't have access to the underground streets. The city of Fuchsia was working on expanding the underground streets, but it being winter and all, and with the ground being frozen, the project would have to wait until next summer. How was she going to get to the former Ella's Enchanted Forest—now the Pink Percolator—without having to walk knee-, and sometimes, waist-deep in this Minnesota blizzard?

Granny shrugged her shoulders and moved toward the lift into Graves's mortuary. Previously, the now Graves' Mortuary building had been Ella's Enchanted Forest, but the City of Fuchsia thought it would be better to relocate the mortuary so it would be more comfortable for mourners to travel, and easier for the funeral home to transport caskets in the comfort of the underground streets from the mausoleum and out to the cemetery.

Since taking over the building, Graves' Mortuary had put a code on the lift, so that every Tom, Dick and Harry couldn't get into the funeral home. Granny supposed she could go to one of the other underground entrances to the downtown Fuchsia stores, but Graves' was closer to Delight's new coffee house. Because she was the one who had found the underground streets and had hooked the crooks working here with one hook of her umbrella, she was given the code for Graves' lift. Of course, getting the lift code might also have had something to do with the fact that she had caught Mr. Graves doing a little snookering with Ivy from over at the Ringlet and Curl Hair Salon when Mr. Graves was supposed to be having his mustache dyed. Granny had a "code no-tell-promise" with him. He gave her the code, and she promised not to tell.

Granny jumped on the lift and punched in the code so the lift would unlock and rise into the mortuary.

At the sound of the lift being activated, Mr. Graves, who was upstairs, turned from arranging the flowers in the former forest room that had been Ella's, to welcoming Granny. He knew it had to be her because no one else had the code.

"Granny, what you are doing out in the middle of a blizzard?" he asked, as he took her hand to help her off the lift.

"That new neighbor of mine, pesky Silas Crickett—don't know why his mother didn't name him Jiminy—rudely woke me up and thought he should use my access to the underground streets. I was up so I decided I should go see Delight at her new shop."

"Uh, Granny, you still have to plow through lots of snow to get there since it's a block from here. The streets haven't been plowed yet and the wind will blow you over. You should go back home."

"Listen, Gravy,"—Granny used the old nickname that Giles Graves had in grade school—"I am bored out of my mind since my son retired me from working for the merchants of Fuchsia. Of course, I must admit I can't be undercover anymore since the last two crimes that I solved made the national news. Granny batted her eyes and gave him the best "feel sorry for me" look that she could muster.

Giles Graves lifted his shoulders and let out a sigh. "Ok, Granny, you always could get me into trouble in grade school with that look. See that machine out front? I could give you a ride on my snowmobile to the Pink Percolator."

Granny let out a laugh. "I knew it. Let's go."

"You need a hat even if we are going just a block. I'll be right back."

Mr. Graves hustled into the back room and came out with a red bomber cap. He plopped it on Granny's head. The flap sides trimmed with fake fur fit down around her ears. The hat had a fake fur flap that was red wool plaid and covered her eyes. The inside of the hat was lined with satin, giving it a little bit of a girly feel. Granny's eyes beamed brightly from under the flap. It was hard to tell it was Granny under the hat, but her purple fur sparkly winter boots gave the secret away to anyone who might wonder who was under the bomber cap.

Granny tapped her head and headed for the door. "Let's go."

Giles Graves grabbed his heavy jacket, stomped into his boots, plopped on his bomber cap, and headed out the door behind Granny.

The streets were deserted. A few abandoned cars sat stuck in the snow on the sides of the streets. Plows didn't come out in Fuchsia until storms were over. Folks didn't get too excited about staying home from their jobs. Fuchsia businesses and factories just automatically called any blizzard a snow holiday so families could spend the day together. If someone wanted to come to work, it was fine. If they wanted to stay home, they weren't penalized. The downtown businesses usually stayed open if the owners could get to their shops. Many owners lived above their businesses or were now connected through the underground streets. Some people, like Granny, became bored and wandered to Main Street through the underground streets. This was a new option and the city was waiting to see how Fuchsia residents would accept the underground streets this winter.

Granny and Giles climbed on the snowmobile. Giles revved the engine and they took off with Granny holding on for dear life. The trip only took a few minutes and, in a flash, they were in front of the Pink Percolator.

Granny got off the snowmobile and asked, "Where did you get this doohickey machine? Think I could drive this? I've never been on one of these before. Do they make them in red?"

Giles Graves gave Granny a look of disbelief, revved the engine, and left without answering her.

Granny opened the door to the Pink Percolator and fell into a wall from the force of the wind pushing her inside.

"Granny, what are you doing here?" Delight asked as she helped Granny away from the wall. "Are you all right?"

Granny stood up, straightened her coat, and pulled off her bomber cap. "How could you tell it was me?"

"Possibly, it was your pink winter coat and your purple sparkly boots that gave you away? Answer my question, why are you out in this weather?"

"I have been put out to pasture and it's a strange pasture at that. What am I supposed to do, take up knitting for real? I suppose I could...could knit a giant wedding quilt for Thor and Heather with my knitting needle cane. I have been told there will be no more skewering of crooks for me," Granny said with a miffed tone as she moved further into Delight's new coffee house. She took a seat by a donut-shaped table that was painted dark brown and covered with what looked like colorful sprinkles.

"Granny, I will get you a cup of your favorite Boneyard Coffee and the pastry I designed for you— Granny's Chocolate Skewer Puff. Maybe that will make you feel better." Delight headed toward the kitchen. Granny heard the patio door open and close. Who would be out on the patio in this storm?

"Delightful day, Delight."

Granny turned to see the face that fit the voice. The voice wasn't anything like what she had heard earlier that morning; it was too nice and sweet.

"Why, Silas, you make even the worst of days sound wonderful," Delight answered back from the kitchen. "Why don't you have a seat next to Granny since you are the only two here and I'll bring you a cup of specialty coffee to warm you up, and a Granny's Chocolate Skewer Puff."

Granny peered at Silas and wished she had her umbrella to hook the chair right out from under him when he sat down.

"See ya decided to follow my lead. Didn't lock the door after me did ya?" asked Silas.

"I did, and you're not getting back in. Find your own way home in this blizzard. In fact, I should report you for unauthorized use of property."

"You do that and I'll report your beasts for trying to eat Radish."

"Radish? My animals hate radishes! Why would they eat them?" Granny asked, confused by the turn of the conversation.

"Exactly; they hate Radish and I will report you for them trying to eat him." Silas leaned forward and pounded the table looking Granny straight in the eyes.

Delight came into the room and, unaware of the tension between the two customers, set the coffee and Skewer Puffs on the table in front of them, breaking up the conversation. .

Silas looked up at Delight and grabbed her empty hand. "My lady, how wonderful of you to prepare this wonderful spot of refreshment in the midst of the glorious storm."

Granny took a sip of her coffee and choked, coughing loudly, when she heard the words that came out of Silas's mouth.

"Oh my, Granny, are you ok?" Delight asked in alarm.

"Fine, fine," Granny answered, glaring at Silas.

"Granny, did you know Silas loves the winter. The cold doesn't bother him. He insisted on sitting out on the donut patio to breath in the beauty of the winter. Can you believe he was able to walk downtown this morning in this blizzard? It goes to show you how all of us, no matter what age we are, can do anything if we keep ourselves in shape," Delight gushed in adoration.

"The Christmas decorations on the patio are outstanding, Delight." Silas winked as he complimented her. "The large Reindeer drinking coffee is so you."

Granny gave Delight a look of amazement right before she stood up, coffee cup in hand, pretending to trip as she stood with the cooled-off coffee, and dumped it straight in Silas's lap.

Silas jumped up but not before he was covered with coffee. Delight tried to wipe away the coffee but Silas stopped her with a glimmer of something in his eyes. "It's fine, my dear Delight. I am sure Granny, feeble as she is,"—Granny skewered him with her look—"is overwhelmed with remorse. I will go and tidy up in the Johnny Gent room."

Granny waited until he was gone to ask Delight a question, "Where can I buy a snowmobile?"

CHAPTER THREE

Delight watched through the front window of the Pink Percolator as Fred Runner, owner of Runner's Skids and Skis, showed Granny the details on how to drive her new Kidoo XYZ Snowmobile. Shaking her head in disbelief, Delight watched Granny intently listening to Fred, all the while withstanding the wind and the snow that was pummeling them. She didn't hear Silas come up behind her so she was startled when she heard his voice.

"What in tarnation is that old woman up to now?"

"I think she just bought herself a snowmobile to get home," said Delight.

Silas threw his scarf around his neck, pulled on his stocking cap, turned and took Delight's hand and brought it to his lips. "A pleasure as always," he said to Delight as he kissed her hand. Before Delight had the chance to respond—she being paralyzed by shock at someone kissing her hand—Silas turned and walked out the door to the snowmobile.

Granny was sitting on the machine ready to take off when Silas plunked down on the seat behind her, grabbing her by the waist so he wouldn't fall off. "Not quite your color is it, Granny?" he asked as he settled down on the yellow and red machine.

"Get off, Silas; I'm going home."

"I assume you locked your door to the underground street so I can't back into your house. I'm not walking all the way home in this blizzard. Do you know how to drive this thing?"

"Nope!" Granny yelled through the blustering wind as she revved the machine and took off.

"I didn't think so," Silas replied as he held on for dear life.

The yellow and red Kidoo XYZ plowed through the drifts on the main street of Fuchsia. Silas almost fell off when Granny took a quick right turn, almost running into a street lamp on the side of the road.

"It's the long way through the cemetery. I can't go by the police station. Thor might be checking out the streets. This snowmobile thing is on a need-to-know basis and he doesn't need to know," Granny yelled through the wind.

"You can't get to your backyard from the cemetery; there's a fence!" yelled Silas.

"There is," Granny answered as she dodged a tree on the side of the boulevard. "Hang on, Silas. I can't see a thing, and if I lose you—well, I lose you. I don't know how to stop this thing so you'd be on your own."

"What do you mean you don't know how to stop this thing?" Silas barked back.

"Fred showed me but I forgot. Now don't bother me; we're almost to the cemetery and once we get to the back by the mausoleum and the fence you have to be quiet."

"Why?" Silas yelled as some snow hit him in the face, making him sputter.

"Because we have to go up the ramp and back down the ramp."

"Ramp? What ramp?"

"The ramp I built for Baskerville, Mrs. Bleaty and the shysters in case they wanted to visit the cemetery. That's how we're going to get home."

"Do you have a death wish?" Silas screamed as the snowmobile hit the ramp and ascended to the top of the fence quickly coming back down the ramp on the other side in Granny's back yard.

Granny maneuvered the snowmobile perfectly straight on the ramp without a hitch until they hit a solid snow-covered patch at the bottom of the ramp in her back yard. The snowmobile veered, its front skis went up and over the mound, while Silas bounced high in the air, coming down hard next to the covered mound in the snow. The snowmobile and Granny stopped a few feet away after stalling out.

"I guess that's how you stop it," Granny calmly observed. "You're home."

The snow was still falling around them and the wind was howling. Silas picked himself up off the ground, looking like a snowman with panic-stricken eyes and his mouth wide open, trying to find words to sputter at Granny. The only thing he was missing was a carrot for his nose and a top hat. His scarf was wrapped tightly around his neck and his cheeks were bright red, warning of the sputtering that was to come.

"Are you trying to kill me?"

"I didn't invite you," Granny said as she turned to tromp through the drifts to get inside her house.

Silas turned and fell over a hard lump in the snow. As he fell, his hand sunk into the drift coming out with a scrappy, half-disintegrated bow tie in his hand. Words failed him as he looked at the tie in his hand. Quickly he moved off the hard mound in the snow.

"Granny, get back here!" he yelled, but Granny had already hustled into her house.

Silas turned back to the mound and gently started digging in the snow. He soon discovered where the bow tie had been attached. He threw snow back on the lump and ran to the house, pounding on Granny's door.

"What now? Go home, Silas. Franklin might get jealous if you keep hanging around and I am not responsible for what he does to you. He was a big New York City Detective, you know."

Silas held up both hands in front of his face trying to silence Granny. He started to speak but couldn't get the words out to interrupt her. Finally, after trying to still his agitating hands that were still in front of Granny's face, he blurted, "You did it now. You killed someone!"

The word *killed* got through to Granny. She pushed Silas's hands away from in front of her face. "Are you daft? Should I call a doctor to look at your head? I didn't kill anyone."

"You should call the police. There's a dead body in your back yard and you ran over it with your snowmobile!"

CHAPTER FOUR

The Fuchsia Police Department led by Granny's son, Thor, was all over her backyard. Franklin, Granny's fiancé, was also in Granny's backyard, discussing the investigation with Thor. Granny had been instructed to stay inside the house, and Silas had been sent home to his house across the street to wait for Thor to question him.

Granny had to block the shysters' pet door, and lock Baskerville and Mrs. Bleaty's window door, so the creatures didn't try to escape and help with the investigation. Granny had tried to see what was in the back yard after Silas announced the dead body to her, after she had called the police, but Thor, who lived across the street, one house over from Silas, and on the opposite corner across from Granny, had heard the police car and had run over before Granny could take a look at the stiff in the back yard. At least she assumed he or she was a stiff because there was a blizzard outside, and it was freezing cold. Detectives in the old detective movies always called the victim a *stiff*. Granny wondered what a dead body was doing in her yard.

"What do you suppose Thor and Franklin are going to say about my snowmobile?" Granny asked the shysters. Little White Poodle seemed to understand what Granny was saying and hid under the couch. Furball stood up and gave Granny a piercing stare with his hair standing up straight as if in fright. Fish and Mrs. Bleaty started meowing and bleating but cut it short and headed for Granny's bedroom when they heard the front door open. Tank and Baskerville slunk low and crawled to Granny's bedroom anticipating a big uproar.

"What did you find out? Was there really someone back there?" Granny inquired of Thor and Franklin as they stepped into the house, brushing the snow that was still falling off their coats.

"You ran over a body all right, Mom," Thor informed her.

"A body that's been dead a long time," Franklin added.

"You mean I didn't kill anyone with the snowmobile?" Granny asked.

"About that snowmobile," Franklin and Thor spoke at the same time.

"First the body, then the snowmobile," Granny informed them, as she lifted the lid on her footstool and took out the fake bottom, grabbing her bottle of wine and the glasses that she kept stashed there away from her daughters' eyes. Thor had discovered her stash a long time ago, and Granny had let Franklin in on that little secret when they became engaged. Granny handed Thor and Franklin each a glass and poured the wine.

"No wine for me, Mom. Working." Thor handed the glass back as he reminded her of the reason he was there.

Franklin lifted the glass to his mouth, but not before catching Thor's eye.

"What?" Granny asked, seeing the look the two men had shared between them.

"Maybe you had better sit down, Hermiony," Franklin said as he took Granny's arm and led her to the sofa.

Granny shifted her arm away from Franklin's grasp. "I'll stand, thank you," Granny informed him with a defiant look in her eye.

"Mom, I don't how to tell you this." Thor looked again at Franklin.

"Tell me what? You just told me I ran over a dead body; I didn't kill anyone so what could be so bad?"

Franklin took over from Thor when he could see that Thor was having a hard time spitting the words out of his mouth.

"The dead body that you ran over—it's your husband, Thor's father."

At this news, Granny did sink down onto the sofa, a look of disbelief on her face. "How do you know that?" Granny challenged both of them just as Tank took that moment to pick up something by the door and jump into Granny's lap, and drop the object in her open hand. Granny looked down at the tattered bow tie in her hand.

"That's his. That's what he was wearing when we buried him in the cemetery. That's how you know, isn't it? Why? How?"

"That's what we have to find out," Thor told her gently. "And because we have had so much snow, we don't know how long his body was out there. If you hadn't run over him with the snowmobile, and Silas Crickett hadn't landed on top of his covered corpse, we might never have found him until spring. We still will have to do some tests on the body to make sure."

Franklin, who had sat down on the couch next to Granny, raised his head when the name Silas was mentioned. "Speaking of Silas, Granny, what were you doing on a snowmobile with the man that you have described since the moment he moved into Sally's house as a disreputable, crotchety, disagreeable skunk?"

"He broke into my house this morning," replied Granny, "tramped down to the basement, unlocked the fireplace door, and made himself at home using my house to get to the underground street so he wouldn't have to go out in the storm. I locked the door after him so he couldn't come back that way." Granny chuckled in satisfaction.

Thor interrupted, "I have to ask you some questions for the investigation, Mom, so let's start from the beginning. "How did you get downtown?"

"I walked the underground streets." Granny stood up and walked over to Thor giving him a stubborn look. "Don't I need a lawyer before you question me?"

A glint came into Franklin's eye. He felt sorry for Thor having to question his own mother—particularly when that mother was the cantankerous Hermiony Vidalia Criony Fiddlestadt.

"No, you don't need a lawyer. Dad was already dead when you mangled him," Thor said in exasperation.

"Thor, watch your language. Is that any way to talk about your father?" Granny countered back.

Franklin decided it was time to step in. "Hermiony, quit giving Thor a bad time and just tell us what you did downtown in this blizzard, and how you happened to be driving a snowmobile so that you ran over your dead husband."

"You two certainly have a way with words," said Granny. "I walked downtown in the underground streets to Graves Mortuary. Mr. Graves gave me a ride on his snowmobile to the Pink Percolator to see Delight. I enjoyed the ride on the snowmobile so much that, after a little forethought, I decided to buy my own snowmobile. You won't let me have my car, Franklin, because my new garage is not built yet, and so I can't come and go as I please." Granny turned to Franklin with a disapproving glance.

"That's the idea," Franklin mumbled. "Keeps you out of trouble," he added under his breath.

"What did you say, Franklin? I didn't quite catch that."

"Go on, Mom," Thor urged.

"Yes, go on," said Franklin. "I want to hear the part where Silas Crickett ended up on the snowmobile with you. Was he driving?"

"That old sourpuss," exclaimed Granny, "I wouldn't let him drive my trike, let alone my snowmobile. They would both break down from his irreparable grouchiness. I was driving."

"And Silas was with you why?" Franklin coaxed.

"He hopped on the back at the last minute. Said he knew I locked the door on him so he couldn't use my house to get to his house and he wasn't going to walk."

"So, Mom," Thor asked with a bit of hesitation, "I'm not sure I want to know this, but I have to ask, why did you go home by way of the cemetery and take the dangerous leap off of the ramp you built for the shysters?"

"Well, um—um." Granny turned around with her back to Thor and in a muffled voice answered, "I didn't want you to see me."

"What did you say, Mom?" Thor asked, leaning in to hear better.

"Yes, Hermiony, what did you say?" Franklin said with one eyebrow raised because he *had* heard her answer.

"We should be worrying about your dear departed father being snatched from his grave and thrown into my backyard. You don't suppose he didn't really die and he was alive and was trying to get to me, do you?" Granny rambled.

Franklin and Thor gave Granny the *look*.

"Um, weren't you with him when he died?" Thor reminded her.

A shadow of the past ran through Granny's head as she remembered covering Ferdinand's head for a few minutes after he died and donning her mini-skirt and taking a twirl, before announcing his death. She remembered the moment of his death being the start of her new life.

"Well, maybe it was his ghost. He's come back to haunt me." Granny said in an alarmed voice.

"Drink your wine, Mom. I'll be back tomorrow. I have to interview Silas Crickett right now. Oh, and you better call off your security team. Mavis and George are peering out their window trying to figure out what is going on. Go on! Wave to them!" Thor remarked as he walked out the front door.

Granny stuck her head out into the cold and the wind and snow, and waved at Mavis and George. Mavis and George were Granny's neighbors. Although they were around Granny's age, she considered them more elderly than she was, and felt she always had to look out for them. Thor was currently renting George's house, which was right next door to Mavis' house, because George was living with Mavis. They were *trying out* their relationship. Mavis had helped Granny solve the most recent shenanigans going on in Fuchsia. Mavis liked reality shows and had had a great time pretending she was in one all the time she was helping Granny. Granny waved at George and Mavis and made a motion with her hand that she would call them soon before turning back into the house and her living room to face Franklin.

"You had better call your daughters and tell them what happened before the newspapers pick it up," Franklin advised. "At least they won't be able to hightail it over here because the highways are closed because of the blizzard. I might not even be able to save you from this." With a twinkle in his eye, Franklin continued in a teasing tone, "You might want to decide which wrinkle farm you might want to reside in. That snowmobile trick and running over your children's dead father might be the straw that breaks the camel's back."

Granny gave Franklin a withering look before replying, "How was I to know that Ferdinand had decided to throw his deteriorated body into the snow at my doorstep. I think I'll let Thor break the news to my children. They might not believe me. But then, who could make up a tale like that? What would I tell them anyway? 'I'm sorry but your dad decided he didn't like being buried anymore, and he decided to visit. I was as surprised as you are when I ran into him?' I think not. I am going into seclusion and think this through. You better leave, Franklin, before you get drifted in, unless of course you want to borrow my new snowmobile to see how much fun it is."

Franklin peered at Granny through skeptical eyes. He knew Granny well enough to know that when she wanted to be alone, trouble was always around the corner. That is what he liked about her. She drove him crazy and made his life interesting. He hadn't had so much fun since he had lived in New York City and had caught the Blue Diamond Stalker. The Blue Diamond Stalker was a very cunning woman, Franklin recalled, but nothing could hold a candle to his Hermiony Vidalia Criony Fiddlestadt.

"You're right; I need to go down to the station anyway and see if my detective skills can help Thor out." Franklin answered.

"You do that. Find out how Ferdinand's body ended up in my yard in the winter time with the ground frozen. I didn't bury him in a heated casket." Granny held the door open for Franklin, as he kissed her on the cheek, ready to walk out the door.

"You let us figure this out, Hermiony, and you put your mind on the double wedding we are going to have on December 26 with Thor and Heather. After all, we just celebrated Thanksgiving, and Christmas isn't too far away," Franklin reminded Granny before disappearing into the snowstorm.

CHAPTER FIVE

Granny decided it must be time for a bowl of ice cream. She needed to think. As she got her ice cream out of the fridge, she also got some yogurt and veggies out and filled the shysters' bowls. Baskerville was the first out of the bedroom and stuck his big nose in the fridge as Granny was grabbing the yogurt. He pulled his own steak out onto the floor. Granny decided not to chastise him as it was probably a hard day for the animals, too, with all the commotion in the back yard. Fish, Little White Poodle, Furball and Tank weren't too far behind Baskerville. Instead of heading for their bowls, they headed out the pet door.

Must have finally had to go, Granny thought. When Granny didn't see Mrs. Bleaty, she headed to the bedroom to see what mischief the goat had gotten into. Granny started laughing out loud when she saw Mrs. Bleaty lolling on her bed with Granny's *Sexy Granny and I Know It,* nightie draped over her while chewing on the book *Fifty Shades of Gray.*

Granny glanced over to the closet and saw that she must have left a crack in her secret cubby in her closet, and Mrs. Bleaty had found it, edged it open and dragged out the stash, making herself comfortable on Granny's bed. As Granny walked over to Mrs. Bleaty and took away the nightie and the book, she threatened the goat. "I can see that it is time for you to have your own home. Perhaps we should find you a Mr. Bleaty."

Granny walked back to her kitchen and was about to eat her melted ice cream when the doorbell rang.

Granny impatiently moved to the door and threw the door open. "Now what?"

"Sorry, Granny, but we couldn't wait any longer," Mavis said as she and George stomped into the house tromping snow all over the floor. Taking off their snow boots and hanging their coats in the closet next to the door, the two walked in and sat down so fast they almost knocked Granny down as they whisked past her. Baskerville hurried over and lapped up the snow on the floor with his tongue. "Now tell us what's going on."

Granny related the entire story to them, about how she had wanted to get out for the day, used the underground streets, got a ride from Mr. Graves on his snowmobile, visited with Delight, bought a snowmobile, and ran over a dead body in her backyard that turned out to be her dead husband that was found when Silas Crickett fell off of the snowmobile.

"Silas Crickett?" Mavis interrupted, "How and when did he get involved in this?"

"Yah," George chirped, looking confused. "All of a sudden, he falls off your snowmobile. When did he get on?"

Granny straightened up her back and answered, "Well, that ornery old man busted into my house early this morning and streaked through the living room to the basement and out my door to the underground streets."

"Streaked?" Mavis shrieked and started laughing at the thought. "It's a little cold to streak in this weather."

Granny looked askance at Mavis. "Ooh, no.....not that; he had his clothes on. I mean he ran through my house. He is the most ornery, cantankerous person I have ever met."

George gave Granny a knowing look. "Did he wink at you?"

"I think he's such a gentleman. I don't know what you could mean by cantankerous, Granny," Mavis added, with a twinkle in her eye.

At that moment, the pet door banged open and all four shysters came running in, covered with snow, stopping in front of where Mavis, George and Granny were sitting. The snow flew around the room sending globs of wet mush right into their faces.

Mavis, wiping her face and eyes with her neck scarf, asked, "How do they know the body was your dead husband?"

"Yah, how do they know?" George echoed Mavis.

"Thor said the clothes on the body matched the clothes that Ferdinand was buried in. Then Baskerville dumped the bow tie in my lap that old Silas picked up when he uncovered the body. It was Ferdinand's all right."

George stood up and held out his hand to Mavis. "Time to go; it's almost supper time and you know we have a *Cooks in the Kitchen* show planned." George was referring to their pretend reality show. Mavis had passed her love of drama on to George after he fell in love with her.

Mavis took George's hand and stood up. She held back as George opened the door letting the crisp air in. Whispering to Granny she said, "I know you'll be investigating. Let me know if I can help." To George she said, "Looks like the snowstorm is letting up. Do you want to make snow angels on the way home?"

Granny closed the door after them and looked at the clock on the wall. It was almost 6:00 p.m. She hadn't noticed that darkness had fallen. Pretty soon it would be December 21 and the days would start getting longer again. Granny decided she had had enough excitement for the day. Since Fish, Little White Poodle, Furball and Tank, along with Baskerville and Mrs. Bleaty, hadn't gone for their daily scamper around the town last night and their time at Franklin's, Granny wondered if they would stay in out of the cold for another night.

It was November 30th, only a few weeks until Thor and Heather would be married. Only a few weeks until she and Franklin would be married. Franklin's proposal last fall had been a surprise. After all, Granny had only made him her pretend fiancé so her kids wouldn't worry about her and want her to move in with them or send her to the wrinkle farm, if she had Franklin there to watch out for her. Then Thor decided to move to Fuchsia right across the street from Granny, so the pretend fiancé thing hadn't been necessary at all. Apparently, however, Franklin had taken it seriously and had proposed after a drug ring and a bunch of murderers had been apprehended with Granny's help.

Thor's announcement was the surprise of the century. Secretly, he had been engaged to Franklin's daughter, Heather. Granny hadn't seen that one coming. She thought Thor was after a certain hussy—and he was—but not in the way Granny had thought. Now Thor was marrying Heather, and Heather's daughter, Angelique, Franklin's granddaughter, would be Granny's grandchild too. It was a mixed up web, and at times, Granny felt like she was the one who was caught in it.

Granny forgot that she had forgotten to cover her snowmobile. Fred Runner had said that she should do that. She was the first to admit that she didn't know much about snowmobiles, but they had made it home alive and that was what counted, and riding the snowmobile had made Granny feel alive! Granny thought about the thrill of the wind, the smell of the crisp winter day, the fluffy snow that had flown up around her as she wove around the streets—and she smiled.

Stuffing her feet into her boots, putting on her bomber hat, and pink coat, and grabbing her flashlight, Granny called to the shysters to come along with her as she opened the door and stepped out into the winter night. She grabbed the snow shovel that sat by the door in case she needed to shovel the snow off the machine. Walking around to the back of the house, she stopped by the temporary storage shed that Thor had built after her garage had burned down, so she would have somewhere to store her lawn mower and snow blower. She knew she had a tarp that she could use to cover her snowmobile temporarily until she could buy a cover.

Grabbing the tarp, Granny plowed through the snow and deep drifts to get to where she had left the snowmobile. She looked around. There was no snowmobile. She shone the flashlight around the yard. No snowmobile.

Granny made her way to the front yard and shone the flashlight around the front yard. No snowmobile. Had Thor or Franklin taken it? Granny turned to walk up the steps onto her porch and into her house to call them when she heard a noise across the street.

The snow had quit falling and it now was a crisp, beautiful night with the moon reflecting off the snow, brightening the darkness. Granny looked toward where she heard the noise. Someone was starting a snowmobile. It was Silas Crickett and it was her snowmobile he was starting—in his yard!

Still holding the shovel, Granny proceeded across the street to what used to be Sally Katilda's house. As she got closer to Silas and the snowmobile, she lowered her shovel and picked up a shovel full of snow. Silas, busy examining the running snowmobile, didn't hear or see Granny approach him. Granny raised the shovel and dumped the entire scoop of wet snow on Silas's head.

As Silas was recovering from the snow avalanche that had been dumped on his head, Granny reached over and pulled the key from the snowmobile, silencing it.

"You thief! You no good, snowmobile-stealing thief! Don't move or this...or this shovel will come down on your head, you cantankerous, ornery, thieving old man! I'm calling the cops." Granny reached for her alarm that she was used to carrying in her pocket when she had worked for the merchants of Fuchsia, only to remember that Thor had taken it, thus putting an end to her undercover security job.

Still holding the shovel over Silas's head, she then reached for her cell phone. It wasn't in her pocket either. She had forgotten it in her house.

"Ornery? You're calling me ornery? Get that shovel away from my head! I'm calling the cops! You attacked me! You're going to the hoosegow." Silas started to reach for the shovel.

Granny lifted the shovel higher to bring it down on Silas's head, when she felt the shovel being taken out of her hand from behind.

CHAPTER SIX

"What do you think you are doing?" Thor asked his mother as he set the shovel down on Silas Crickett's driveway.

"Where did you come from?" demanded Granny. "I'm glad you're here. Arrest him, he stole my snowmobile."

Thor gave a big sigh. "He didn't steal your snowmobile; he was fixing it. He does part-time work at Runner's Skids and Skis. He's fixing it after you used it for ramp diving."

"Just a few things needed straightening out," said Silas. "And, Hermiony, I do know what I'm doing. They use them harder than this in Alaska where I had my shop." Silas gave Granny a withering look before telling Thor, "I won't press charges this time. I realize she's a confused old lady."

At the word *old*, Granny tried to pick up the shovel again, but Thor had it stuck deep in the snow and was still holding on to it.

"I was just coming over to talk to you," he said, "when I saw you tromping through the snow to get to Silas."

"Haven't you seen enough of me today?" Granny asked Thor. "Don't you want to go kiss Heather? I'm sure she's missing you."

Thor grabbed Granny's arm to escort her back across the street to her house. A loud voice came out of nowhere, "Unhand her this minute! Unhand her this minute!" As Thor turned to see where the voice was coming from, a large gray bird with specks of red under his tail flew out the door of the house that Silas had left open, and landed on Thor's head. Just as the bird landed, the side window that Granny had turned into a door on her house so Baskerville could come and go, popped open. Seeing the gray bird on Thor's head, Baskerville made a mad dash for Thor as Thor was trying to get the bird off his head. Coming from a dead start in the deep snow, Baskerville hit Thor head on, knocking him into Silas. Silas, who had been standing by the snowmobile, fell over the snowmobile, landing on the other side in the deep snow. Thor ended up on top of the snowmobile with the bird still attached to the cap on his head. Granny jumped on top of Baskerville as he came back down from jumping on Thor. Granny and Baskerville were now lying in the snow next to the snowmobile. The gray bird was still shouting "Unhand her! Unhand her!"

Hearing all the noise, Mavis looked out her window. Seeing the bodies on the ground, she snapped a picture through her window before running through her front door and out into the fray. She grabbed the gray bird off Thor's head. "Hi, Mavis," the bird said as it gave Mavis a little peck on her nose.

"You know this bird?" Thor asked as he checked his head to make sure it wasn't spouting blood.

"Of course she does. Mavis is one of Radish's favorite people. Isn't that right, Radish?" Silas answered for Mavis.

"This is Radish? The Radish you are always going on about when you're complaining that my animals are always trying to eat Radish?" Granny confronted Silas while still using her full weight to keep Baskerville on the ground. Radish flew off Mavis and tweaked Baskerville on the nose before flying back into the house. Silas followed Radish, turned, and said to the group, "Been nice. See you soon, Mavis." With a wink at Mavis, he closed the door on the watchers.

Granny shook her head in disgust and grabbed the shovel. "It's time for bed. My dreams have to be better than this."

"We have to talk, Mom," said Thor. "Mavis, you might as well get George and come along too. It will save Mom having to relay all the news and I can lay the law down to all of you at once." Thor walked across the street after Granny. "Come on, Baskerville—you too."

Baskerville, instead of following Granny and Thor, planted himself firmly on the steps leading into Silas's house and gave a loud howl.

"Leave him there, Thor. He'll come when he wants to," Granny advised. "Serves Silas right if he howls all night, and keeps that cantankerous old man awake."

George and Mavis arrived at Granny's house minutes later, brushing snow off their feet while Thor and Granny searched the house for Fish, Little White Poodle, Furball, and Tank.

"No sign of 'em," Granny announced, "they must have decided the weather was good enough for their nightly rounds again. They'll head to Franklin's after that and get back to their usual routine. Mrs. Bleaty seems to have made herself comfortable on my bed and is snoring away."

Granny took one look at George and let out a large laugh. "Star Wars fan are ya, George?" referring to the flannel pajamas that George hadn't bothered changing out of when Mavis woke him to come to Granny's.

George ignored Granny's jibe. "What's going on, Thor?"

"Just wanted to tell you that we are putting extra patrols in the neighborhood again because of the body found in Mom's back yard. Although we know the body was tossed there before it snowed, it had to have been put there in the last couple of days because last night was our first snow storm of the year. We might be looking for a grave robber."

"Why would they dig up Ferdinand's grave?" Granny asked in puzzlement.

"They didn't," Thor answered.

Granny jumped up from the chair she had been sitting in, standing up so quickly that the chair went backwards and would have fallen over had Mavis not grabbed it. "Then how did your dad get in my back yard, Thor?"

"They didn't rob his grave; they robbed yours." Thor backed away a little from his mother, waiting for her reaction.

"My grave! I don't have a grave. I'm here. I'm not dead, in case you haven't noticed," Granny informed him as she stomped one foot on the floor.

"Well—the mausoleum was broken into and the interior crypt that you bought when dad died was broken into. Apparently, dad was buried in there."

"I didn't buy myself no grave. I kind of have this aversion to death, and I wouldn't do that until I figured out what epitaph I want on my tombstone. And if your father was in my burial crypt that I didn't even have, then who is in his grave? Who did we bury there? I threw dirt on that casket after they lowered it in the ground. Who did I waste my dirt on?" Granny asked, her voice getting louder and more upset with each question.

Mavis walked over to Granny and handed her a glass of wine that Mavis had dug out of Granny's hiding place. Granny looked at the glass. "You know about my hiding place, too?"

"Drink up, Granny," Mavis advised. "It was a stressful time when your husband died. Maybe you forgot that you bought a place in the mausoleum."

"Mavis, I think you and I had better go on home and grab Baskerville from Silas's doorstep. Granny might need him tonight to protect her," George said as he grabbed Mavis's arm leading her to the door. "Thor, it might be a good idea if you lock Baskerville's side window door so no one else can get in."

"Good idea, George," Thor agreed.

Granny raised her eyes at all of them being so concerned. "Since I'm alive and the criminal appears to be a grave robber, I suspect I'm in no danger. Besides, he already robbed the grave I didn't know I had." Granny walked over and followed Mavis and George outside.

Thor followed Granny. "And what are you doing now, Mom?"

Granny grabbed the shovel she had set down outside the door on the porch. "I'm getting my trusty shovel. Never know when it might come in handy to ding a digger."

Thor took the shovel out of his mother's hands, "Or to shovel Silas? Good night, Mother." Thor walked down the steps carrying the shovel in his hand. "Think I'll keep this at my house for all Fuchsia citizens' safety. Call if you need it."

Granny watched Thor walk across the street to his house, shovel lowered, shoveling a path to his house. Baskerville trotted over from his post outside of Silas's door, following George, who lured him across the street with a steak and preceded Granny into her house. "Thanks, George," said Granny, acknowledging his act of kindness. She went inside the house, locked Baskerville and Mrs. Bleaty's door, turned out the lights and headed back to her bedroom.

She made sure her special *weapons*—her knitting needle, cane, and umbrella—were by her bed in case she needed protection during the night. Mrs. Bleaty was snoring softly on the side of her bed. Granny sat down on her side, intending to change her clothes but it had been such an exciting day that she lay back for a moment to catch her breath and instantly fell asleep.

CHAPTER SEVEN

A howl, then a bleat, broke into Granny's dream. She opened one eye and then quickly opened the other. Instead of being snuggled in her blankets, she was still laying half on, half off the bed. She hadn't moved all night since falling asleep. Granny sat up and since she hadn't taken off her fuzzy slippers, she jumped up and hustled down the hallway to see what the noise was all about.

Mrs. Bleaty was head butting the side glass panel door that was over the pet door. Baskerville was howling, trying to open the large pet door before Mrs. Bleaty butted her way through it. *So much for keeping me safe,* Granny thought. The pet door might have kept grave robbers out, but it kept the two animals in. It was a good thing they were very well house trained or someone would have to pay for them going to the bathroom in the house and it wasn't going to be her.

Granny checked the clock on the wall in the kitchen––9:00 a.m.—way past the time she usually got up. She looked down at the red sweatshirt and jeans that she still had on from yesterday. Granny decided they weren't really her style. Since she didn't have to pretend that she was senile and limpy anymore, perhaps it was time to get a new wardrobe. Maybe she would ask Mavis to go shopping with her in Allure. After all, Mavis hadn't done too badly with her makeover last fall. Besides, she needed to get something to wear for the wedding shindig when Thor and Heather got married. Granny couldn't quite wrap her mind around the fact that she and Franklin were getting married that day, too.

The sun gleamed through the cracks in the curtain. Granny pulled the curtain aside and looked out onto her front lawn. Her snowmobile was parked right by the stairs to her porch and it had acquired a cover. After her shower, she would take a ride downtown and possibly through the cemetery, to see the place where apparently she was supposed to have been buried.

Granny grabbed her coffee before heading to the shower. She turned on her radio so she could listen to *Wedding Bell Blues* sung by the *Fifth Dimension* and other music she might want for her wedding. She was still humming *Wedding Bell Blues* as she exited the bathroom and dressed in red corduroy pants and a velour top with a picture of a steaming coffee cup on the front announcing, "You Steam It, I'll Cream It!"

"Are you ready?"

Granny jumped and almost fell back into the bathroom at the voice. "What are you doing here?" Granny grabbed the door to steady herself.

"I thought we would go downtown and finalize our wedding plans. I have a surprise for you," Franklin said with a wide grin on his face.

"You're going to ride with me on my snowmobile?"

"No—I thought we would go in my car. We can stop by Runner's Skids and Skis and see if Fred will take your snowmobile back."

Granny moved past Franklin in a huff. "You worried I'll run over you?"

"It's dangerous—a woman of your age driving a snowmobile."

"What's dangerous is what will happen to you if you think you can take my snowmobile away," Granny warned as she put on her coat and boots.

Franklin dropped his shoulders in defeat. "We'll talk about this some other time. I have something for you to see." Franklin relented, as he held the door open for Granny.

"Can we go through the cemetery?" Granny asked as she buckled her seatbelt in the front seat of Franklin's four-wheel drive Escalade. "Where's your '57 Chevy?"

"Don't you remember? I parked both of our cars for the winter. This one will get us through the thick snow when we need it. We are not going to the cemetery. Thor would be livid and you are on a need-to-know basis. We know what you need to know—and the cemetery is not on the need-to-know list."

"I want to find out where I'm supposed to be buried. I want to see my final resting place. I always thought I would be scattered over Blue Bird Pond or perhaps in the underground streets. Then maybe I'd come back as a ghost and catch crooks that way." Granny laughed as she considered the remote possibility.

"We have more important things to do today," Franklin informed Granny.

"Such as......?"

"You'll see. Details, my dear Hermiony, details."

Franklin drove through the main street of Fuchsia, having to stop a time or two as the street crews were lifting the snowmen and reindeers that would be lighted up for Christmas onto the light posts of Fuchsia.

"Look, Franklin! Angel will love these decorations. This will be her first year to celebrate Christmas in Fuchsia," Granny remarked.

"Mine, too, Hermiony. What are those wires for?"

"The snowmen glide up and down the poles and the reindeers travel from pole to pole on the wires. Our decorations are animated."

"What is happening on top of all the buildings?" Franklin asked in confusion.

"Every building has a Christmas tree that is lit up on top of it. Each tree plays a different Christmas tune and the trees take turns with the music," Granny explained.

"That's a little over the top, isn't it?" Franklin commented.

"Wait till you see it. Christmas in Fuchsia is unforgettable. Where are we going? We are clear across town."

Franklin drove to the very edge of town and pulled into a circular driveway in front of a large Victorian house with turrets and a wraparound porch.

"Why are we visiting the Mayor?" Granny asked.

"We aren't. The Mayor sold this house to me," Franklin said as he turned to look at Granny.

Granny eyed the house. "Did you buy this for Heather and Thor?"

"No, I bought it for us."

"Us? But we both have houses." Granny pointed out.

"We can sell them and move in here when we get married."

Granny opened the car door and stepped out. She looked at the house and turned back to Franklin who was still sitting in the car. "Well, I hope you'll be happy in your house," Granny said sweetly as she started to close the door, "because you're going to be living here by yourself." Granny slammed the door to the Escalade and started walking down the street toward town.

Franklin quickly started the Escalade and drove out of the driveway and after Granny. When he caught up with her, he slowed down so he could talk to her since she wouldn't stop. "What's the matter with you? It's a beautiful house. I did it for us. I wanted to surprise you."

"Well, I guess the surprise was on you. Did it ever occur to you that I might not want to move? Did it ever occur to you that the shysters might not want to move?

Did it ever occur to you that you are not my husband yet!" Granny yelled in frustration.

At that moment, a car pulled up to the curb near Granny. Granny saw that it was Franklin's daughter and Thor's fiancée, Heather, along with Franklin's granddaughter, Angel. Granny moved to the open window of the car. She loved little Angel.

Franklin called out to his daughter, "Heather, can you talk some sense into Granny? I have to get to the police station."

Granny gave Franklin a glare and got into the car with Heather and Angel as Franklin drove away. "Granny, did you and my grandpa have a fight?" Angel asked innocently, as innocently as a four-year-old does.

"Honey, we were just having a slight difference of opinion, nothing for you to worry about," Granny reassured Angel.

"My momma said that you two are hot heads. Can I feel your head? Is it hot?"

"What are you and your momma doing today, Angel?" Granny asked, turning the conversation to another topic.

"Momma is going to take me to find a dress for the weddings because I am going to be her flower girl and your flower girl. Can I have two dresses for two weddings?"

Heather and Granny laughed. Heather advised her daughter, "I think we better find one dress first. Do you want to go along, Hermiony?"

"No, I believe I need to stay here today. You heard what happened last night?" Granny answered, forgetting that Angel was listening.

"No; what happened, Granny?" Angel asked giving Granny a wondering look.

"Nothing to worry your little head about, dear," Granny assured Angel while trying to think of an answer to the question. "Mr. Crickett just had a little snowmobile accident, but he is fine."

Heather raised her eyebrows at the answer. "Anywhere we can drop you, Granny?"

"Nail's Hardware. I heard it has a new owner and I need to pick something up."

"Maybe you should wait with that. Let me drop you off at home," Heather advised.

"Why would I want to do that?" Granny asked. "Why shouldn't I go to Nail's Hardware?"

"You won't like the answer, Granny," Angel piped up, just as her mom stopped in front of Nail's and grabbed Angel's shoulder lightly and gave her a look that said she was not to say anymore.

Granny turned and blew Angel a kiss. "Have fun shopping, Angel. I guess I'll find out what I don't like." With a final wink at Heather, Granny closed the car door and waved them off.

Granny listened as the nail wind chimes on the door of Nail's announced her arrival. She heard a voice call from the back of the store. "Be right with you."

As Granny waited for someone to help her, she started fingering the snow shovels, lifting each carefully and pretending she was shoveling snow. She also tested the weight of each snow shovel to see if she could lift it over her head.

"Can I help you?" A familiar voice asked.

Granny turned around to stare straight into the face of her son-in-law Butch, Penelope's husband. "What are you doing here?"

"Um…ah….we were going to tell you soon. This is my first day."

"Tell me what? Why aren't you over in your own town running your security business?"

"Because he bought Nail's Hardware and we are moving to Fuchsia," Penelope informed her mother as she walked to the front of the store from the backroom.

"You didn't think to tell me, your own mother?"

Butch shuffled around, a little nervously before answering, "Actually we were going to tell you yesterday, but there was this blizzard. You remember the blizzard, where you ran over Penelope's father?"

Penelope started sniffling as Butch put his arm around her. Penelope kissed him on the cheek and walked over and hugged her mother. "I'm so sorry that happened to you, Mom. You must be so upset. If we live here we can help you out more."

Granny gave Penelope a quick hug back and backed to the door. "I....ah....have to have a little time to get used to this news. We'll talk later." Granny hurriedly left the store. Once back on the street, she pulled out her cell phone. "Heather, have you left town yet? Good. Can you swing by and pick me up? I think I *will* help you out with the shopping for Angel, and I need to stop at the hardware store in Allure and pick up a new snow shovel."

CHAPTER EIGHT

"Bye, Granny; thank you for letting me get two flower girl dresses. I can't wait till your wedding," said Angel.

Granny removed the pink shovel out of Heather's trunk, and turned to Heather and Angel still in the warm car. "Thanks for the lift. I appreciate it."

"That certainly is a strange shovel, Granny," Heather commented, "I have never seen a shovel with a rubber cover that will make it stand on end. And pink on top of it."

"They customized it just for me," Granny said proudly. "It's a good thing it took you gals a lot of time to make up your mind in choosing your dresses, so I don't have to go back to Allure anytime soon."

Heather, noticing cars parked by Granny's house, said, "It looks like you've got lots of visitors, Thor included, Granny. I think I'll get Angel home to bed and let you take care of your company."

"Can't we stay and help Granny with the shysters, Mom? There's Grandpa, and they're in the back of his car," Angel pleaded.

Heather—seeing her dad, Thor, Penelope, Penelope's husband Butch, Starshine, Granny's other daughter, and Mr. Crickett, all converging outside of Granny's house—said, "It looks to me like home might be the best place for us right now. Bye, Granny." Heather drove away without giving Angel the chance to beg to stay some more.

Granny, seeing all the people who were now waiting for her on her porch, walked to the porch and leaned on her shovel with the flat-bottomed cover holding up part of her weight. She didn't imagine anyone was here for a party.

"Could you help me up the steps? Hurt my ankle a little. Shopping is hard on the bones. I think I need to lie down and rest. It was real nice of you all to check up on me. You can go home now, once you help me in the house. I'm going to lie down and rest. We can all talk some other day," Granny informed her company.

"Good idea. I don't know why I'm here anyway," Silas remarked.

Franklin helped Granny up the steps and into the house. The shysters were already inside having used their pet door. Thor, Penelope, Butch, Starshine and Silas followed, making themselves at home in Granny's living room.

Granny looked at Franklin. "Did you give up on the idea of the house?"

"House? What are you talking about?" Thor asked.

Yah, what is everyone doing here?" Penelope asked. "We thought we'd better come over and explain about the hardware store."

"Hardware store? What about a hardware store?" Starshine asked. "I came over to tell Mom that I'm engaged."

"Engaged?" Granny said, startled.

"I came over to talk about the house," Franklin explained.

"House? What house?" Thor asked. "I'm here because I need to talk to Mom about the murder investigation."

"Murder? What murder investigation?" Granny asked, perplexed. "I didn't murder your dad when I ran him over; he was already dead."

"Now that we've established why everyone *else* is here," Silas Crickett interrupted, "will someone please tell me why *I'm* here amongst all you confused people?"

Baskerville and Mrs. Bleaty chose that moment to come out of Granny's bedroom. Once they saw Silas Crickett, they ran over and greeted him with barks and bleats, nuzzling his hand as he tried to fend them off.

With eyes skewered into little slits, Granny glared at Silas. "I thought you didn't like them and they didn't like you, Silas—something about them killing Radish."

Silas, as usual, ignored Granny's inquiries and turned again to Thor. "Do you mind telling me why you asked me to come over?"

"You asked him to come over here," said Granny, "after he broke into my place yesterday morning and tried to hijack my snowmobile!" Granny advanced on Thor with a pointed finger.

"He what?" Penelope and Starshine advanced on Silas.

Thor held up his hands and in a loud voice said, "Enough! If you will all calm down, no matter what reason you came here, you all should hear this!"

That got everyone's attention and they all claimed a chair or a couch and all sat down—all except Granny. She reached down and picked up Little White Poodle who was standing by her feet.

Thor walked over to Granny and looked into her eyes. "The body that you ran over yesterday that was dressed like dad was dressed when he was buried, wasn't dad, Mom. But, it was buried in your tomb in the mausoleum."

Thor looked into the shocked faces of his sisters and the other occupants of the room. He appeared to be gauging the look on Silas Crickett's face in particular.

"Why are you looking at me?" Silas asked Thor. "I'm new in this town and this woman got me involved in this mess by her crazy driving."

Franklin then stood up, and walked over to Granny and put his arm around her, apparently knowing from his earlier detective days that there was more to come.

"The autopsy revealed," continued Thor, "that the body you ran over, Mom, had been *murdered* years ago."

Granny broke away from Franklin's arm, walked to the kitchen counter and grabbed a donut that had been on a covered plate. She broke off a little piece and gave it to Little White Poodle before she set him down on the floor. He took the piece of donut and walked over to Fish, Furball and Tank, gave a little bark to tease them, and ran off down to the basement. Baskerville and Mrs. Bleaty started barking and bleating and ran after him followed by Fish, Furball and Tank.

Since it was the start of Christmas season, Granny had taken all the pictures down from her walls, and off the tabletops, and put them in the hutch made of barn wood that stood in the corner of her living room, intending to replace them with Christmas paraphernalia. Granny now walked to the hutch and took out a picture, gazed at it for a few minutes, and walked over to Thor and Franklin, while the others watched wondering what Granny was going to do with this news that she had just been given. Taking the picture and shoving it at Thor's chest, she asked, "Well, then, Thor, who is the dead man in my husband's clothes? And what was the stiff doing in my crypt that I didn't know I had? And…who is *he*?"

Thor took the picture from Granny and looked at it intently. "I don't know yet, Mom. I don't have any answers. I barely remember Dad or anything about his funeral; I was so young."

"I was barely into my teens, but I don't remember anything strange either," said Penelope. "You didn't have an open casket, Mom, so we didn't see how Dad was dressed—or that he was even in there. Oooh, this is creepy." Penelope buried her head in her husband's chest.

"I guess I'll be going. You don't need me around during this weird family discussion," Silas announced, backing toward the door.

"Thanks for coming, Silas. I thought since you were inadvertently dragged into this that you should hear the news," said Thor, walking over and patting Silas on the back. "I'll walk out with you." Turning to the rest of the room, he added, "I think I'll go see Heather and bring her up to speed. Good luck with your news." Thor winked at Penelope as he opened the door for Silas. "And congratulations, Starshine, I hope we meet your fiancé sometime soon. Come on, Silas, it would be wise to be a little way away from here when Penelope and Butch give Mom their news."

Granny watched as they walked out the door. At that moment, there was a ruckus and the menagerie of animals ran up the stairs. Mrs. Bleaty was in the lead and she had Little White Poodle's stuffed toy in her mouth. She ran for the side window door. As she reached the door, Baskerville gave his howl so the door would open and the two ran out into the night. The rest of the shysters followed suit through the pet door.

Turning to Penelope, Granny waited in silence with her I'm-not-going-to-like-this-am-I look.

"You already know that Butch bought Nail's Hardware, Mom," said Penelope. "He was looking for a new adventure now that we are empty nesters. What you don't know is that we're moving to Fuchsia."

"Across town in the Mayor's house, right?" Granny asked sarcastically, looking at Franklin.

"No, why would you think we could afford the Mayor's house?" Penelope asked. "We're buying George's house across the street. He's decided that he and Mavis are going to travel the make-believe reality show circuit for the rest of their lives, so he's going to sell his house. When Thor marries Heather at the double wedding with you and Franklin in December, the sale will be finalized and we'll move in. We're going to be neighbors! Isn't that wonderful, Mom? Butch and I, and you and Franklin can spend lots of time together."

Eyes wide with what her daughters perceived to be an awestruck look—and it was, but not for the same reason they were thinking—Granny asked Starshine, "And you're engaged?" She simply wasn't able to get any words out about having more of her children across the street.

"I am," Starshine answered, holding out her hand for Granny to see her star-shaped diamond engagement ring. "Isn't it beautiful? Lars had it made to signify my name because he said that I'm the shining star in his life."

"Have you met this guy?" Granny asked Penelope.

"No, she's been keeping him a secret."

Granny knew all about secrets, but Starshine was a hippie Aquarius type—free spirited and blabby. Granny had named her after the hippie movement.

Franklin stepped forward and hugged Starshine. "My new, almost daughter-in-law, do you want to have a triple wedding, and share the day with Thor and your mother?"

"No, we might stay engaged forever and just commune together." Starshine answered.

Franklin, seeing Granny had had enough surprises for the night and that the word *commune* might push her off the edge, quickly moved Starshine to the door. "It's time for you all to go now. Past your mother's bedtime. You know how frail she sometimes gets."

Penelope and Thor were already halfway out the door, having started to leave at the word *commune,* knowing what Granny's reaction might be. Starshine quickly followed and closed the door before Granny could say a word.

"Commune! Commune! What the heck does that mean? The stiff I found was murdered and my daughter's moving in next door!" Granny yelled. "And….you think I'm going to move. You decided that we're moving! Go home, Franklin. How much do you think an old woman can take in one day?" Granny walked to the door and held it open. She picked up her new pink shovel with the flat bottom and raised it into the air. "Leave now or I will not be responsible where this shovel lands."

Franklin chuckled and winked at Granny as he retreated through the door. When Granny shut the door behind him, she didn't hear the loud laugh or the whistle coming out of Franklin's lips. "Yup, my Hermiony Vidalia Criony Fiddlestadt is back and it's going to get interesting," he said to himself as he walked through the cold crisp winter night.

CHAPTER NINE

Granny looked at the time displayed on her cell phone that she kept by her bedside—midnight. Since all the noisy fur creatures that shared her house were gone for the night, Granny decided to try to get the events of the day out of her mind by cozying up with a good book and a box of chocolates that she'd forgotten she'd hidden in her secret closet.

The Sinister Sitcom Caper by Sally Carpenter seemed the perfect fit to get Granny's mind off the fact that someone dead was masquerading as her husband and wearing his clothes. But now, looking at the time, Granny knew she would never get to sleep until she visited the grave where she had buried her husband, or at least took a look at the spot in the mausoleum that was supposed to be her grave.

Throwing back the covers on her bed, Granny grabbed the bedpost and slowly stood up so she wouldn't tip over as she sometimes did when she got up in the morning. Sometimes she tipped one way; sometimes she tipped the other. Granny chuckled, "I'm a good tipper, and no one knows it."

Knowing that they wouldn't let her near the cemetery during the day, now seemed like as good a time as any to explore. Grabbing her flashlight, she headed to the closet by the front door. Plopping her bomber hat on her head and putting on her winter coat, she arranged the coat to hide her winter PJs. Tonight she was wearing her red velvet PJ tops and bottoms embroidered with purple sequins and red feathers. *No one will see what I have under my coat anyway*, she thought.

After stepping into her purple boots, she peeked through the curtain of the front window. There didn't seem to be any lights on in the neighborhood. The coast was clear.

Picking up her pink shovel, she proceeded to the back door of her house. She didn't use it very often but it came in handy if she needed to sneak out unnoticed. No one would ever suspect her of sneaking out her back door. Granny made sure all the lights were out in her house before she left.

Once outside, Granny looked around to make sure there was no one watching. She hoped everyone was sound asleep and wouldn't hear her snowmobile. If they did, they'd probably think they'd just heard the snowmobile club's drive-by patrol. Sometimes they rode around this neighborhood taking the path through the grove at the end of the street to avoid the town police, especially if they'd been imbibing at the Fuchsia Sip 'n' Spit, the local pub. It hadn't happened much lately since Thor had become the chief of police, and now lived on the street. It was probably because the club members weren't sure how the new man in town would enforce the Fuchsia community rules.

Granny hopped on her snowmobile, gently revved the engine, and took off toward the ramp at the back of her yard. As she got to the top of the ramp, she didn't see any movement in the cemetery and decided the coast was clear. *No ghosts out tonight,* she thought.

Slowly, she maneuvered the pathways in the cemetery until she came near the tombstone of her dead husband, Ferdinand Fiddlestadt. She heard the sound first. It sounded like a motor running. Cautiously, Granny stopped the snowmobile on the path by a large headstone, giving cover to the snowmobile. Granny cut the engine, grabbed her pink shovel, and cautiously made her way over to where the noise broke the stillness of the night. Peering around a neighboring tombstone, Granny saw that a generator sat alone in the night by her husband's grave purring softly. On top of Ferdinand's grave was a large blanket.

Moving slowly closer through the deep snow, holding on to her shovel for protection, Granny stopped by the grave. Reaching down, she touched the blanket. It was warm to the touch. Granny pulled her hand back, shining the flashlight into the darkness. There appeared to be no other movement in the cemetery. Granny eyed the blanket in speculation. Why were they apparently thawing out Ferdinand's grave? What else weren't they telling her?

Reading Ferdinand's epitaph on his tombstone, *I had a wife, she was very nice; I had some children too, But now I'm dead, she'll keep them fed, She knows it's the right thing to do,* Granny shook her head. Even in death, Ferdinand made sure to remind her of the right thing to do. Granny took the pink shovel, picked up some snow, and threw it towards the gravestone at the epitaph engraved on the stone, that marked the spot where her husband should be.

Turning back and stepping through the deep snow, using the shovel for traction, Granny decided to visit the mausoleum on the way back to her house. Just maybe someone forgot to lock the door. It was a long shot, but then, this was Fuchsia. Granny took one long look around the tombstone that was hiding her snowmobile at Ferdinand's grave. She got back on her snowmobile, revved the engine and took off, "This one's for you, Ferdinand; it's the right thing to do, for me, not you!"

Granny cut the engine and stopped a little way away from the mausoleum. Since it was next to Granny's property and close to the ramp, she wanted to make sure it was ready to go if she needed a fast getaway. After all, the mausoleum was what had gotten broken into. The door probably would be locked anyway.

Shining her flashlight on the door of the mausoleum, she moved forward and tried the handle. The handle clicked and the big oversized ornate mausoleum door opened. Granny stuck her head in slightly to peer around to the other side of the door. It was strange that the door was unlocked. Her eyes darted to behind the door and into the dark room. She couldn't see a thing, so she pushed the door open a little more and took hold of her pink shovel with both hands, holding it in front of her while still juggling the flashlight and the shovel. Moving forward, she shone the flashlight on the crypts in the walls, trying to find her supposed resting place. All of a sudden, she heard the door to the mausoleum behind her slam shut. Granny jumped. Then, she heard footsteps.

"I'll ding you with this shovel and your head will ring if you come any closer," Granny warned the unknown person, keeping the shovel raised with one hand, while shining the flashlight toward the sound of the footsteps.

The footsteps came closer and suddenly, Silas Crickett revealed himself in the light. "Woman, don't you know it's dangerous out here. See that crypt over there? I could pick you up and seal you in it and then it really would be your grave!" Silas yelled in an exasperated loud voice.

"Stay where you are!" Granny warned, "I'm calling Thor."

"With your cell phone?" Silas asked in a persnickety tone. "The cell phone I have in my hand that I picked up at your house?" Silas advanced on Granny.

Granny gripped the shovel tighter. *Where were the shysters when you needed them?* Granny heard scratching at the mausoleum door at the same time Silas did. As Granny was plotting how to get the best of Silas, Silas unexpectedly turned and walked back to the mausoleum door and opened it. Baskerville, Fish, Little White Poodle, Furball and Tank bounded into the room and surrounded Granny. Only Mrs. Bleaty was missing.

"Attack!" Granny commanded her furry friends. Baskerville moved forward and started licking Silas on the hand. Furball jumped up on Granny's head and started purring, making Granny drop the shovel. Fish walked over and lay down at the feet of the statue of the founder of Fuchsia, and Tank sat down in the scoop of the fallen shovel.

Silas held up the phone again. "Do you want me to call your kids?" With a laugh, he walked over to Granny and picked her up to carry her out the mausoleum door.

Furball fell off her head as Granny was lifted from the ground. Granny reached inside her coat and grabbed her inside pocket. She still carried a small version of her knitting needle cane with her in case she ever found any crooks. She lifted the knitting needle and hit Silas in the arm, barely puncturing his heavy coat, but the movement surprised him and he dropped Granny.

"I'm not the enemy," yelled Silas. "We need to get out of here. Since all the shenanigans that have been going on in the cemetery, the police are checking it now every hour. You'd know this if you paid attention to what your son tells you."

"And why are you here?" Granny asked suspiciously.

"I saw you leave and was curious what you were doing. When I realized where you were going, I thought

I would follow; after all, my days have been too dull lately," Silas answered sarcastically.

Granny stood up and looked around, shining her flashlight and ignoring Silas now that she realized he wasn't a threat. "Which crypt do you think is mine?"

"You'll find out soon if we don't get out of here," Silas warned. "You'll have to hide in it to avoid the police."

The sound of a car pulling up outside by the snowmobile interrupted their conversation. Silas put his finger to his mouth to indicate that Granny should be quiet. He slowly moved over to the door of the mausoleum and silently closed it and clicked the locks.

"Now what, Mister you'll-find-out-soon-if–we-don't-get-out-of-here man?" Granny taunted. "My crypt should be empty now since the anonymous clothes-stealing stiff isn't in here. Ornery men before ladies," Granny quipped as she swept her arms toward the crypts in the wall.

Silas led Granny over to where the lift came up through the underground streets and in a whisper called to Granny's animals. Fish, Little White Poodle, Furball, Tank and Baskerville scurried to the lift and sat in a huddle as if they already knew the lift was going to move. Silas pulled himself and Granny onto the lift and punched in the Graves' Mortuary Code. Granny eyed him suspiciously as she was under the impression that she was the only other person besides Mr. Graves who had the code. The lift lowered into the underground street. Granny, Silas, and the shysters, plus Baskerville, stepped from the lift into the lighted street. Fuchsia kept the lights on at all hours in case the residents wanted to take a nighttime walk in the underground streets in the winter. It was 3:00 a.m. and this night Granny, Silas and the furry ones had lucked out. The streets were deserted.

"Now what? How are we going to get home?" Granny asked. "My door to the streets is locked."

Silas gave Granny a wicked grin, "No, it isn't. How do you think I got into the mausoleum?"

Before Granny could answer, Silas took her arm and led her down the street to her door. He opened the door and gestured for Granny and the furry ones to go first.

Granny gave Silas a shrewd look before entering the room under her house. "You broke into my house again?" Granny accused, pointing a finger at his chest.

"Not exactly," Silas answered, as he headed for the fireplace door.

"I'm calling Franklin. This harassment has got to stop," Granny yelled as she followed him through the door and up the steps.

She stopped when she encountered a sight at the top of the stairs. Mrs. Bleaty was waiting for them and, sitting on the top of her head, was Radish, the gray parrot from Silas's house.

"Bleat, unhand her; Bleat, unhand her," Radish squawked.

"What is she doing in my house and why are the only words she knows *unhand her*? Does she have to tell you to do that a lot?" Granny asked as she walked over, unlocked her front door and opened it, gesturing for Silas to leave.

Silas answered, "No; she knows the word *bleat* that your creature has taught her. That's why I was on my way over when I saw you on the snowmobile. I'll tell you what has to stop—this has to stop! Your animals have to stop being a bad influence on Radish. And—I'll leave the way I came." Silas ordered Baskerville, "Baskerville, howl!"

Baskerville sat by his pet door and let out a howl. The door popped open. The long window by the side of the door had been turned into a pet door because

Granny's original pet door was not large enough for Baskerville. It had been set to open when he howled.

Silas walked over, grabbed Radish, and squeezed through the pet door, having to turn his body sideways, which was the only way he could fit through, but not before he winked at Granny.

CHAPTER TEN

Granny woke the next morning to the loud noise of someone yelling and pounding somewhere in her neighborhood. It was so loud she could hear it with her windows and doors closed. She slowly opened one eye and glanced at the window over her bed. Daylight was peeking through the shades. She opened the other eye and didn't bother checking the color of her big toe. It was winter and it was cold. She could feel the cold air piercing through her blankets. Was her heat not working?

Granny threw back her blankets and slowly sat up. She hoisted her feet over the bed and checked to see what she was wearing. At times, she surprised herself when she woke up in the morning, not remembering which of her Red Hot Momma's purchases she had put on the night before.

Yup, she still had on the red velvet PJs that she had kept on before her nightly scamp into the cemetery. It was a good thing that Silas didn't know what she had on under her coat. *Why was it so cold in here?*

The pounding and yelling continued. Granny grabbed the bedpost to steady herself and put on her feathered slippers before she shuffled down the hallway to see where the cold air was coming from. When Granny got out to her living room, she saw that Baskerville's pet door was standing open. It was standing open because there was a small evergreen tree lying on the ground outside which was stuck in the door. Baskerville was inside trying to pull the evergreen tree through the door into Granny's house. Mrs. Bleaty was on the other side of the door, head butting the tree, trying to get it into the house. Fish, Little White Poodle, Furball and Tank were all sitting on the edge of the couch, watching as the two critters tried to get the tree through the door.

"Where did you get that tree? Take it back," Granny ordered as she tried to move Baskerville so she could push the tree back out the pet door. "This isn't my tree."

Baskerville took one look at Granny and planted his big body right on top of the tree and wouldn't move.

At that moment, Granny heard a loud yell followed by what sounded like Mavis shouting, "Someone call 911!"

Granny grabbed the coat that she had thrown off on the couch last night—or early this morning—being too tired to hang it in the closet. Stepping into her boots, Granny ran outside to find Mavis in front of her house across the street, still yelling, "Call 911! Call 911!"

George lay in the snow-covered bushes by the house, floundering, trying to get out of the bushes. A ladder lay in the snow by the bushes.

"Mavis," George said to her, "I'm ok, I'm ok."

Mavis still continued to yell, "Call 911! Call 911!" and so she couldn't hear what George was saying to her while she was yelling and jumping up and down excitedly in the snow.

Granny, seeing that George was okay and that Mavis out of control, reached down to the ground with her bare, no-gloved hands and picked up some snow. She walked over to Mavis and dumped the snow on her head. The shock of the snow immediately stopped Mavis's pleas for someone to call 911. By this time, George was out of the bushes. He grabbed Mavis and planted a kiss on her lips, which stopped her from continuing her frantic plea.

George turned to Granny, "Thank you, Granny. Mavis, you're in your reality show *Christmas Concoctions on the Roof.* Get a grip for your audience."

"What are you two doing with all the pounding?" Granny inquired.

"We're putting up Christmas lights and making a DIY video for our new video channel on FuchsiaStrobe.com. And...we are demonstrating how to attach a Christmas tree to the roof of your house for decoration." George looked around. "Where did our Christmas tree go?"

Granny rolled her eyes. "I think it's attached to Baskerville's door on my house." Granny indicated with a nod of her head the door across the street.

"Maybe you should go get the tree, George," Mavis advised as she noticed two cars driving toward them.

"What do they want now so early in the morning?" Granny moaned. "A woman can't even have her coffee and donuts without interruption."

"Uh, Granny, it's not early," Mavis said, pointing to the watch on her wrist.

Granny peeked at the watch. "One o'clock p.m.; I just got up!"

Mavis put her hand on Granny's forehead. "Are you feeling okay? You never sleep this late."

Granny didn't want to admit to what she'd been doing last night. "Now that you mention it, maybe I do feel a little feverish," Granny said as she watched the cars pulling up to the curb. "If they're coming to see me, tell them I had to go home and lie down and I don't want to be disturbed."

Granny sprinted across the snowy street and back into her house. George followed to get the evergreen tree, leaving Mavis to talk to Thor and Franklin, the occupants of the two cars.

Once back in her house, Granny locked the door and headed for her bedroom. The shysters headed out their pet door, meeting Franklin and Thor on the sidewalk, barking and meowing a welcoming, but continuing on their way to whatever mischief they were plotting in their shyster minds.

Granny plodded to her bedroom and kicked off her snow boots, not caring that she had tracked snow all over the floor. *There were times when a quick getaway was more important than a clean floor*, she mused. She threw her coat on the bed and rummaged in her closet for her old undercover Granny clothes. She knew Thor and Franklin were here for a reason—maybe reverting back to her undercover Granny clothes would throw them off whatever reason they were here for. As Granny was donning her polyester skirt and her granny blouse, she heard the click of the lock on the door. Tying her red sparkly high top tennis shoes, she remembered that both Franklin and Thor had a key.

Granny heard plates rattle in the kitchen. She heard the sound of the coffee maker, gurgling as it made coffee. She hadn't had any today since she'd gotten up so late, and the grinding of coffee beans and the gurgle of the coffee pot made her stomach roll with longing for the velvety smoothness of the liquid going down her throat. The aroma of the coffee led her down the hallway. Thor and Franklin were sitting at the table with a plate of donuts in the center and coffee cups set for three at the table.

Suspiciously, Granny made her way into the kitchen and eyed her self-invited guests. This was something new. They didn't like her eating donuts—something about it being bad for her health—and now here they were, ready to feed her donuts.

Franklin got up and held out a chair, indicating Granny should sit down. Tiredness from being out all night kept Granny from bristling and thinking of a snappy comeback. *Maybe my age is getting to me,* she thought as she sat down in the chair.

Franklin poured Granny a cup of coffee. "I thought I'd come over and pick you up, so that you and I can go over to the We Save You Christian Church and talk to Pastor Snicks about our wedding. After all, it is coming up soon. I talked to him this morning and he's available."

Granny took a sip of coffee before she answered. "I've been neglecting you, haven't I, Franklin? You're right, we need to do that." Glancing at Thor, Granny stood up. "I'll get my coat from the bedroom. We can leave now. Thor, you can let yourself out."

Thor got up and led his mother back to her chair. "Have a donut first, Mom; we have some things to discuss," he announced, sharing a look with Franklin.

"You want to discuss our wedding, our double wedding. Sure, what do you want to discuss?" Granny asked her son with a wide-eyed innocent look.

"Where were you last night, Mom, between the hours of midnight and 4:00 a.m.?"

"Where do you think I was? Most people are in bed."

Thor got up from the table, walked to the front door, opened it, stepped out onto the porch and came back in carrying Granny's pink shovel.

"You're bringing me my shovel off the front porch?"

"No, I'm bringing you the shovel that we found in the locked mausoleum in the cemetery—and your snowmobile—which is now sitting in the back yard. I put the cover on it for you."

"Someone stole my shovel and my snowmobile? Who would do something like that?" Granny innocently asked her son.

"And the prints in the snow we found by dad's grave match your purple boots." Thor walked to Granny's bedroom and came out with Granny's purple boots.

Granny looked at Franklin who said, "Hermiony, your skills are getting a little rusty." Franklin sealed his comment with a wink to take the sting out of the words that he knew would raise Granny's ire.

Granny stood up and took a bite of donut with a swig of coffee before replying with a glint in her eye. "Rusty are those old hinges on the mausoleum door. Rusty is an anchor at the bottom of the sea. Rusty is Rin Tin Tin's owner. Hinges open doors, anchors hold a ship steady and Rusty and Rin Tin Tin took care of each other. I am rusty, rusty and trusty—not dusty. I am the hinge of our family. I am the anchor when you are all sinking and I and my furry friends make it all work. If someone is going to stuff themselves in my crypt that I didn't even knew I had, and then end up a stiff in my backyard after stealing my husband's clothes, I'm going to make dang sure I'm not next."

Thor and Franklin exchanged looks. "You visited dad's grave and saw that we were going to exhume it to make sure that it's him in the grave, since his clothes ended up somewhere else."

"Well, you two hotshots wouldn't let me anywhere near it, and I needed to find out if he was still there— and where someone planned for me to end up too!"

"Did you notice the dead body we found this morning under the warming blanket on Dad's grave? Were you alone in the cemetery?" Thor asked in a tired tone.

"Dead body? What are you talking about?"

"They found a dead body under the warming blanket this morning when they went to exhume the body. He had been hit with a shovel."

"My shovel?" Granny said with an alarmed tone.

"No, your shovel was found locked in the mausoleum and doesn't match the marks on the body."

"You keep saying body. Whose body?" Granny asked.

"We can't tell you yet, Hermiony. We have to notify the family," Franklin answered for Thor.

Franklin turned to Thor. "She and I are going to be late for our appointment with Pastor Snicks at three. I know you still need to question her. We'll meet you at Rack's Restaurant at five, unless you want us to meet you at the police station?"

Thor stood up. "I'll meet you at Rack's. I need to bring in another detective. You and I are too close to this situation. I'll make some phone calls and see you there."

Thor kissed his mom on the cheek and said to Franklin as he walked out the door, "Keep her out of trouble."

CHAPTER ELEVEN

Pastor Hester Snicks stood up from behind his desk at the We Save You Christian Church and extended a hand to Franklin. "Franklin, good to see you." He turned to Granny. "How is my collection plate keeper, Granny?" referring to the fact that before Tricky Travis Trawler had ended up in jail, Granny had made it her mission each Sunday to stop him from pilfering from the collection plate.

Granny acknowledged Pastor Snicks' words with a smile. "Kind of miss the old pilferer; made church a little more exciting, if you know what I mean," Granny answered with raised eyebrows, giving the impression that occasionally Pastor Snicks' sermons were a little on the boring side.

Pastor Snicks was on a preaching rotation at We Save You Christian Church. We Save You was the only church in town, so each Sunday was a surprise as to what denomination would be holding the service on that particular day. If you went to We Save You Christian Church, you might find yourself at a Lutheran, Catholic, Methodist, Baptist, or a non-denominational service. The pastors and priests didn't post the schedule; it was always a surprise, and that seemed to be the way the people of Fuchsia liked it because the church was always full.

Granny, Franklin, Heather and Thor chose Pastor Snicks for their wedding ceremonies as he was there when the proposals happened, and he seemed to be able to read Granny very well, something that occasionally made Granny uncomfortable. He always made her feel like she had to confess something even when she didn't have anything to confess. At times, she thought she should confess something when Pastor Snicks gave her that certain look.

Looking at his calendar, the pastor confirmed, "December 26 at 2:00 p.m., Franklin Jester Gatsby and Hermiony Vidalia Criony Fiddlestadt are going to be married in a double ceremony along with Thor Ferdinand Fiddlestadt and Heather Angelique Gatsby Farr. Is that correct?" he asked, raising his glance to Granny and Franklin.

"Well, not exactly," Granny informed him.

Pastor Snicks gave her a questioning look.

Franklin explained, "We thought it would be nice if we each had our own ceremony. Thor and Heather will get married first with their own vows, music, and things that they want at their wedding. When they've said their 'I do's' to each other and walked back down the aisle, then our wedding would start. So basically, it would be two weddings."

"Uh huh." Pastor Snicks nodded his head. "This will be a first for me, but I guess we can do it that way. In any case, let's start planning the ceremony. How many people will be in your wedding party?"

"Angelique, our granddaughter; the shysters; Baskerville; and Mrs. Bleaty," Granny answered, counting off the numbers on her fingers. "That makes five plus."

"Uh huh, I...ah..meant people—not animals," Pastor Snicks mumbled.

Franklin tried to clear up the Pastor's confusion and ward off any roadblocks for the wedding. "Pastor, Hermiony has three children, I have two daughters, and we decided we didn't want to play favorites. Hermiony has two other grandchildren who are grown. They will be in Thor and Heather's ceremony. Of course, we want to include Angel in our wedding because she's the youngest and is a lot like Hermiony, but the animals are our family, too. They are what brought us together." He took the time to wink at Granny. "Is there a problem with that?" he asked as he gave a stern look at the Pastor.

"No, of course, not, um...it's just a rather unusual request. Should we continue? Do you have any special hymns or songs picked out?"

"How about *Wild Thing*? You know the song that was sung by the Trogs?" Granny asked as she turned to Franklin and belted out a verse of the song.

Franklin leaned back into a hearty laugh. "How about *I Got You Babe* by Sonny and Cher?" He turned to Granny and sang a part of that song off key.

"Okay, okay; I think perhaps I will have our music director call you to discuss some appropriate choices," Pastor Snicks said as he broke up Franklin's rendition of the Sonny and Cher song. Let's move on to the vows. Will you write your own?"

"Yes," Franklin answered.

"I have to think about it," said Granny.

Franklin turned to Granny with a puzzled look on his face. "What do you mean you have to think about it?"

"I want to keep you guessing. It will be a surprise." Granny countered back.

"Moving on," Pastor Snicks interjected before Franklin could answer. "Will you be having the reception in the church basement? If so, we'll put it on the calendar."

"No, the reception will be at Rack's Restaurant," Franklin answered.

"You are mistaken, Franklin," Granny informed him. "The reception will be at the Pink Percolator."

Pastor Snicks, sensing things might be getting a tad out of control, changed the subject. "Granny, I hear there has been a little excitement in your neighborhood. It must have been devastating for you to find a body wearing your dead husband's clothes. If you need to talk about it, feel free to call me, day or night."

Granny was about to answer when Franklin stood up abruptly with a suspicious look in his eye. "I think we have it all down now, Pastor Snicks. How is your wife, by the way?"

"Franklin, you've been here almost a year now," said Granny. "Pastor Snicks isn't married."

"Pardon me, Pastor Snicks." Franklin took Granny's arm to lead her out the door and, turning to Pastor Snicks, he said, "I will take night duty if needed. We don't want to interrupt your evenings."

"Franklin, that was rude," Granny chastised him.

"That coming from a woman who told Father John he would look more like a priest if he shaved his head," Franklin reminded Granny.

"Let's go meet Thor and see if he has any news for us." Granny hustled into the car for the short drive to Rack's Restaurant.

Franklin pulled into the lot at Rack's, parking under the weird weeping willow tree. It was safe to park under it in the winter. It was only in the summer that the tree would weep at night and darkness descended, trapping anything underneath it until morning.

Thor and Heather were waiting for Franklin and Granny. They had secured a spot at Granny's favorite booth in the back of the restaurant. During her undercover days, Granny had claimed this booth as her own so she could keep an eye on the occupants of the restaurant in case there was any hanky-panky going on.

"We've ordered for all of us," Heather informed the two. "We know what you both love so we took the liberty."

Granny sighed. When she wasn't with her kids, she ordered deep-fried chicken, mashed potatoes and gravy, deep-fried onion rings, and topped it all off with a hot fudge sundae with a chocolate donut on top. Her kids always ordered her a healthy meal—usually broiled walleye, some kind of a vegetable, and some fruit. Some things never changed.

After Franklin and Granny got comfortable in the booth and were sipping their coffee, Thor pulled out a picture. "Do you know this person, Mom?"

Granny looked at the picture that Thor had set in front of her. She brought the picture closer to her face and looked at it with squinty eyes. "He looks vaguely familiar. Do you know him, Franklin?"

Franklin shook his head. "Can't say that I do. Who is he?"

"He's the body under the warming blanket in the cemetery on Dad's grave," Thor informed them. "And there's something else you need to know. Someone was trying to dig up the grave while the ground was warm before we got back to it today. It must have happened this morning—early this morning."

"You think this stiff was trying to dig up your dad's grave? But why?" Granny asked in a puzzled voice.

"No, we think he surprised someone else who was trying to dig up the grave early this morning right before dawn. That's when the coroner put the time of death," Thor explained.

Before Granny had a chance to respond, a shadow towered over her. She looked up and fainted dead away.

CHAPTER TWELVE

The bright light blinded Granny for a moment. This time she knew she wasn't at the big concert in the sky; she was in the emergency room again. She looked into the eyes of Dr. Dreamboat, the same doctor who had treated her the day she collapsed when she was awarded the key to the City of Fuchsia.

"I'm in heaven, aren't I? And you are the angel sent to kiss me to wake me up," Hermiony said in her weak Granny voice. She looked into Dr. Dreamboat's eyes as he was examining her.

"You appear to be fine, Granny. Can you tell me what happened right before you fainted?" Dr. Dreamboat inquired.

"I got scared my memory was really failing me this time. I looked up and saw someone who looked like the Big Guy, only younger, like the Big Guy might have looked twenty years ago and he was staring straight at me. That's all I remember until I looked into your eyes." Granny looked up even higher to see the eyes of Thor, Heather and Franklin fixed firmly on the ground.

"What? What?" she said.

"Let's get you home," Franklin informed Granny, "and then Thor will explain. It's getting late. Rack's is going to send our meals to your house. Mavis said she would go over and put them in the oven to keep them warm. Thor told her where to find a key."

"I left Angel with Mavis. I'll pick her up and take her home while all of you chat," Heather said, picking up Granny's coat and helping her put it on. "Thor and I will meet you there."

As they came out of the Fuchsia hospital, Granny noticed that all the Christmas lights were lit. The trees on the tops of the buildings were taking their turns playing Christmas songs. The reindeer and snowmen glided along on their wires from post to post and up and down the posts. The manger scene in the center of town glowed with warmth, giving off a radiance into the cold winter night.

"Look Franklin, isn't it beautiful? How can all these things be happening in our little town during the best holiday of the year?"

Franklin gave Granny a skeptical look. It wasn't like her to be so mellow, especially with all that was happening. Maybe the Christmas season truly had the effect of peace and calm on even the most skeptical people.

His thoughts about Hermiony mellowing out lasted until they drove down the street to her house. He had barely stopped the car when Granny's feet hit the ground, and she hurried up the walk to her house. Grabbing the ladder that was perched against her house, she started to rattle it. The man at the top of the ladder grabbed hold of the roof and the eaves to steady himself to keep from falling.

Franklin caught up to Granny just as she was going to shake the ladder again and moved her away from the ladder, keeping a firm arm around her. The man on the ladder climbed down to confront Granny.

Granny pulled herself out of Franklins grasp. "Find Thor, Franklin; have him arrest this man."

"Arrest me for what?" Silas Crickett raged back at Granny.

"For trying to knock down my house with a hammer."

"I was putting up Christmas decorations," Silas sputtered.

"On my house?" Granny sputtered back.

"What's the matter with you? Don't you have any Christmas spirit? Don't you even have a tree? Well, Ms. Bah Humbug, your neighbors were just trying to do you a favor. I told 'em that doing anything nice for someone as cantankerous as you was a waste of time." Silas threw the hammer on the ground and stomped off, just as Franklin stepped forward with a threatening look on his face ready to stop the tirade.

Mavis came running out of Granny's house, followed by George and Angel. "Granny, Franklin, stop! Silas is in my reality show and we're taping."

Granny was ready to let out another yell to Silas, but seeing Angel out of the corner of her eye, she stepped back and took a breath.

"Hi, Granny. We put your tree up. I got to put on all the glass bulbs. I was really careful. Little White Poodle tried to eat the ornament that looks like a bone. Do you think Santa will stop here?"

Silas heard Angel's question from out in the street and yelled back, answering Angel before Granny could, "Not if he knows what's good for him!"

Angel asked in concern, "You wouldn't do anything bad to Santa would you, Granny?"

Granny bent down to Angel's height and looked in her eyes. "No, Angel, we wouldn't do anything to Santa.

Heather arrived with Thor and stepped forward. Sizing up the situation, she held out her hand to Angel. "It's time to go home, Angel; it's almost your bedtime. I'll run in the house and pick up my dinner out of the oven and take it home with me."

"We'll help you," Mavis offered, anxious that she and George be able to stay and hear what was going on.

If they were already in the house, maybe they could scoop the action for their pretend reality television show.

Granny watched as the four of them stepped into the house. She turned to Thor. "Aren't you going home with Heather? Franklin can fill me in on my scare at the restaurant."

"No, I'll stay and fill you in, and give you the latest update. We can eat together. You might need to get out your wine for us for this one," Thor informed his mother.

As they were talking, Franklin was staring thoughtfully across the street at Silas Crickett's house. "What do you know about him, Thor? He seems to have taken a dislike to your mother."

"And I to him," Granny countered back.

"That's all part of what I have to tell you," Thor said and walked over, kissed Heather, and hugged Angel as they came out of Granny's house.

"Good luck," Heather said to Thor, giving him an anxious look.

Granny saw that Mavis had set the table for all of them—herself and George included. *It's good Mavis is here,* thought Granny. Mavis had helped Granny out in the past, and she had turned out to be a pretty good sidekick when Granny needed a little help throwing her family off the track of her investigations.

Granny opened her mouth to ask a question, but both Thor and Franklin held up their hands at the same time. "We eat first, then we talk," Thor instructed his mother, "We don't need another distraction."

Granny sat back in her chair. "Well, I was going to ask if anyone had seen the shysters, Baskerville, and Mrs. Bleaty."

"Mrs. Bleaty is on your bed resting," Mavis informed Granny. "Don't know where the others are.

Mrs. Bleaty seems to have a thing for that Radish creature across the street so she doesn't go far."

"I am concerned," Franklin added to the conversation. "They haven't been on their usual schedule lately. They're here when they're usually supposed to be at my house; they're at my house when they're supposed to be at your house, and they don't seem to be seen at their usual haunts around town."

The conversation continued until Thor put his fork down and wiped his mouth with his napkin. He checked to see if everyone was done eating. When he saw that they were, he decided it was as good a time as any to bring up the subject of what had made his mom faint at Rack's Restaurant.

Granny watched Thor closely. When she saw the fork go down and the napkin touch his mouth, she started in, "Was I seeing things? That man looked just like the Big Guy," referring to the former Chief of Police and Chief Detective in the Fuchsia Police Department. "Come to think of it, the apparition *was* a little bit different—he was skinnier and younger, but the face was almost the same. Was I seeing things?"

Mavis and George seemed to hold their breath waiting for Thor to answer.

"Maybe I should get you a glass of wine," Thor said to his mother, getting up from the table.

"Dining and wining me is not going to get you off the hook. Spill it," Granny said, standing up and walking around the table to confront Thor.

"He's the new detective I brought in on the case to help solve this ghoulish crime. He's uh," Thor gave a little cough looking to Franklin for support, "he's, uh—the Big Guy's younger brother." Thor stepped back waiting for Granny's reaction.

Mavis jumped up so fast that her chair tipped over as she anticipated Granny's reaction. "One Stricknine wasn't enough? He has a brother?"

"His name is Ephraim Cornelius Stricknine, and there's more you're not going to like," Thor warned, looking at his mother.

"So Cornelius Ephraim Stricknine has a brother named Ephraim Cornelius Stricknine?" Franklin asked, thinking he hadn't heard correctly.

"Right; apparently their mother liked the name so much she just switched the first name and the middle name when she had her last son."

"And you hired him to help you? How do you know you can trust him?" Granny barked at Thor.

"He comes highly recommended; there's nothing in his background to indicate he might have the same problems as his brother did, and he was coming to town anyway to visit his father. Both boys followed in their father's footsteps by becoming detectives."

By now, everyone was up from the table. Granny moved into the living room and walked over to her footstool, removed the fake bottom and pulled out her bottle of wine. "Since you all know about my wine stash, do you want some?" Turning to Thor she asked, "Am I going to need this?"

Thor walked over and took the bottle of wine away from Granny. He handed the bottle to Mavis. "Why don't you pour her a glass?"

"Oh," Granny said, sitting down on the couch. "Get on with it. Since you're trying to get me drunk with wine, this must be really bad. Will I need another weapon when I go out?"

Franklin laughed; he'd been getting worried that Granny's fainting had knocked the stuffing out of her, but now her feistiness was coming back. He looked closely at Hermiony. Or—was she was putting on her helpless act? He really would have to pay more attention so he could read her better after they were married to keep her out of trouble.

"Let's start with Ephraim Cornelius's father," Granny suggested. "What's his name? What's his name? Do I know him?"

They all looked at Thor eagerly. Thor turned to examine a spot on the wall near the door. They heard him answer but couldn't quite make out what he said.

"We can't hear you!" Granny yelled, trying to get the point across.

Thor turned and cleared his throat. "The brothers' father's name is Silas Crickett."

Granny jumped up. "Silas Crickett? My Silas Crickett? The cantankerous, old coot across the street?"

Franklin gave Granny a strange look when he heard the words *my Silas Crickett* come out of her mouth.

"Granny, don't say that 'bout Silas; he's so nice and such a gentleman." Mavis sighed.

George gave Mavis a hard look, and then lifted his eyebrows and caught Franklin's eye.

"How can that be?" Granny railed. "He has a different last name. You told me he owned his own snowmobile shop in Alaska, that he was working for Runner's Skids and Ski's."

"Silas explained it to me earlier today when I visited with him and Ephraim," Thor answered. "Silas was a high level detective up in Alaska. Things in Alaska when he worked the streets were pretty raw, and he wanted to protect his wife and children. So his wife kept her last name, and when their kids were born, they took her last name. It was their way of protecting their children and their family—which were kept very separate from Silas's professional life. Even his co-workers had no idea he was married and had kids. Unfortunately, Silas got shot one night while working a case and was held hostage. Before he was rescued, and while still with his kidnappers, he became delirious and started talking about his family. The kidnappers got away during the police rescue, but not before they got the names of Silas's wife and kids."

Thor paused and the others were silent waiting for him to finish his story. "Unfortunately, when Silas was rescued by the police, he was unconscious, and the police had no idea he had a family. By the time Silas came to in the hospital and vaguely remembered his delirium, it was too late for his wife. They found her the next day in their home. She had been shot. Luckily, the kids were out of state visiting her parents at the time or they would have been killed, too. To make this long story short, Silas vowed he would bring this case to an end and he did. He found his kidnappers and his wife's murderer. He left his kids to live with his wife's parents for their safety and went back into his life as a detective with very few people knowing he still had a family somewhere. When the kids were of age, they reconnected and the boys took on the same career as their father in law enforcement. Apparently, Silas did own his own business, but it was a business he used as an undercover front, and he still works at Runner's Skids and Ski's, helping them out when needed."

The silence in the room was deafening. Even Granny couldn't think of anything to say. She took her glass of wine and downed it in one gulp. The others, still in shock at the story, retrieved more wine glasses and poured themselves glasses of wine, giving them all a moment to digest what they had just heard.

"I'm afraid there's even more we have to deal with tonight," Thor informed the group.

"More? More? What could possibly top that?" Granny said in an exasperated tone.

"Why don't we all sit down, take a powder, and calm down," Franklin suggested, leading Mavis and George over to the sofa in hopes that Granny would follow and plop down in her chair.

Granny remained standing.

"We need to talk about the reason I had to bring in another detective," Thor explained.

"You already told us," Granny reminded him, "You're too close to the case of the stiff that landed in my back yard dead in your father's clothes. You would have thought the ghost wearing Ferdinand's clothes would have warned me since it's Christmas. Do you suppose he's trying to be the ghost of Christmas past?"

Thor felt better continuing with what he had to say as Granny started getting back to her crabby old self.

"Well, the tests came back on the body in your back yard. It was Delbert Delure—Delight Delure's husband."

Granny's eyes got wide and she sat down with a plop in her easy chair. Mavis had a look of horror on her face while George gulped down his wine at the news.

"Have you talked to Delight about the days surrounding Delbert's death?" Franklin asked Thor, his detective personality kicking in—retired or not.

"We have and we're going to talk to her again," Thor answered.

"How did he get Ferdinand's clothes? I didn't know Delight back then. I still lived on the farm and I didn't get to town much. When did Delbert die?" Still in shock over the news, Granny rattled off her questions.

"He died the same week we buried Dad."

"Did you exhume Ferdinand's grave today?" Franklin continued with the questions.

"No, we were too busy trying to figure out how the body got under the warming blanket, trying to track down who was in the cemetery last night." Thor gave his mother a steely look. "and we didn't want to disturb the crime scene."

Granny stood up. "Is there anything more or can this old woman go to bed? It's late and it's time for all of you to go."

"One more thing." Thor held out the picture he had shown Granny earlier at the restaurant. "Does anyone recognize this man?" One by one, they shook their heads, except for Granny. She was staring intently at the photo.

"I've seen him somewhere before."

All eyes were now on Granny.

"Maybe he just looks familiar," Mavis suggested, "We've never seen him around here before."

"Go home, all of you," Granny instructed. "Franklin, we need to figure out where our menagerie is going and what they're doing. They could be getting in trouble. Tomorrow, we track them." Granny walked to the door, opened it and gestured that they should all leave. "It's been nice, but let's not do this again," Granny told them as they all left her house. Closing the door, Granny turned out the lights, walked back to her bedroom, opened her secret cabinet, pulled out her chocolates, turned to Mrs. Bleaty who was still lounging on the bed and said, "Move over. You bleat, I'll eat, and tomorrow we'll solve this crime easy and sweet."

CHAPTER THIRTEEN

Pastor Snicks was waiting for Franklin to put the ring on Granny's finger before he pronounced the couple man and wife. Granny looked down at the ring that Franklin was putting on her finger, then looked up––straight into the face of Silas Crickett. Granny woke with a start out of her dream. She sat up in bed and looked at the clock on the cell phone sitting by her bed––5:00 a.m.

Granny laid her head back down on her pillow and snuggled into her warm bed. It had been a long time since she'd had a nightmare, and what other way could she classify the dream that had just rocked her out of a deep sleep, except to say it was a nightmare? Why else would she dream about Silas?

She let her mind wander as she tried to get back to sleep, the image of the face on the picture Franklin had shown her last night drifting through her head. Closing her eyes, the face came to her again under the darkness of her eyelids. It was the face of the man she'd caught watching her and taking her picture earlier in the year when she'd gone to Allure, Minnesota, to replace her cell phone. She had even told the young whippersnapper clerk in the store to call the police, but he hadn't seemed too concerned—and then he had called the police on Granny!

Granny sat up and grabbed her cell phone. She shouted the word *Mavis* into her phone. The phone started dialing Mavis's number. Granny heard the phone pick up. "Mavis, are you there? Mavis?"

"Wha..? Ya, just a minute. Who is this?" Mavis sleepily muttered into the phone.

"Mavis, I know who that dead body was in the cemetery!"

"Uh huh, I...ah...know there was a dead body in the cemetery. Now go back to sleep until at least 6:00, Granny." Mavis hung up the phone.

"Mavis, don't you hang up. Get up!" Granny looked at the phone. The connection said *terminated*.

Granny tossed the phone on the bed. Mrs. Bleaty was no longer there. Granny picked the phone back up, trying to decide if she should call someone else. It wasn't even light out yet. In Minnesota, in the winter, it got dark earlier, and light later in the morning. Granny thought about Delight and wondered how she was coping with the news that the stiff in Granny's back yard was her husband. Granny decided to find out. Throwing the covers to the bottom of the bed, and swinging her legs over the side, she grabbed the bedpost to keep herself steady as she stood up, while noticing that sometime during the night, Mrs. Bleaty had moved from the bed to the floor and was now snoring soundly.

Waking herself up with a quick shower that melted the cobwebs out of her eyes, she dressed in her old Granny garb, putting the bad dream about Silas out of her head. Granny looked down at what she was wearing and decided before she headed home she would stop at AbStract and see if she could find a new more stylish wardrobe that fit her personality, since she didn't have to wear her polyester undercover clothes anymore. She decided to use the underground streets instead of the snowmobile to get to town. Slipping into her red sparkly hightops, she tied the laces. The streets and sidewalks had been plowed so it would be easy to get from one store to the other above ground once she got downtown. She would use the lift at Graves' Funeral Home.

Pulling on her coat, Granny picked up her pocketbook and, for good measure, decided to take her pink snow shovel cane too. It just might come in handy if she had to snow a snatcher.

There were no animals in sight. Maybe they were at Franklin's where they usually were at this time of day. Granny peeked out the front window to see if all was quiet. It was as good a time as any to leave the house before she had to deal with the supercilious Silas. What a good word! That's what she was going to call him— supercilious! With a smile, Granny tromped down the basement stairs and exited her house into the underground streets.

Since it was so early in the morning, the streets were deserted. Granny made her way to the lift at Graves' Mortuary, and punched in her code. The lift moved quietly up to the main level, only making a noise when it finally jolted to a stop. Granny was caught off guard by the darkness of the store. Then she remembered, it was only 6:00 a.m. Graves' Mortuary was still closed and Gravy was probably tucked snug in his bed. Granny hoped she would be able to unlock the door from the inside and get out so she could walk down the street to the Pink Percolator.

Granny made her way through the darkness of the mortuary to the front door. The Christmas lights of downtown Fuchsia shone through the window, illuminating her path. She extended her arm to try to turn the lock on the store's front door, when a voice came out of the darkness, "Is someone there? I hear you breathing."

Granny scowled. There was no way anyone could hear her breathing. "Stop or I'll shang you with this shovel!" Granny warned the voice.

"What does *shang* mean? There's no such word as *shang*." The lights turned on, flooding the room.

"Mother Fiddlestadt! What are you doing here?" exclaimed the voice.

Mother Fiddlestadt? Only one person called her that. "Butch, what are you doing in Graves' Mortuary?"

"Didn't I just ask you that question?" her son-in-law Butch countered back.

"I'm supposed to be here. I have the code," Granny challenged.

"I'm supposed to be here, too. I have the key." Butch held up the key in his hand.

"Why do you have the key?" Granny asked suspiciously.

"Because I used to work for Mr. Graves when I was in high school and since Penelope and I are moving back, I'm going to help him out from time to time. Penelope can handle the hardware store while I'm gone for a little while. Mr. Graves asked me to move some caskets around this morning in the casket room. They are getting too much for him. I wanted to do it before I opened the hardware store. Your turn."

"I wanted to go to the Pink Percolator for coffee and I didn't want to use my snowmobile. I took a shortcut through the funeral home."

Butch sighed. "It's a good thing I caught you before you turned that lock and opened the door or you'd have had the entire Fuchsia Police Department here. You would have heard a *ding, ding, ding* and it wouldn't have been in your head. Mr. Graves installed an alarm system yesterday after someone robbed your grave."

"It's not my grave! I'm—not dead! So it's not my grave!"

Butch walked over, turned off the alarm, and opened the door for Granny. "And I won't tell your daughter that you're roaming around in a funeral home at 6:00 a.m. You're welcome."

Granny turned to say something to Butch before exiting the building, thought better of it, and walked out into the cold.

Butch closed the door, reset the alarm, and shook his head, no doubt thinking about the strange family he was a part of.

Delight was turning on the Christmas lights inside of the Pink Percolator when Granny entered the coffee house. The aroma of fresh baked goods and roasted coffee filled the air. When Delight turned and saw Granny, she rushed over, threw her arms around the petite woman, and started sobbing.

"Oh, Granny, I'm so sorry that Delbert stole your husband's clothes! I know he didn't do it on purpose. He was a good man."

Granny patted Delight on the back while extricating herself from Delight's tight grip. She held Delight at arm's length and looked her straight in the eye. "Delight, he was dead; he didn't do it on purpose," she said, trying to help Delight get a grip on her grief.

Delight looked back into Granny's eyes, gave a final sniff, wiped her eyes, and stepped back out of Granny's grasp. "You're right. Delbert has been gone a long time. How this did happen and how did Delbert get in your grave? They don't seem to know."

"Again, I'm not dead so it *isn't* my grave or my crypt and I don't know anything about it," Granny explained in exasperation. "What we need to do is figure this out."

"I'll get you some coffee and a donut." Delight moved toward the counter. "We can talk before I get busy, and the others come in to work."

Granny sat down near the window so she could see what was happening on the streets. She lay the snow shovel down on the ground underneath the table. Delight brought over the coffee and the donuts and sat down across from Granny.

Granny moved her gaze from the window to her coffee cup. She read the saying on the side of the cup out loud and laughed. "'Yesterday is gone, today is here; drink your coffee, not a beer.' Got something against beer, Delight?"

"No, but I was trying to think of something that rhymed with *here,* and *beer* was the only thing I could think of. I don't have your gift of rhyme, Granny."

"It's fine, Delight. I probably would have ended it like this, 'Yesterday is gone, today is here; drink your coffee, it'll help you look in the mirror.'"

"Oh, Granny, that's wonderful! I think I'll change my cups to that the next time I order them. Do you mind?"

Granny ignored Delight's cup comment enthusiasm and got down to the subject most on her mind. "When did your husband die, Delight, and what were the circumstances? I didn't know you then. Did you actually see him in the casket?"

"Well, according to your son, Thor, they died the same week and were buried on the same day. Your husband was buried in the morning and my husband was buried in the afternoon. We had a closed casket because I couldn't bear to look at him dead, so I never actually saw him after he died. Also I didn't want to upset Ella by having her look at her dead dad."

"How did he die?" Granny asked.

"He was on a business trip for his job and he stepped off the street right in front of a motorcycle. It was a fitting death because he always wanted to ride a motorcycle," Delight reminisced. "He was thrown up on the motorcycle behind the driver, and when the driver came to an abrupt stop, he was thrown into a nearby tree."

Granny nodded and patted Delight on the hand. "At least he died doing something he enjoyed."

"But now, they're saying that the new autopsy they conducted indicated that he was murdered," Delight reminded Granny, just as the door opened and Franklin hurried into the Pink Percolator and stood over Granny, interrupting their conversation.

"Have you seen the shysters, Granny? They didn't come to my house last night. Were they with you?"

Granny stood up. "No, I assumed they were on their nightly rounds and were with you. Where are they disappearing to these days?"

"We need to find them. Have you seen Baskerville? Do you suppose he's with the shysters? He doesn't always hang out with them," Franklin reminded Granny.

"Mrs. Bleaty was still snoring loudly on the floor of my bedroom when I left. We have to go to the police station first, Franklin. I know who the stiff under the warming blanket is."

Delight had been listening to the conversation while savoring her coffee and said: "They're exhuming Delbert's body today. I signed the papers yesterday. If you hear anything about the results of his autopsy while you're at the police station, let me know."

Granny bent over and pulled her shovel out from underneath the table. "Hang tight, Delight. We may have answers by tonight."

Delight could hear Franklin questioning Granny about the dead stiff as they exited the Pink Percolator. She smiled, as it was clear Granny wasn't goin' to tell what she knew until she got to the police station. The last words she heard Granny say to Franklin her cranky tone before the door closed were, "You and Thor are too close to the case. Remember your decision. I'll tell the Big Guy's doppelganger and only his doppelganger. You are not on a need-to-know basis."

CHAPTER FOURTEEN

Thor was standing by the front desk in the police station, chatting with another officer when Granny and Franklin entered. Seeing his mother, Thor nodded to the other officer, and met Granny before she could get any farther into the station.

"Mother, what brings you here today?"

"Are you the officer in charge of the Grave Robber Case?"

"I'm working on it, but the officer in charge is Ephraim. But you know that."

"Then there's no sense in asking me why I'm here. I'm here to talk to the officer in charge and that happens to be the Tall Guy."

Thor raised his eyebrows at the name. "The Tall Guy?"

"Well, he's the Big Guy's brother and I can't call him the Big Guy, so I have to call him the Tall Guy, because if I called him the Small Guy, it would be a big exaggeration since he's no wally-smally," Granny pointed out.

Thor looked at Franklin. Franklin shrugged his shoulders and shook his head.

"I'll tell him you're here and need to talk to him, but you need to leave the shovel out here." Thor took the shovel from Granny's hands and handed it to the desk sergeant before walking down the hallway, stopping to knock on a door farther down. Opening the door, he poked his head in and said something that Granny couldn't hear. Then Thor raised his hand and indicated that Granny and Franklin should come his way. When they reached the doorway, Thor ushered them into the room. Ephraim Cornelius Stricknine was sitting behind a desk. He looked up when they entered.

"What can I do for you, Granny? Your reputation precedes you."

"And ya better believe it, unless they're poisoning your mind with untrue tales," Granny answered, as she gave Thor a shrewd glance.

Ignoring the barb, Ephraim indicated they should sit down. "Have a chair and tell me why you needed to see me."

"I know the guy in the picture."

Before Ephraim Stricknine could get the question out himself, Thor asked, "You know him? How? And what's his name?"

"I don't know his name but I know him," Granny reiterated. "He's the guy who was following me when I went to Allure to get my new cell phone. He was taking pictures of me but that young pip in the cell phone store wouldn't take me seriously."

"Is that the same store where they had to call the police for you—something about you harassing the clerk?" Thor reminded his mother.

Granny frowned at Thor. "The guy was taking pictures of me. It was him," Granny insisted. "Tall Guy, you have to believe me!"

Ephraim laughed When Granny called him the Tall Guy. "My brother warned me about you. No matter his faults, he always had a soft spot for you, Granny, and he told me to watch out for you. Big Guy, Tall Guy. We would have made a great team if he hadn't gotten so greedy. He really liked being a detective and he thought that by doing detective work it would make up for his shady past. So, don't worry. I've got your back, Granny."

Granny flinched at those words. Then, she sat up taller and smiled at Franklin and Thor, as if to say *ah ha.* "Does that mean I can work for the merchants of Fuchsia again?" Granny asked with hope in her voice.

"NO!!" Franklin and Thor shouted at the same time.

The Tall Guy looked at both of them, and then said, "For the moment—no. But before we even think about that, let's solve this crime first. Thank you for coming, Granny." He gestured to the door, indicating the meeting was over.

Reaching the lobby of the police station first, Granny retrieved her shovel from the desk sergeant before Franklin or Thor could object. Leaning on it for support, she turned and said to the two men who had finally caught up with her, "That visit wore me out; I knew I needed my shovel cane for support before my wobbly legs let me down." Her voice seemed to weaken as she talked.

Franklin looked at Granny intently. He was never sure when she was using her Granny routine or when she actually was having a weak moment. He could have sworn it was all an act, but after hauling her to the ER twice in the last year from fainting spells, Franklin wasn't sure he could read the situation accurately.

"We have to go anyway. We have to find the shysters and Baskerville," Franklin reminded Granny.

Granny shuffled to the door with her shovel cane, "Where's your car, Franklin?"

Franklin held the door for Granny, both saying good bye to Thor.

"Let me know what's happening," Granny yelled back to Thor.

Franklin took Granny's arm and helped her into his car. "We should check my house first to see if they finally got there. Keep an eye out on the streets. I'll drive through the alley behind AbStract to see if they might be hanging out there."

Not finding the shysters or Baskerville in the alleys, park, or at Franklin's, they headed for Granny's house. Pulling up out front, Granny noticed Mrs. Bleaty, bleating in front of Silas Crickett's house. "That goat sure has got a thing for that bird Radish. We better get her home," Granny concluded.

Reaching Silas Crickett's door, Granny grabbed the collar she had put on Mrs. Bleaty so she could lead her around once in awhile when Mrs. Bleaty was being stubborn. Now was one of those times. As Franklin grabbed the collar gently to help her, they heard barking and a bird screeching and cats meowing from inside Silas Crickett's house.

"He's kidnapped the shysters and Baskerville! Mrs. Bleaty is trying to rescue them!" Granny started pounding on Silas's door. "Silas, I know you're in there and you're holding my furry ones hostage. Let me in!" Granny kept pounding.

Franklin, still holding on to Mrs. Bleaty, tried the knob on the door. Mavis and George, hearing the racket coming from their neighbor's house, came over to see what the noise was about. "Is something wrong with Silas?" Mavis asked in a concerned voice.

"He's dognapped and catnapped my animals," Granny answered.

"It's fine, Granny," said Mavis. "Silas loves your animals. In fact, he's made them a great place to play in his basement. He has cat ramps and agility courses for your dogs. And Radish loves them too."

Granny stopped pounding as she turned and looked at Mavis, "Have you lost your marbles? He's always complaining about them."

At that moment, the door opened and Silas Crickett stuck his head out the door, scowling at Granny and asked, "What in tarnation are you doing, woman? You're making enough racket to raise the dead." Seeing Mavis, his face crinkled into a big smile. "Mavis, George, how nice of you to visit. You, too, Franklin, come on in."

At the nice tone, Granny elbowed her way past Silas and inside his house. Not seeing her furry creatures, she turned to the basement steps.

"Silas, I don't like your tone when talking to Hermiony," Franklin warned, while still holding on to Mrs. Bleaty. Giving Silas a stern look, he joined the others in entering the house trying to catch up with Granny.

"Let Mrs. Bleaty go join the others, Franklin. She wasn't here when they came over. She wants to have fun with the others," Silas instructed.

Mavis followed Granny down the basement steps, trying to calm her. "See, Granny! Look what Silas has done for your furry ones."

Granny was speechless as she looked around Silas's basement at the scene in front of her. What had previously been Sally's basement, and the Hussy and The Big Guy's den of illegal activities, was now a large playground for animals. Silas had opened the door to the old tornado shelter and the hidden underground room connected to the tunnels that led to the lake, and had built catwalks, dog agility courses and swings for Silas's gray parrot, Radish. It was heated with the generators that had previously kept plants warm and alive.

Little White Poodle ran up and jumped at Granny's ankles. Fish wove in and out and around her feet. Furball jumped up into Franklin's arms as he and Mrs. Bleaty got to the bottom of the stairs, and Tank ran and snorted at his feet. Baskerville sat in the center of the room and let out a howl. When he howled, the trap door on a cage tethered to the ceiling opened just enough to let a few treats drop to the ground. When that happened, the shysters left Granny and Franklin and headed to the treats. Mrs. Bleaty, not wanting to be left out, gave a jerk and got free of Franklin's grasp. At the same time, Radish was nibbling on a radish while perched on a swing high up out of reach.

"Where's my shovel, Franklin? I have to snow shovel a sneak. He snatched my animals!"

"Can it, Granny," said Silas. "They love it here. I leave the door by the lake open so they can come and go as they please. The snow has melted enough that they can get in and out."

"I warned you, Silas," Franklin barked as he advanced on Silas, "You don't talk to my fiancé that way."

Silas took a step toward Franklin. At that moment, Granny yelled "Attack!" and pointed to Silas and Franklin. Baskerville jumped on Silas with the full force of his weight, knocking him down. Furball gave a leap and jumped on Franklin's head; Fish, Little White Poodle, and Tank launched their own attack, knocking Franklin off balance and, with a little help from a light head-butt from Mrs. Bleaty, Franklin fell to the floor. Radish, still sitting on his swing, started screeching, "Fight! Fight! Fight!"

Granny looked at the two men trying to extricate themselves from the animals and announced, "I'm going home. Good job, shysters and Baskerville. My training paid off. Silas, you cantankerous thieving old man, I'm reporting you to the Tall Guy and if that doesn't work, I'm taking you to the town council. Franklin, I can take care of myself."

Turning to the animals, she pointed to the stairs, "Home!" The shysters and Baskerville followed Granny up the steps. Mrs. Bleaty turned, let out a bleat, and ran up the stairs after Granny.

George walked over to Silas and extended a hand to help him up. Then he turned to Franklin and helped him up, too. "I think she's a little angry." Turning to Mavis, he added, "This would be a good script for our pretend reality TV show. 'Flipped Over The Older Woman.'"

"You're right; let's go, George."

Turning to the two men, George issued a stern warning, or as stern as George could get, "Behave."

Franklin and Silas were silent for a few minutes and then Franklin held out his hand to Silas. Silas pondered the gesture for a minute before holding out his hand to Franklin.

"She drives me crazy, Franklin," Silas Crickett explained to Franklin.

"I know," Franklin agreed, "That's why I love her."

CHAPTER FIFTEEN

Granny's stomach was rumbling as she opened the door to her house. Apparently, the shysters, Baskerville and Mrs. Bleaty had the same rumblings in their stomachs because they almost knocked Granny over entering the house in a rush for their food dishes.

Stepping into the kitchen, Granny opened the refrigerator and pulled out a steak for Baskerville and Mrs. Bleaty, figuring they deserved some sort of treat for coming home. Instead of the usual yogurt and vegetables that she usually fed to the shysters, Granny opened a can of tuna for Fish and Furball. Not wanting to leave Little White Poodle and Tank out of the treat fun, she opened a package of hot dogs and flipped them in the air to be caught by the excited dogs. Maybe they would want to come home if she fed them something dogilicious.

The doorbell rang and Granny listened to it play *Santa Got Run Over By A Reindeer. Who had changed her tune to THAT song?* Granny wondered as she headed for the door. Granny opened the door to Angel looking up at her with the beautiful blue eyes that Angel had inherited from her mother.

"Hi, Granny, this is for you." Angel plopped a present in Granny's arms before walking past Granny into the house and sitting down on the floor next to Baskerville.

"We heard from Dad that you had a rough morning," Heather informed Granny as she followed Angel into the house. We thought you might need some lunch."

Granny set the present down on the kitchen table and inhaled the fumes coming from the package.

"It's your favorite, Granny, but Mommy said we should keep this between us. Why? I wanted to tell Aunt Penelope when we met her at Rack's restaurant, but Mommy said we couldn't tell her because it was a surprise. Is it a surprise?"

Granny pulled away the paper revealing her favorite fried chicken, mashed potatoes and gravy, and deep-fried onion rings. "It is definitely a big surprise," Granny answered, sitting down to her favorite meal.

"I have another surprise," Heather announced, pulling out an insulated bag. Opening it, she set the contents on the table in front of Granny. A big smile lit up Granny's face as she saw the chocolate fudge ice cream with a chocolate donut on top.

Angel jumped up and down with excitement, "Surprise, surprise, surprise!"

Laughter filled the room as Heather, Angel and Granny laughed. Granny looked at Heather with a questioning look.

"Well, you are going to be my mother-in-law and my step-mother so I thought I better get on your good side," Heather joked.

"Do you have a bad side, Granny?" Angel asked with a puzzled expression.

The doorbell saved Granny from answering the question. "What is this, no rest for the good and who put that song on my doorbell?" Granny started to get up to answer the door, but Heather stopped her and ran to the door instead.

"Surprise—oh, Angel, why are you here?" Thor asked Heather as he stepped into the room with a carryout bag from Rack's restaurant with the same aroma as the box Angel had just given to Granny.

Thor stopped by the table. "Oh, what's that you're eating?"

"Ah, ah, my dinner?"

"Yah, and it's our secret, so you better not tell. We want Aunt Penelope to be surprised."

Thor walked over and hugged Angel. "She certainly would be surprised, especially if she knew what I brought Granny, too." He winked at Angel. Opening the bag, he took out fried chicken, mashed potatoes and gravy, deep-fried onion rings, and, in a Styrofoam container, chocolate fudge ice cream with a chocolate donut on top.

Granny looked at Thor suspiciously. "Am I ill? Is this my last meal and I don't know it?" Never in her late life could she remember any of her children feeding her anything but organic and wholesome food.

"I hear you've had a hard day." Thor shook his head as he spoke trying to have a sympathetic tone. "I hear you had another altercation with Silas."

"Where did you hear that? Franklin! He had to go and tell you. Did he tell you that despicable man stole my animals! Did he tell you that *he* and Silas almost got into a fight?" Granny was on a roll now. "Did he tell you that that he almost popped Silas? And you think I'm out of control. Did he tell you that Silas Crickett held my animals hostage and I had to rescue them? Did he? Did he? Did he?" Granny's voice got louder with each *did he*.

Angel walked over next to Granny and looked into Granny's face with a sweet little smile. "Are you talking about that nice man across the street? He promised to let me play with his bird someday if I come over. He said I could call him Grand because he's old and he's not my Grandpa, but he is *grand*."

Granny stood up quickly, then realized that she had to set an example for Angel. "Yes, sweetheart, I am talking about Mr. Old Grand. He has another name, but I think it's too long for you to say. It is *supercilious* but I think you should just stick to calling him Old Grand for now. I'm sure he would like that. Why don't you go play with the shysters and Baskerville. It looks like Mrs. Bleaty is going to my bedroom to take a nap."

"Ok, should I call you young Grand then?" Angel asked as she headed down the basement stairs followed by the shysters and Baskerville, not waiting for an answer.

"Grand! Grand! And now he's trying to steal my new granddaughter! Wait until I get ahold of him," Granny ranted. "You all might as well have some of this since you decided to feed me."

Thor and Heather joined Granny at the table. Thor was quiet for a few minutes, watching Granny intently.

"What? Why are you staring at me? Have you never seen me eat fried chicken before?"

Actually, I can't stay," said Thor. "I'm headed to the cemetery. They're about to open up Delbert Delight's grave. It will be interesting to find out if there's anything or anyone in there."

"I'll go with you," said Granny.

Heather broke into the conversation. "Actually, Granny, I thought you and I could visit Pastor Snicks. I've made an appointment so we can talk about the weddings. There are a few things that need to be coordinated between us. Then I thought we might do some Christmas shopping. It will be a good bonding time for us. I've made arrangements for Mavis to come over and watch Angel. They're going to work on the Christmas pageant for Christmas Eve."

Granny eyed both Heather and Thor. "You planned this. Butter me up and then go in for the kill."

"No, really, I had no idea what Thor was doing. He said he was going to be busy all day."

"The only reason I stopped in was to tell you that we know the name of the man who was found under the warming blanket on Dad's grave." Thor assured Granny.

"Well?" Granny prompted.

"Felix Smart."

"Why would this guy Felix Smart be taking pictures of me?"

"Perhaps because he's a private investigator?"

"Who would investigate me? I'm just a little old lady almost ready for the wrinkle farm. Do you think I did something I can't remember?" Granny asked in alarm.

"Did you?" Thor asked, studying Granny's face to see if she was pulling her I-am-a-feeble-old-lady act. He had a hard time telling, unlike his sisters who always believed that Granny was frail and helpless and needed taking care of. Maybe that was what daughters did. He didn't know.

Granny skewered him with a dirty look.

Thor let out a big sigh. "All we know at the moment is that he was a private investigator and he rented Neil Nail's house from Neil. Since Neil is no longer able to live in his house, he decided to rent it out. We're doing some checking. I've got to go and see what they're finding out in the cemetery."

"Isn't the Tall Guy in charge now?" Granny reminded him.

"Yes, but I'm working the case with him." Thor walked out the door, calling back to Heather, "Good luck, this afternoon! Don't bond too much; you might turn into my mother!"

CHAPTER SIXTEEN

Pastor Snicks was studying something on his desk so intently that he didn't see or hear Heather and Granny enter the room until Granny pounded her snow shovel cane on the floor. With a start, he quickly covered the papers he'd been studying.

"Tryin' to hide something?" Granny blurted out in a suspicious tone.

With a little laugh and a covered cough, Pastor Snicks indicated that the women should have scats in the two chairs in front of his desk. "Yes, Granny, I am; I'm hiding the records of another parishioner. Privacy Act, you know. You can't see what I know."

"Well, I know what you can't see," Granny countered back.

"Pastor Snicks," Heather had decided to break up the conversation so they didn't upset the Pastor—after all, they needed him. He was on the books for weddings the month of December for the We Save You Christian Church and, although he and Granny usually got along, you never knew what conclusions Granny might stoop to if she thought he was hiding anything about his other parishioners. "I want to finalize our wedding party and music, Pastor," said Heather. "I brought Granny along in case any of our decisions impacted their wedding."

"No problem, there," Granny piped in, "whatever you do is fine with me. We're going to march in to the *Wedding Bell Blues*, say *I do* and let the party begin."

Ignoring Granny, Pastor Snicks looked at the papers he'd taken out of his drawer. "Yes, but we do need to name the Matron of Honor and the Best Man. You two have to discuss this before making a decision."

"Yes," Heather answered. Heather turned to look at Granny. "Granny, I would like you to be my Matron of Honor."

Granny looked at Heather and at first was speechless, which was an odd thing for Granny. It took her a few moments to answer. "Me? Matron of Honor? I've never been a Matron of Honor. Don't you want your sister or a friend? I'm old. Do you know what I would look like in one of those frou-frou dresses?"

"Granny, my mother is dead. Since I've met you, you have accepted me and I feel like you are my mother, too. By being my Matron of Honor, it will be like our ceremony, too—becoming mother and daughter."

Granny cleared her throat and turned away from Heather and Pastor Snicks to let out a little pretend cough, sneaking a hand across her eyes to hide the tears that were welling up in her eyes. Turning back to Heather, she answered in barely a whisper, "I...ah...I... ah...I suppose I can. But what will your father say?"

Heather smiled. "He's going to be Thor's best man. It will be our ceremony uniting Thor and me and making you both our new parents."

Pastor Snicks had been watching this exchange. "All right now," he said, clearing his throat. His eyes were a little misty at the exchange between the crusty Hermiony Vidalia Fiddlestadt and the young Heather. "We have that settled; anything else, Heather?"

"Yes, Thor and I have decided that we would arrange for music for the guests to enjoy while they are waiting for my dad and Granny's wedding to begin. After all, Angel has to change and Granny will have to get her flowers, and if she may want to change dresses– –although i's perfectly fine if she wears her wedding dress for our wedding too. We'll need a little time in between to get ready."

"Wedding dress? I don't have a wedding dress yet," Granny said in a panic. "Can I get a wedding dress in two weeks? I haven't had time to shop, what with all the hoopla about Delbert and the dead stiff in the cemetery. Speaking of the cemetery, can we go there?"

"Why would you want to go to the cemetery today?" Pastor Snicks queried.

"They're digging up Delbert Delure's body."

Pastor Snicks quickly looked down at his watch. "I'm sorry; I have to go. You need to stay away from the cemetery, Granny. Leave the detectives to do their work. You can let yourself out, right, ladies?" Pastor Snicks grabbed his coat off the coat tree, along with his hat and exited his office at a quick pace.

Heather and Granny buttoned their coats and put on their gloves. Granny looked at her shovel and laughed. "Want me to shovel you a way out?" indicating that the cover had slipped off the sharp scoop of the shovel.

"That's a pretty cute shovel, Granny. It was a good idea. It keeps you stable on the ice with those four little sharp teeth at the bottom of the shovel cover. It has a sleek handle and is kind of pretty," Heather mused.

"They made it to my specifications."

"You know, you should show it to Butch. Maybe he could market them and you could go into the unique cane business. It would keep you busy."

"Heather, would you mind dropping me off at the Pink Percolator instead of us going Christmas shopping? I think I should spend some time with Delight. After all, it's her husband's grave they're digging up," said Granny as they drove away from the church.

"Maybe we both could do that."

"No, no; I think you should do your Christmas shopping. It's going to snow again tomorrow and Christmas isn't too far away. Maybe you should go to Allure," Granny suggested.

Heather looked at Granny with a thoughtful face. "I think I should stay with you."

Granny did her best to give Heather a sad look. "I feel so bad for Delight and I'm sure she would talk to me better in private."

Heather stopped the car in front of the Pink Percolator. "Ok, but I'm calling my dad. He can pick you up later."

"I will be so glad when I get my car back and get my garage rebuilt. I miss my wheels. Tell him to bring my snowmobile to pick me up. It'll give him a thrill."

Granny waved good-by to almost daughter-in-law as she opened the door to the Pink Percolator. She stood inside the door and watched Heather drive away.

"Hi Granny," Delight's daughter Ella greeted her. "Do you want coffee? Mom left you some donuts from the morning rush. She thought you might come in."

"No, thanks, Ella; I know your mom is at home waiting for the news from the cemetery. I'll catch her later and….if Franklin comes looking for me later, stall him. You have my cell phone number. Call me and I'll get back here. Tell him I'm in conference with your mother up in the office and we can't be disturbed."

"But Mom's at home," Ella answered, confused at Granny's instructions.

"I know that, but he doesn't."

Granny stepped onto the sidewalk and made her way down the street, leaning on her shovel to keep from falling on the icy spots. That was the problem with Minnesota winters. Once the snow started melting, it would get colder and freeze again leaving ice patches on the sidewalks. Granny made her way down the street to AbStract Department Store, which carried almost anything, and it had a good line of Minnesota goods, too.

Justine, one of the clerks in AbStract, smiled when she saw Granny enter the store. "Are you ready for your wedding, Granny? Or are you here to shop for that perfect piece of jewelry or pair of shoes to wear on your special day?"

"Thanks, Justine; I'll shop later. I just came through to use your door to the underground streets. Oh, and you didn't see me, if anyone asks."

Justine didn't answer.

"Did you hear me?" Granny yelled because she didn't get an answer.

"Is someone there?" replied Justine, looking around.

Granny laughed and opened the secret door and went down the steps to the underground streets. It was crowded today. Fuschians were using the warmth of the underground to shop the stores of Fuchsia. Granny admired some of the wares that were set out in front of the shops. It was almost like the Farmer's Market in the summer except Christmas cheer was all around.

Granny walked for a little while until she passed her door and got to the lift for the mausoleum in the cemetery. This far out, the underground streets were deserted. She looked around to make sure no one saw her before pushing the code to come up on the lift into the mausoleum. She didn't think they would be using the lift to transport the exhumed body because a dead body didn't care if it was cold or not and the others would have their cars by the grave. She couldn't believe the police hadn't had Gravy change the code to keep her out, but it was still the same. Maybe they didn't know she had the code. She'd have to thank Gravy.

Once inside the mausoleum, Granny noted that the heaters weren't running. Pulling her coat tighter to keep warm, she edged toward the outside door and unlocked it, turning the latch. Slowly opening the door, she peered out through a crack to see if Thor and the Tall Guy were there, along with the crew that was bringing up the casket. She could see cars, but she was too far away to see who was there and what was happening. Taking her snow shovel, she put it through the crack in the door and gently nudged the door farther open. No one noticed. Stepping into the cold air, she moved forward out of the mausoleum.

Walking quietly, using the spikes on the bottom of the shovel cover for traction, she moved forward slowly, taking cover behind a big tree not far from the scene of the exhumation. She could see and hear everything. Delbert had been buried not far from where Ferdinand was buried. She still wondered how their clothes had gotten mixed up. She could see that they had the vault that housed the coffin out of the ground. Granny saw the gold inscription on the vault. *He liked his coffee. He liked his tea. He even liked me. Rest in peace, Delbert Delure.*

Delight must have written Delbert's epitaph, Granny surmised with a chuckle. She happened to look down at the ground and saw that hers weren't the only footsteps in the snow around the tree. She put her foot into one of the footprints and saw that the print was much larger than hers. It seemed to be recent. Her eye caught something sticking out of the snow by one footprint. Quietly so as not to call attention to herself, she bent down and picked up what appeared to be a crystal from a wristwatch. Turning it over in her hand, she examined it closely. Then, hearing the crew talking, she quickly pocketed the crystal and peered around the tree. It looked like things were wrapping up. Darkness was starting to fall. Granny reached into the pocket of her coat to check the time on her cell phone but her phone wasn't there. Then, she remembered that she'd forgotten it on her table at home.

Quietly and carefully, she made her way back to the mausoleum. She had to get back to the Pink Percolator. Franklin would be looking for her and there was no way for Ella to call her if she didn't have her phone. Stepping into the mausoleum, she locked the door from the inside. Just as she locked the door, she heard a car pull up outside. Drat! The police were checking the mausoleum before they left. She'd have to get out!

Granny stood on the lift and tapped the code for the lift to take her into the streets underneath. Nothing happened. It appeared to have no electricity. Granny tapped again, still no action. *Darn Fuchsia Power Company,* Granny thought. They were probably on overload because of all the extra Christmas lights. It wasn't usually a problem because the residents of Fuchsia liked using the old fashioned oil lanterns from long ago when the power went out. However, today it was a problem. Granny couldn't get out through the streets and the daylight that had been shining through the windows high up in the mausoleum was fading. And Granny didn't have her flashlight.

Using the shovel as a guide so she wouldn't trip over any of the statues, she made her way over to the door. Before she moved to unlock the door, she listened for sounds from the car that had just arrived. What she heard was the car driving away. She turned the latch. It didn't move. She put her face close to the lock to make sure she was turning it the right way. It still didn't move. Picking up her shovel, she hit the lock. She had seen that work in movies. The sharp bang of the shovel didn't faze the lock on the door. It was cold in the mausoleum. Granny gave a shiver, whether because she was cold or because she had just realized that she was locked in the mausoleum and no one knew where she was.

CHAPTER SEVENTEEN

Hopping up and down to keep warm, Granny spun around slowly in a circle to see if there might be another way out of the mausoleum. The descending darkness hampered her investigation. She found the crypt that was supposedly hers. Maybe she would need it sooner than she thought. It, too, was closed and locked tight.

Grabbing her shovel, Granny walked with determination over to the lift from the underground street. Punching in the code still had no effect. There was still no power. Granny lifted the shovel high and started pounding on the lift floor. Perhaps someone would be passing by the end of the tunnel and would hear her pounding. She knew it was a long shot because she lived at the end of the tunnels with the turn in the tunnel going to the cemetery at the back of her house and a dead end.

"A whiff, a stiff are not going to get me into a tiff." She hollered to the cold air and the now dark night, as she banged on the lift referring to the whiff of chemicals she had inhaled the last time she had been kidnapped in the underground streets.

All of a sudden the lift came to life knocking Granny and her shovel to the floor as the lift moved downward into the underground street. The face of Silas Crickett came into view and he had a big scowl on his face.

"What are you trying to do? Turn yourself into a stiff? What were you doing in the mausoleum in this cold weather at night?" Silas scolded.

Granny stood up, tidied her coat and hat and planted her shovel cane on the floor of the lift and then stepped off the lift next to Silas. Haughtily, she said, "I was taking a walk in the cemetery breathing in the fresh crispness of the night. What are you doing here?"

"I happened to be coming home from town and I was going to use the shortcut through your house since I didn't want to walk in the cold. I pounded on your door and you didn't answer, then I heard the pounding coming from the lift."

"It must be late, Heather must have picked up Angel and Mavis must have gone home. They were at my house earlier."

"It's seven pm. How long were you up there?"

"If I had a watch do you think I would ask you the time? Granny shook her head at what she thought had been obvious. "There was no power to get back down on the lift."

"That's because someone disconnected the wires from the lift connection box. I had to fix it before I could get it running again."

"Who would do that?"

"Someone who knew you were there and wanted to make sure you stayed there?"

Granny was silent for a minute. "Did you do that Silas Crickett? Are you trying to get rid of me?"

"I want to get rid of you but I'm not into stiff making." Silas cranked back at Granny.

Granny moved toward her basement door.

Silas followed, "Why didn't you go out the mausoleum door into the cemetery? It locks from the inside?"

"I had been out checking on the exhumation but when it was over I was going to go through the mausoleum back home and I couldn't get down the lift. Then I heard the police car and they locked the door from the outside." Granny unlocked her underground door and started to shut it on Silas.

"I save you and you slam the door in my face?"

"I shut the door, there is a difference, do you want to see how I slam a door?" Granny gripped the door tighter, ready to slam it shut.

Silas put out his hand to stop her and moved his body into the half-closed door. "I guess I'll go down to the police station and talk to Franklin and Thor and tell them about your adventure this evening. I'll ask why they locked you in the mausoleum." A crafty smile lit up Silas face.

Eyebrows raised and with pursed lips, Granny slowly opened the door. Silas walked past Granny and sprinted up the steps in an unwobbly fashion. Maybe he wasn't as old as she thought; Granny surmised as she watched him and then followed him up and into her living room.

"Let's go." Silas ordered Granny.

"Go? Go where? I just got home and why should I go anywhere with a cantankerous old man like you, Mr. Supercilious."

"Supercilious? Silas asked confused. "We need to check the cemetery. I was at the police station when they came back from exhuming the grave to meet my son. They didn't check the mausoleum. In their haste they forgot. They decided they didn't need to check it since they had been in the cemetery all day. The patrol was going to check it various hours through the night. They didn't lock you in. We need to find out why you couldn't get out."

"You're helping me after threatening to blow my cover?"

"Look, I miss Alaska. I miss my detective days and my sons seem to think they don't need my help. They want to put me out to pasture. They'll accept Franklin's help and he is only a year younger than me. I suspect they worry about my safety since I left them for someone else. They think they're protecting me. As ornery as you are, I would hate to see you end up like that stiff. After all, I am already helping you with those corrupting furry creatures and I don't want to take care of them full time. Just don't ask me to be nice to you. You're not my type." Silas turned and walked through the house to Granny's back door. "Are you coming? Oh, and bring your shovel, we might need it. I left my gun at home."

The snowmobile was already running by the time Granny got to her back yard. Silas was in the driver's seat.

"I'm driving." Granny told him.

"Over my dead body, I remember that last ride."

"That can be arranged, I mean the dead part." Granny hitched herself behind Silas on the snowmobile grabbing him by the waist.

Silas maneuvered the snowmobile up and over the ramp and into the cemetery coming to a stop by the mausoleum. The cemetery was quiet.

Silas had remembered to pick up the flashlight that had been by Granny's back door. He walked to the mausoleum door and shined the flashlight at the door and the lock. Granny joined him. When she saw what the flashlight was shining on she gave a gasp.

"Someone jammed the lock and piled snow against the door." Granny leaned closer to see what was on the lock.

"They super glued the lock shut." Silas concluded. "Then they shoveled a snow bank up against the door so even if you could have somehow got the glue out of the lock, you couldn't have gotten out."

"What do I know, that I don't know that I know, that someone wants me dead?" Granny wondered.

"I'm sure you forgot, because if you remembered I am sure you would tell Ephraim. I hear you remember what you forgot, when you remember that we need to know, what you didn't know, that you actually knew."

"What? Granny asked in a confused tone. That makes absolutely no sense."

"Exactly," Silas answered back, a smirky smile on his face.

Silas got back on the snowmobile and indicated Granny should follow suit. "It's time to call Ephraim, your son, and I suppose we should warn your Franklin that somebody's after you."

"Ah, maybe we could wait awhile with that? How about if you and I investigate the case and keep this our little secret?" Granny cajoled.

"Let's go home."

Granny hopped on the snowmobile and Silas drove it up the ramp and back down in Granny's backyard without incident. Waiting for them in the driveway where Granny's garage had been was a police car and Franklin's car.

"You called them?"

"No, what did you do now?" Silas asked.

"Why does everyone always think I did something?" Exasperation peppered Granny's voice as she went to meet the men that were waiting for her. It had already been a long day.

CHAPTER EIGHTEEN

The Tall Guy and Thor didn't inquire as to where Granny and Silas had been. They appeared to have something more pressing on their minds. On the other hand, Franklin looked none too pleased and had been about to ask questions about Granny's not being at The Pink Percolator when Thor led everyone into the house and asked them to sit down.

"This looks like a family discussion. I think I'll go." Silas stated and walked towards the door.

His son, Ephraim Cornelius, stopped him. "I think you should stay since this all started with you and Granny's ride home from town the other day."

Thor cleared his throat before addressing Granny." Can I get you some water or something stronger to drink?

"What's up. You're offering me liquor or wine again? Are you running a fever?" Granny stood up and, stalling for time, felt his head. This could only be bad news.

"I'm fine." Thor led his mother back to her seat. "The body we dug up in Delbert Delure's grave was Dad's."

Granny threw her arms in the air, stood up, walked to the refrigerator, took out the ice cream and proceeded to get a bowl out of the cupboard. "I'm hungry, anyone want some ice cream? I missed my supper."

Thor walked over to Granny and took the ice cream out of her hands. Franklin and The Tall Guy exchanged glances. "Did you hear me?"

"I did. Someone mixed up their graves. It's no big deal. He's still dead, just with someone else's clothes." Granny put a scoop of ice cream in her mouth.

"Aren't you curious what is in Dad's grave, why Delbert ended up in your grave, and how Dad ended up in Delbert's grave and why and how Delbert ended up in your yard?

"Read my lips. I don't have a grave. I have never bought a grave and I don't plan on using one soon." Granny ranted ignoring Thor's questions.

Silas stood in the background with a gleam in his eyes as he watched the verbal exchange between the people in the room.

Franklin moved by Granny's side, put his arms around her and turned to her inquisitor. "Enough, can't you see she's frail and tired. I can read the signs. It's time for all of you to go and we'll talk tomorrow."

Granny looked up at Franklin batting her eyelids. "Yes, oh Franklin, can you hold on to me, I am feeling weak all of sudden. The news must have been too much for me."

Silas looked at Granny with shrewd eyes. "Yup, I'm out of here. We'll catch up tomorrow."

Franklin opened the door for Silas, "You and I will catch up tomorrow too. I want to know about your little snowmobile trip tonight and if Hermiony needs any help she can call on me. Two weeks and she will be my responsibility. By the way, she's moving, so if you know anyone who wants to buy a house, Hermiony's is for sale."

Silas winked at Granny before closing the door behind him. Granny was looking at Franklin's stern expression. Thor took stock of the looks going between Franklin and his mother and said to the Tall Guy. "I think it's time we leave while it's still safe."

Granny turned to Franklin after the two left. "First my undercover sleuth job for the merchants of Fuchsia is gone. I thought that was Thor but now I'm not so sure he didn't do that without some convincing. Then I'm moving?"

Franklin smiled at Granny, gave her a wink, and moved toward her to take her into his arms. At that moment both pet doors slammed open and closed as the shysters and Baskerville along with Mrs. Bleaty bounded into the room knocking Franklin and Granny apart. Little White Poodle had a notebook page in his mouth and Baskerville and Tank were chasing him. Little White Poodle kept winding in and out of Franklin's and Granny's legs to keep away from his followers. Franklin grabbed Granny to hold her steady so she wouldn't fall. All of sudden a howl cut through the air and then the words "Stop him, stop him. He's a thief!" Radish flew in through Baskerville's pet door after imitating Baskerville's howl and grabbed the paper out of Little White Poodle's mouth. Radish flew around the room with the shysters and Baskerville chasing him. Mrs. Bleaty, having enough of the bedlam, retreated to Granny's bedroom.

Franklin let go of Granny to try and get the paper out of Radish's claws but Radish was too quick and flew out the door leaving only a piece of the document in Franklin's hands. The shysters and Baskerville, seeing the chase was over, settled down on the floor to take a nap.

Franklin looked at the piece of paper in his hand.

"Since when do parrots like winter?" Granny asked as Franklin continued his scrutiny of the paper.

"His name is Radish, he belongs to someone from Alaska who is, in your description, despicable, and they live in the strange town of Fuchsia, Minnesota. Does that answer your question? When does anyone in

Fuchsia do anything normal?" Franklin reminded Granny as he held out the piece of paper for her to see.

"This looks like it has my name on it. My maiden name."

"It looks like a birth certificate."

"Why would that bird have my birth certificate?" Granny wrinkled her nose at the thought.

She lifted her eyes to Franklin's, stiffened her back, grabbed her shovel cane and pounded it on the floor. "That man! That despicable, cantankerous old man is investigating me. He's spying on me." Granny grabbed her coat that she had thrown over the kitchen chair on her return earlier and was ready to stomp out of the house when Franklin stopped her.

"Where are you going?"

"Where do you think I'm going? I'm going to get to the bottom of this."

"Calm down, it's late. Let me take this to Thor and he can do the questioning. You stay away from that man. Get some sleep and dream of our wedding. I'll talk to you later." Franklin leaned over and kissed Granny, gave her a hug, and walked out the door.

The calendar on the wall by Granny's bed had a big red circle around December 26. Putting on her *Sexy Granny and I Know It* PJs, Granny glanced at the calendar and realized that she still hadn't picked out what she was going to wear for her wedding to Franklin and, as she found out tonight, they still hadn't settled where they wanted to live. Franklin had bought the Mayor's big Victorian house and put his house on the market. Fuchsia Mayor, Horatio Helicourt, had moved to a smaller home closer to downtown and the mayor's office.

Climbing into bed with a new book and her chocolates, Granny wondered if she wanted to move. It seemed Franklin was making the decisions for her and

Granny worried that she might be falling back into her old ways as when she was married to Ferdinand. When she had been married to Ferdinand, he had made all the decisions and she liked her independence now. Was she afraid she would turn back into her former self, letting Franklin control her life? Was that what he wanted to do? It seemed since he had bought her a new car and she had accepted his ring, things had changed. She found herself agreeing occasionally to things that she didn't want. Was she mellowing? She missed the forgetful, cunning part of herself that she had used for her undercover role. Maybe that was more a part of her than she thought. Her children were no longer threatening her with the wrinkle farm and she missed the game of trying to stay out of the hoosegow or the wrinkle farm. Now that had been living she thought as she drifted off to sleep.

CHAPTER NINETEEN

There appeared to be no movement anywhere on Granny's street, no human movement anyway. The only thing Granny could see as she peered into the binoculars that she had perched on the sill in her kitchen window was the movement of snowflakes falling from the heavens and the wind gracefully blowing those snowflakes into white swirls that mimicked the waves on the oceans. It was snowing again in Fuchsia.

The shysters, Baskerville, and Mrs. Bleaty, had been gone by the time Granny woke up from another nightmare about Silas. This time in the nightmare, Silas was interrupting her wedding, claiming that she was his snow baby. Granny awakened shouting, "I am not your snow baby! I am not your snow baby!" It took her a few minutes to get her eyes open wide enough to realize it had all been a nightmare. When she did, she realized that there were no warm creatures sharing her bed. Thinking they might have wandered back into their normal routine, she decided to check if there was any evidence that they had escaped to Silas Crickett's house.

Training the binoculars on Silas's window, there didn't seem to be any evidence of movement. Adjusting her surveillance to the basement window, she could see no light and no tracks in the snow, although the wind could have covered their tracks. She was about to put the binoculars down to go and change clothes to confront Silas, when her cell phone rang. It was still in the bedroom so Granny shuffled fast to answer it before it went to voicemail. People always got upset at her voicemail message: *It's a bark not a lark.* Then the Little White Poodle and Tank would bark before the next part of the message: *It's a phone, I'm not home. Don't cry foul, leave a howl.* Then Baskerville would howl and it would be time for the caller to leave a message. Granny couldn't understand why no one left messages.

As Granny picked up her phone, Eye Time popped up and Franklin appeared in her vision. "Good morning, Hermiony, and what delectable nightwear are you wearing this morning?"

Granny glared into Franklin's eyes though the Eye Time screen and held the phone up high so Franklin could not see her *Sexy Granny and I Know It* PJs.

"I am wearing what I always wear in the winter—my PJs with the feet built in, you know, the one piece kind," Granny told him in a crusty voice.

Franklin's grin faded at the thought of Granny in the old-fashioned foot pajamas. "Just wanted you to know all the furry crew made it here to my house during the night before the snow started falling. They must be back to their routine. Didn't want you to worry."

"I was just looking for them. What do you suppose they are up to now going back to their normal routine? Think they're trying to throw us off the scent of clues?"

Franklin sighed, "They're animals, our loveable animals, they like routine and they are back to it. No clues, no mystery. And you should take their cue. Let the Tall Guy and Thor—and me, when they want my help—solve the problems in the cemetery."

Granny thought for minute before making a suggestion, "Maybe you all should bring Silas Crickett in on the investigation since he was such a hotshot in Alaska."

"I get the impression from the Tall Guy that when Silas hung up his hat as a detective in Alaska, it was for good. The last case he had was a pretty brutal one. So much so that Ephraim says he won't talk about it. Keep your distance, Hermiony. There's a lot we don't know about him," Franklin warned.

"Got to go." Granny abruptly hung up the cell phone.

Granny walked back to the kitchen with her binoculars and pointed them at Silas's house. She hadn't really wanted him in on the investigation, she just wanted him out of her hair so she could continue snooping. Everything was dark. He didn't appear to be home.

Granny picked up her cell phone and barked into it, "Mavis!" The phone dialed Mavis's number.

"Are you up?" Granny queried.

"I am now."

"Where's George?"

"He's in Contrary, Iowa, visiting his daughter. He left before the snow. Why?"

"Ever been on a snowmobile?"

"Uh, no," Mavis answered with a hesitation in her voice.

"Have you seen Thor this morning?"

"I saw him leave his house early this morning. I assume to go to work. Do you need your son?"

"Perfect, dress warm. I'll pick you up in ten minutes." Granny slammed down the phone and hustled to prepare for the trip.

Granny watched as Mavis shuffled down the steps and through the snow that had piled up on her front steps. On Mavis's head was a bomber hat with earflaps that reached almost to her eyes. The hat sat down low on her head coming down to the top of her eyes. All that seemed to be peeking out from underneath the cap was a tiny nose and an anonymous chin. She had on a pair of adult snowpants that were a little too big for her, tucked into tall black rubber snow boots. Her coat was bulky black fur that reached down to her knees. Granny concluded it looked like a good undercover disguise. No one would know it was Mavis underneath all that bulk. Granny, on the other hand, stood out like a red thumb with her pink coat, purple boots and red bomber hat.

"Nice duds," Granny complimented Mavis, trying to keep from laughing at the picture Mavis presented in her winter outfit.

"They're George's. It's called undercover. No one will know who I am; they'll think I'm George."

"Good thinking. Maybe they'll arrest George instead of you if we get caught." She led Mavis to the snowmobile.

"How do I get on this thing?" Mavis asked, looking the machine over.

"Just plop down behind me."

"Where's the seat belt?" Mavis asked, positioning her body behind Granny.

"I'm your seatbelt. Hold on."

Mavis grabbed Granny tightly.

"Mavis, I didn't say squeeze the life out of me."

The hands that gripped Granny around the waist loosened a little.

"Here we go, hold on." Granny instructed.

"Where we going?" Mavis asked, as the blowing snow flew into her face.

"Back to the crime scene."

"We're going to the cemetery?" Mavis yelled over the wind.

"No, we're going to old Mrs. Periwinkle's former house, the one that's now owned by Neil Nail," Granny yelled back.

"That's the last crime scene. You solved that one."

"Yes, but the new dead stiff was renting that house and I want to find out why he's investigating me. No one else seems to be concerned about that little tidbit."

Mavis was silent, concerned that while Granny was talking, the snowmobile was weaving in and out of some trees. Granny had decided to take the back way by Blue Bird Lake where there was no path, but they would come upon Neil's back yard unseen from the street.

Granny slowed down when she neared Neil's back yard. She pulled up by the garage on the back of the property and indicated Mavis should get off. Granny cut the engine on the snowmobile and joined Mavis who was now gazing at the house.

"Um. Granny, how do you plan to get in?"

"Maybe the doors are unlocked. Remember last time the basement window was unlatched."

Mavis looked doubtful and pointed out to Granny, "That was a fluke and if this guy was a private investigator and he's dead, the police have probably been here and locked it up tight."

"Where's your adventuresome spirit?" Granny asked Mavis as she walked back to the snowmobile and pulled out her shovel. "See these tiny prongs on the bottom. I bet we can pick the lock."

"You know how to pick locks?"

"Um, no. But there's always a first time for everything. Where there's a will, there's a way. If you believe you can do it, anything's possible. If..."

Granny was about to add something more, but Mavis put her hand up to still Granny's recitation. "All right, all right; I get the point."

"Mavis." Granny gave her a confused look. "There's no point. I don't have my knitting needle cane." Granny shook her head and moved through the snow to the back door, indicating Mavis should follow.

First Granny tried the knob. It didn't turn. She peered at the deadbolt lock halfway up the door. She reached to the bottom of her shovel cover and pulled out the spike that apparently was made to unscrew from the bottom of the shovel cover. She took the narrow sharp object and inserted it in the door lock, turned it and leaned her entire little body into the door.

Mavis watched, skeptical that this would work.

As Granny leaned into the door, it opened and Granny fell forward, straight into the arms of Silas Crickett.

"Fallin' for me are ya, Granny?" Silas cackled. "I thought you only fell for Franklin," referring to the fact that Granny had fallen into Franklin's arms the first time they had met.

"How did you know that?" Granny sputtered, pulling herself away from Silas, grabbing the wall for support. Realizing that Silas was here when he wasn't supposed to be, she quickly forgot about her first question. "What are you doing here and how did you get in and why did your annoying bird have my birth certificate? I'm calling the police." Granny reached in her pocket to get her cell phone.

Mavis quickly entered the house and put a hand over Granny's mouth before she could bark into the cell phone "Police Station" and start the cell phone dialing system.

A muffled sound came from Granny's covered mouth.

"Granny, you can't call the police. We're not supposed to be here either." Mavis grabbed the shovel out of Granny's hands and held it in front of her. Grabbing Granny, she pushed her behind her, keeping the shovel centered on Silas. Silas watched all this with an amused grin.

"Silas, what are doing here? You're usually so nice. Are you a villain?" Mavis pleaded for an answer from Silas.

Granny pushed Mavis out of the way and walked up to Silas, nose to nose. "I told you he was despicable. You didn't believe me about Mr. Supercilious."

Silas grabbed both of them by the arm, catching Mavis off guard. Mavis dropped the shovel. He propelled them further into the kitchen of the house. "Will you two be quiet? Someone's going to know we're here if you two don't keep the lid on it." He smiled at Mavis. "Mavis, dear, I'm on your side. I'm just trying to help your dear friend, Granny, even if she is the most stubborn, persnickety, crabby old woman I have ever met."

Granny pulled away from Silas. "You can leave now Supercilious. We have work to do and how did you get in?" Granny asked wrinkling her forehead.

Silas held up a key and with a smirk, quietly said, "I have the key to the lake door. I came in through the basement and the tunnel," referring to the underground old tornado shelter room and the underground cavern and tunnel that led to the lake.

Silas walked through the door to the living room and stopped by the desk. He picked up a three-ring notebook and held it up. "I believe this is what you're looking for." He tossed the notebook to Granny.

Granny caught the notebook and motioned Mavis to join her on the couch. One by one, she paged through the documents and pictures. "This is my life, Silas, my entire life, from birth till now. Why is it here and how did you get it? And how did Radish get my birth certificate? The police must have been here."

"Actually, I don't think they checked the tunnel," said Silas. "Must have thought it didn't have anything to do with the death of Mr. Private Investigator, Felix Smart. I stumbled over it as I was walking through the old tornado shelter yesterday when I knew the coast was clear. I took it back home to study it. Radish must have stolen your birth certificate in one of his snits. He loves to tear paper."

"This has nothing to do with you," Granny reminded him.

"I'm bored. I came to Fuchsia to rest up. I thought it was a quiet little town in Minnesota that had snow in the winter so it would remind me of Alaska. I wanted to spend some time with my son. If I had spent more time with Cornelius maybe he wouldn't have ended up where he is today. I blame myself, so I moved here after I retired. After my last case, I needed a new perspective," Silas explained uncharacteristically serious and with a low toned voice. "I miss the thrill of the chase and I sense when something isn't right. I knew my son and Thor would be at the cemetery digging up your husband's grave so they wouldn't be here and I wanted to bring the book back. I was curious why it ended up where it did and not upstairs."

The words "husband's grave" got Granny's attention. "They didn't tell me. Are you sure?"

"Yes, I'm sure. They didn't tell you. Thor wants to keep you safe and Franklin wants to turn you into a mellow woman." Silas pointed out a fact that had been weighing on Granny's mind.

"He does not," Mavis piped up. "He likes her as she is."

Silas got a gleam in his eye, "Ah, does he?"

"You're changing the subject," said Granny. "I knew nothing about them digging up a grave."

"Apparently, word at the police station is that someone else was there again. They brought their own warming blanket and had it half thawed out. They must have gotten interrupted since the blanket was still there this morning and there were shovel marks where they had tried to shovel the hard dirt. Someone is desperate, maybe the same someone who locked you up in the mausoleum," Silas reminded Granny.

Giving Silas a shrewd look, Granny asked, "We're off the subject. How did you get the key to get in here?"

"I wasn't undercover all those years for nothing. I stole from the evidence drawer in the police station."

"That doesn't explain why you're investigating the dead stiff private investigator," Granny pointed out.

"Granny, Granny, Granny. You're the female version of me. Not only did I want to return the history of your life, I knew you'd show up here if you didn't think anyone was watching you. You need my help. Let's all team up and work on this together. No one will suspect. After all, you don't like me and I don't like you. We drive each other crazy but....we are both cunning; they think we're old. We can solve this and find out who's robbing the graves."

"Granny," Mavis interrupted in a low voice, "I...ah...don't think Franklin would approve?" Mavis stepped back a little waiting for Granny's answer knowing it was a risk to ask that question.

"Approve!" Granny belted out in a loud voice, "Approve! He doesn't have to approve. We're getting married in less than two weeks. We have to get this out of the way before Christmas, before the Fuchsia Pink Flamingo Christmas Parade. He's going to be my husband, not my keeper."

Granny turned to Silas, "Ok, you can help. Just don't get in my way, don't steal my donuts and keep the shysters and Baskerville and Mrs. Bleaty out of your house away from that creature you call Radish."

While this exchange was going on, Mavis had gone back to studying the notebook. She hesitantly pointed to something in the book. "Ah, Granny, I didn't know you had a twin sister."

At the words *twin sister*, Granny grabbed the book from Mavis and closed it so hard it made a large clap when the covers came together. Mavis's eyes opened wide, worrying about what was going to come next.

Granny ignored Mavis's question and answered with one of her own for Silas. "Do you have a theory about what this Felix Smart was doing by Ferdinand's grave?"

"I do and so does Ephraim. He thinks he was a casualty of being in the wrong place at the wrong time. That's all he would tell me, but I did a little digging on my own. I am sure Ephraim and Thor know this too. He works for Magellan, Magellan and Smart. They were hired by the Amelia Corporation and the Amelia Corporation rented this house."

At the word *Amelia*, Granny's face blanched.

Mavis, noticing the change of color in Granny's face, quickly moved to Granny's side. "Are you ok? You look like you're seen a ghost."

Granny was silent for a moment before she answered, fanning her face, "No, no, no. I just feel a little weak. The heat's too high in here and we have these big bulky clothes on. When I get hot, instead of turning red, I turn white, something that's been with me all these years. Let's go Mavis; they might be looking for us and I need some cold air."

Granny grabbed Mavis and pushed her through the door before Mavis could answer, hollering back to Silas, "Don't forget to lock up."

CHAPTER TWENTY

"Do you mind if we take a side trip by Nail's Hardware before we go home?" Granny asked Mavis as she started the snowmobile.

"Can you drop me at Pickle's Grocery and pick me back up. I think I can hold on to a carton of Egg Nog on this contraption. I'm getting pretty good at balancing as we go in and out of the trees," replied Mavis.

Granny dropped Mavis off at Pickle's Grocery store putting her head down low, as Franklin drove by in his Escalade. He didn't appear to notice Granny and Mavis stopped in front of the grocery store.

Granny cut the engine of the snowmobile, and took a moment to listen to the musical trees on the tops of their respective buildings, serenading the Christmas shoppers.

Approaching the door of Nail's, Granny took a look inside through the glass door before entering. She saw Penelope and Butch in a heated discussion about something. Penelope saw Granny's face at the door and stopped what she was saying, to wave at Granny and walk toward the door.

When Granny entered, Butch gave a wave, walked through the back room and out the back door. "What was that all about?" Granny questioned, seeing that Penelope had fire in her eyes.

"Revelation, revelation!" Penelope informed her mother in a raised voice.

"You're studying Revelations? I didn't know Pastor Snicks was having a Bible study group on Revelations."

"We were arguing about what should be revealed and what is better forgotten," said Penelope.

Granny slowly shook her head. "I see. Something needs to be revealed." Holding out her hand, Granny indicated that Penelope should proceed with her explanation.

"Butch knows something that others don't know, that—should they know, it might help them know more about what they don't know," Penelope told her mother in one breath.

Granny's eyebrows raised. "Ah, don't take this wrong, dear, but…uh, uh…" Granny proceeded slowly, not really sure of Penelope's reaction, "but…uh…you…sound…a little like me."

Penelope stared at her mother, eyes wide with fear.

"I actually know just what you're talking about," Granny told her with conviction. "It makes perfect sense to me." Patting Penelope's hand, she continued, "Tell your mom all about it. What does Butch know that he's scared to tell."

Realizing what was happening, Penelope jerked her hand out of her mother's. "What brings you here, Mom?

Knowing that she was going to learn no more about what Butch needed to reveal to someone, Granny moved on to her reason for visiting Nails. "My wedding is almost here and I don't have a dress. I thought that maybe I've been a little standoffish. Busy. How would you like to go shopping with me and help me find a dress for my wedding?"

"You want me to help you find a dress?" Penelope asked hesitantly. "Ok? But…we don't have the same taste."

"Well, your taste is a little boring and my taste is not, so we should be able to come to an agreement about something in between. I suppose I should tone it down a little for Franklin. I was thinking something red with sparkling beads. After all, it is Christmas. Then I could wear my high tops under my gown so I can sprint away fast if I need to for whatever reason."

Penelope looked skeptical. "Ah, red? High tops? Sprint away? Where would you sprint to if you're the bride? Are you sure you want me along?"

Granny walked over to Penelope, grabbed her shoulders, looked her straight in the eye and said, "You can do it! It's time we bonded. By the way, I know of a big Victorian house you could buy from the new owner instead of living in George's tiny house across the street, after Thor moves out."

Butch came through the back door as Granny was finishing this sentence. He saw Granny, turned around, and walked back out.

"Something I did?" Granny asked, watching Butch walk out the door.

"No, something he did. It looks like Franklin is waiting for you outside by your snowmobile. You better find out what he wants. He looks none too pleased."

CHAPTER TWENTY-ONE

Granny was now the one looking none too pleased to be sitting in the interrogation room of the Fuchsia Police Department. Franklin had been waiting for her when she left Nail's Hardware. Apparently, the police had found something when they exhumed Ferdinand's grave and Granny was needed for questioning.

"What do they think I did that they put me in this room, Franklin?" Granny looked to the wall on the far left. She knew the police would be watching her. Granny was convinced the mirror, although small, was really a window so other detectives could watch the interrogation process. Granny made a face at the mirror waiting for Franklin's answer.

"I'm not privy to that information. They didn't tell me. They just told me to bring you in. Will you quit making faces at that mirror," Franklin instructed.

Granny got up and walked over to the mirror, moved closer, and made squinty eyes to see if she could see the people she knew were standing on the other side. "They make these things pretty good; looks like a real mirror."

At that moment, the door opened and the Tall Guy and Thor entered the room.

"What are you doing peering into the mirror, Mom?" Thor asked.

"Trying to see who's watching me on the other side. I know how you guys work when you interrogate someone. I've watched those detective shows." Granny raised an eyebrow and gave Thor and the Tall Guy a knowing look.

"That's a mirror, Mom, and this isn't the interrogation room. This is going to be my new office. Ephraim has agreed to stay on as co-chief of police and detective. We find we work very well together and we asked the City Council if we could share the job. They like what we've been doing, so they said yes."

"No offense," Granny remarked to Ephraim, "but does that mean your dad is staying too?"

Ephraim chose to ignore her question and held the chair out, indicating Granny should sit down. "Mrs. Fiddlestadt, did you actually see your husband's body in the casket before he was buried?"

Granny raised her eyebrows at the "Mrs. Fiddlestadt."

"Nope."

"Would you like to expand on that statement, Mom?"

"Nope."

"Hermiony, you need to answer the question," Franklin instructed.

"I just did. I didn't see his body. The last time I saw Ferdinand's body was when he died at home and Graves' Mortuary came to collect it."

"Did you pick out the casket? What about the epitaph that was on the plaque on his coffin? And why didn't you have the casket in a burial vault?"

Granny raised her hands upward in confusion. "What difference does it make? Fuchsia doesn't require burial vaults. And, yes, I ordered the epitaph. What is this all about?"

Franklin pulled out a chair, sat down by Granny, and took her hand. Granny looked down at her hand in his and looked Franklin in the eyes. "What is this all about?"

Thor cleared his throat and exchanged a look with the Tall Guy. "We dug up Dad's grave today."

Granny pulled her hand out of Franklin's and stood up. "Is that all? I knew that. It had to be empty since Delight's husband was in the anonymous crypt that you keep saying is mine, in Ferdinand's clothes, and Ferdinand was in Delbert's grave in Delbert's clothes— so Ferdinand's grave had to be empty. Come on, Franklin; take me home so I can see if Mavis got my snowmobile home ok." Granny started for the door.

"Ah, not exactly," the Tall Guy informed Granny.

Granny turned to give the Tall Guy a questioning look.

"It had something in it," Thor answered, watching Granny closely.

"Like another dead stiff?"

"No," the Tall Guy said slowly, "more like two million dollars. Do you know where it might have come from?"

"Probably the bank over in Allure that I knocked off a few years back," Granny answered sarcastically, "right before I picked you up from school so they'd never suspect I was a bank robber. I used you as my cover. What do you think? Stupidest question I ever had anyone ask me."

"May I remind you that you never picked us up from school; you always had to stay home on the farm," Thor reminded her, "but dad did, and the money was buried in his coffin."

"So I was burying money instead of Ferdinand when I threw the handfuls of dirt on his coffin at his funeral? Too bad we didn't know. Pastor Snicks could have had a blessing of the green and I would have changed the epitaph to read, *The Buck Stops Here,*" Granny chuckled.

"The money didn't come from the bank in Allure. It came from a bank in Fish, a small town up in northern Minnesota. Since this was in a time before the internet, if you didn't get the newspaper, you probably wouldn't have heard of it. No one was hurt, but the money was never found—until today." Ephraim Cornelius Stricknine related the story to Franklin and Granny while Thor went behind his desk, poured a cup of coffee, and handed it to Granny.

At the news about the bank robbery and the money, Granny grabbed the cup of coffee and took a gulp. She coughed. "Are you trying to poison me? You call this coffee?" She handed the cup back to Thor.

"She doesn't know anything. Do you need her anymore?" Franklin asked. "I think I should take her home; she's had enough excitement for one day."

Granny looked up at Franklin; *if he only knew,* she thought.

It was still snowing lightly as Franklin escorted Granny out of the Fuchsia Police Station. Franklin checked his watch. "It's lunch time. Do you want to stop at Rack's and have something to eat? We should talk about some of our wedding details. Don't worry about the honeymoon; I've got it all planned."

Before Granny could reply, she felt something cold pelt her back, and a little giggle followed the pelt. Granny turned around to see Angel with another handful of snow. Granny bent down, picked up a handful of snow, and playfully threw it back at Angel, returning her giggle.

Heather interrupted the little snow fight. "Hi, Dad and Granny; we were doing a little Christmas shopping. The snow is so light and fluffy that it makes shopping more fun."

"Granny, did you see Santa?" asked Angel. "He's over in front of Rack's restaurant. We were just going there to eat. Can I talk to Santa, Mommy, and tell him what I want for Christmas?"

Franklin laughed and picked up his granddaughter in his arms. "Let's go see Santa and find you some chicken nuggets." He turned to Granny and Heather, "Coming?"

At Rack's, Angel stopped to tell Santa what she wanted for Christmas and accepted a gift of a candy cane from him.

As Granny walked past Santa to go into the restaurant, he shook his jingle bells at her and, with a twinkle in his eye, he slipped a chocolate donut into her pocket. Granny turned to look at him. His eyes looked suspiciously like Silas Crickett's eyes underneath the suit.

Once the group was settled in Granny's favorite booth and they all had ordered, the conversation turned toward the Christmas Flamingo Parade that always took place in Fuchsia the week before Christmas.

"Why flamingos? Craziest thing I ever heard of at Christmas time!" Franklin remarked to Heather.

"Why not flamingos?" Granny asked. "Haven't you noticed it's cold outside? Horatio Helicourt and the City Council along with the Fuchsia Community Holiday Committee felt it was perfect. Flamingos remind you of warm weather and it's always cold the day of the parade. So if you think pink, you won't feel so cold when the street's like an ice rink."

"Ice rink?" cried Angel. "I can skate Granny! Is the parade at the ice rink?"

"No, sweetie; they flood the streets with water and it turns to ice for the parade, and everyone and everything is on skates on Main Street. The plastic flamingos and the floats are sleds. I must admit, it's a challenge for the Fuchsia Blue Bird High School Band and the Fuchsia Community Band to skate while they're playing their instruments. We've only had one casualty all these years and that was when Donnie Drum, the band instructor, turned a corner too quickly and started sliding. He slid into a majorette, who slid into the first row of the band, who slid into the second row of the band and you get my drift. We had the sliding trombones meeting the frozen flutes. It was an amazing site—almost like synchronized swimming in the summertime, but on ice." Granny had a faraway look in her eyes remembering the scene.

As the waitress set the food in front of them, Granny looked at her plate in amazement. It was her favorite fried chicken, mashed potatoes, gravy, and deep-fried onion rings. She looked at Franklin with a question in her eyes.

"Hot fudge ice cream and donuts, coming soon." With a smile, Franklin gave Granny a hug and a kiss on the cheek which caused Angel to giggle.

Thor came in as they were finishing their meal. Heather stood up, put on her coat and helped Angel on with hers. "We'll see you later; we need to do some shopping, don't we Angel?"

"I'm going to get you a present, Granny. But it's a secret. Right, Mommy?" Angel looked up at her mother for confirmation.

"Yes, see you later."

Thor took Heather's place in the booth.

"Boy, that money threw us for a loop. We didn't expect to find that." Thor shook his head, "We're following up leads, but this is crazy for all of this to have happened years ago and no one ever suspected."

"Have you found out how Delight's husband Delbert was murdered? Delight didn't know anything about that. At least, that's what she told me." Her eyes on Thor, Granny waited for an answer.

"Apparently, at the time, they thought Delbert's death was an accident. There was no autopsy and no reason to suspect murder, but when you found his body in your yard, and the autopsy was done, it showed a knife wound that was the cause of death."

"Why didn't they find the knife wound at the time of his death?" Franklin asked perplexed.

"His injuries from landing on the motorcycle and hitting the tree were pretty extensive, so they must not have noticed the knife wound. No autopsy was done because they thought it was just an accident. Ephraim figures that Delbert was standing on the curb and someone stuck a knife into him and threw him toward the motorcycle."

Granny asked the question playing around in her head. "Do you think he had something to do with the bank robbery?"

Thor shook his head. "It's too early to tell."

"My, look at the time!" Granny looked under the sleeve of her coat, pretending to look at a watch that wasn't there. Franklin, can you drive me home?"

Franklin winked at Granny and stood up. "Maybe we can talk about our wedding on the way home. We seem to have gotten sidetracked over dinner. He threw a tip on the table for the waitress and headed for the door. Granny hung back a minute with a final word for Thor.

"You might want to check out and arrest the Santa by the door. It's not the real Santa. You need to arrest him for stealing Santa's identity."

Granny winked at Thor as she followed Franklin through the door, whispering to Santa as she walked by him, "A donut a day, doesn't keep the cops away from YOU!"

CHAPTER TWENTY-TWO

Granny was ready and waiting for Penelope to pick her up for their shopping trip. After Franklin had driven her home the previous day, he came in and they talked about the details of their wedding without interruption, until the Shysters, Baskerville, and Mrs. Bleaty came home late in the afternoon, wanting their evening meal. They had interrupted the discussion about where Granny and Franklin were going to live after their marriage. Franklin was pointing out that Granny's daughter would be living across the street once Thor got married, and the despicable Silas Crickett would still be ensconced in the corner house that belonged to Sally Katilda. The menagerie of furry creatures arrived just in time to stop Granny from admitting that Franklin might be right about moving.

Penelope pulled up in front of the house. Granny checked to make sure she had her pocketbook, cell phone and shovel. Mavis had dropped the shovel off along with the snowmobile. Franklin had insisted that Granny couldn't take it with her to the police station.

"I'm glad you brought your shovel cane, Mom," said Penelope. "You have such unique canes. That nice Silas Crickett mentioned all the cute canes you have yesterday when he stopped by the hardware store. Such a nice man."

Granny slammed the car door and turned up the radio as she mumbled an answer.

"I'm sorry I didn't hear you," said Penelope. "Where shall we go for your dress? Do you want to drive over to the Bridal Shop in Taffeta? It's a little longer drive, about an hour. This is going to be so much fun!" Penelope clapped her hands in excitement, swerving the car when her hands came off the wheel.

"Do you want me to drive?" Granny asked, as she held onto the dashboard for support. She might need her crypt sooner than she thought.

The trip to Taffeta was uneventful. The Bridal Shop was aptly named *The Taffeta*. Granny eyed the gowns in the shop with a skeptical eye. They certainly didn't look like what Granny had in mind for her wedding dress.

"So, what are you looking for?" the tall, buxom blonde sales girl asked.

"Something, possibly in beige, with a high neck, possibly a belt around the waist and below the knee in length," Penelope answered for her mother. "Maybe soft wool, since it's winter?" she added as an afterthought.

"I was thinking red silk or possibly velour and to the floor, with sparkling red beads around the neck and on the bodice. I'll know it when I see it," Granny informed the two, as she walked to the back of the store where there were racks of red dresses.

"Don't you want something a little more sedate for your wedding?" Penelope held out a soft beige and white wool suit trimmed with black velvet.

Granny reached into the rack and pulled out a long slim-to-the-floor silk skirt with a panel of red velvet in the front and the back. Hanging with the skirt was a short red velvet tapered jacket, lined with red silk to match the skirt. The front had little patches of silk sewn over the velvet; with red sequins shimmering on the edges of the lapels and collar. With a stubborn look on her face, Granny announced, "This is my wedding dress."

Seeing the look on Penelope's face, the sales clerk turned and pulled out a matching red sequined top made out of a sheer silk. It was fully peppered with sequins to hide anything that might show underneath.

A look of triumph lit up Granny's face. "That's it!"

Penelope swallowed and said slowly, "Well .... if ...you're ...sure."

"I'm sure. I was going to wear my red high tops, but did you see those sequined red boots over there? They look like me. Do you have my size?"

After Granny got fitted and arrangements were made to pick up the dress, mother and daughter decided to stop at The Pink Percolator when they got back to Fuchsia and order the flowers for the wedding. Though the forest was no longer part of Delight's shop as it had been at Ella's Enchanted Forest, Delight and Ella still did special arrangements for weddings and funerals.

Ella served Granny and Penelope a Twisted Hot Caramel Fuchsia Latte as they waited for Delight to bring them some flower options for the wedding.

Nonchalantly, Granny inquired, "So did you and Butch settle your differences the other day?"

"No, and we won't until he comes clean," replied Penelope.

"Comes clean about what?" asked Granny.

"Comes clean about what he wants to forget that he knows that he wishes I didn't know," said Penelope.

Granny laughed so hard she almost spilled her latte.

"What are you laughing about? It's not funny," Penelope informed her mother in a miffed tone.

At that moment, Delight joined them. "What's so funny?"

"Watching myself across the table." Chortling, Granny could barely get the words out.

Delight looked at Penelope. "By the way," Delight said, "when I see Butch helping out at Graves'

Mortuary, it brings back memories of when he used to work there. I remember he was so young, just out of high school, but he had a way with those bodies. He should have been a mortician instead of in security."

Penelope, seeing Silas Crickett come in the door, jumped up and called Silas over. "Silas, I just remembered, I have to leave. Can you take my mother home? Thank you." Penelope made a beeline for the door, calling back to her mother, "It's been fun!" and practically ran out the door.

"Something I said?" Delight asked, confused, "We didn't do anything with the flowers."

"I have a feeling it *was* something you said, Delight, but I'm not sure what," Granny answered in a thoughtful tone. "And she left with my shovel."

Silas sat down across from Granny. "Good, I'm safe."

With a withering look at Silas, Granny turned to Delight. "We'll talk about the flowers later. Delight, did the police question you?"

"Not so much question as much informed me of what really happened to Delbert. He was murdered. They said he was stabbed and then pushed off the curb, hitting the motorcycle which threw him onto it and then into the tree. Who would do something like that?"

"Where was your husband when he was murdered?" Silas joined the questioning.

"He was in a town in northern Minnesota on business. I think it was called Fish."

"That's where the money that was in Ferdinand's grave came from!" Granny brought her hands down hard on the table in discovery. "Would your husband have robbed the bank?"

Delight started sobbing.

"Now look what you've done," Silas chastised Granny. "You've made this poor woman cry." He handed Delight a napkin to wipe her tears while glaring at Granny.

Granny changed her questioning. "What were you saying, Delight, about Butch being good with dead bodies? I knew he helped out when he was a kid but ...."

Delight looked around, making sure none of the other customers could hear what she was about to say. "I remember that he sometimes had to dress the bodies and see that the inscription plaques were put on correctly. Gravy was a little, um, discombobulated, if you know what I mean." Delight winked as she said the word *discombobulated*.

"No, I don't know what that means. Can't you women talk English?" Silas shook his head in disgust.

Delight's whisper became quieter. "It means he liked the moonshine a little too much."

"So, don't we all from time to time," Silas grouched.

"But at that time he liked it all the time. Most people didn't know that there was a reason Gravy was always so happy. That all stopped when he got married." Delight's tone got quieter yet.

Granny pondered that thought for a few moments.

Silas got to his feet, "Let's go home. I need to talk to you." He held out his hand to help Granny up.

Looking at his hand, Granny turned to Delight. "I never take handouts. I'll call you about the flowers, Delight. I have a special request for my bouquet."

Silas laughed, withdrew his hand from Granny's reach, and turned to Delight, taking her hand. "I'm sure *you* would take a handout." He leaned down and kissed her hand. Delight giggled and blushed like a schoolgirl.

Granny took one look at Silas and the giggling Delight and stomped out of The Pink Percolator. She was halfway to the hardware store when Silas caught up with her in his car.

"Where are you going? Home's the other way."

"I need my shovel. Penelope's car is parked in front of the hardware store."

"Get in; I want to talk to you about Felix Smart. We'll get your shovel."

As Silas parked in front of the hardware store, they could see Penelope and Butch having an argument through the window. It appeared to be pretty animated, accompanied by frantic, gesturing arms.

"I'll get the shovel; I think it's best we don't disturb them," Silas suggested. "Do you know what they might be arguing about?"

"According to Penelope, it's something someone needs to know, that they don't know, that they should know, that they maybe will never know." Granny shook her head matter-of-factly.

"Never mind, I shouldn't have asked."

Silas retrieved Granny's pink shovel cane out of Penelope's car and drove through the streets of Fuchsia, eventually coming to a stop in his own driveway. "You need to come in."

"Your house? Why?" Granny asked suspiciously.

"I have some information I want to show you."

"This better not be a trick, Silas Crickett." Granny warned as she got out of the car.

Silas unlocked the door to his house and ushered her in. He indicated that Granny should proceed to the living room. When he joined her, he had two glasses of wine in his hands. He held one out to Granny.

Granny hesitantly took the glass in her hand. "Are you planning on getting me drunk?"

"I think better when I'm more relaxed, and you might listen better if you're more relaxed."

Silas took out some papers and spread them on the coffee table before them. "These are all the companies that are subsidiaries of the Amelia Corporation. They are a big conglomerate but you never hear about them. For some reason, they prefer to fly under the radar. We just happened to get lucky finding those papers that your detective stiff left."

At the word *Amelia*, Granny blanched. Seeing this happen again, Silas challenged Granny, "Spill it. Who is the Amelia Company, and why are they investigating you? Do you know they also own the land outside of town under the name Foofidleyfah Fortunes? There's a rumor they're going to build on that land. Again I ask, what does that have to do with you?"

Granny took a drink of her wine, draining the glass. "I have to go home; I feel weak, and I'm not feeling so good. Where's my shovel cane?" Granny tried to stand up, but Silas grabbed her hand pulling her back down next to him.

"That doesn't work with me. You're fine. Now spill it." He looked deep into her eyes.

"Why should I tell you anything, Mr. Supercilious!"

"Because if you don't, I'm going to find out what you're hiding and tell Thor and Franklin."

"Unhand him! Robbers! Unhand him!" Radish screeched as he flew in from the kitchen window. At the same time, they heard a commotion across the street. Baskerville was howling, the cats were hissing, Little White Poodle was barking and barking, and Tank growled loud enough to be heard in Silas's house. Granny and Silas ran to the kitchen window just as they heard George and Mavis yelling, "Stop or I'll shoot!"

The sound of a gunshot interrupted the barking, growling and meowing that was coming from across the street at Granny's house.

CHAPTER TWENTY-THREE

Hearing the gunshot, Granny grabbed her coat, along with her pink shovel cane, and ran out of the house. Silas ran after Granny yelling, "Hermiony, stop!" concerned at what danger she might be headed into.

The first thing Granny saw was George lying on the ground with the large Christmas tree from his roof planted firmly on top of him. Mavis lay in the snow too with her shotgun in her lap.

Alarmed, Granny ran to Mavis while Silas, taking in the scene, ran to George. At the same time, the noise across the street abated as Baskerville, Little White Poodle, Tank and Mrs. Bleaty headed into the woods by the side of Granny's house, giving chase to what looked like a man in black garb and a black stocking cap over his head.

"Mavis, Mavis, speak to me! Are you dead?" Granny asked in alarm while gently slapping the sides of Mavis face.

"Enough," Mavis answered, swatting Granny's hands away. "I think I shot George. I was trying to wound the guy, or maybe it was a gal, running out of your house, but when I let the shot go, my shotgun kicked back and knocked me on the ground. I heard George yell. Did I kill him? I can't bear to look." Mavis covered her eyes and burrowed deeper into the snow with her back.

"You didn't kill him, wound him or maim him," Silas barked from behind them. "You treed him."

"Treed him?" Mavis quickly sat up and turned around. Granny, too, turned in the direction of the voice.

"Next time you decide to shoot that thing, Mavis, you'd better lean against the house so you actually hit the thing that you want to hit," George advised, extricating himself from the evergreen tree.

Silas walked over to Mavis and took the shotgun from Mavis's lap. Granny gave Mavis a hand and helped her up. "You shot the tree, Mavis."

"I'm confiscating this. You're dangerous. You're *all* dangerous!" Silas blathered in a loud voice. "Someone should have warned me before I moved in. At least, *I* know how to shoot a gun."

The sound of a snowmobile starting up and taking off in the woods diverted Silas's attention. The dogs were still barking and a faint bleat could be heard under the roar of the snowmobile. "Do you mind telling me what this is all about?"

Mavis looked at Granny. "What were you doing in Silas's house?"

"Mavis, focus! Why did you try and shoot someone?" Granny clicked her fingers in front of Mavis's face to get her to focus on Granny's question instead of her own about Granny's little sojourn to Silas's house.

"Someone must have broken into your house, Granny. Your animals came home, ran into your house, and then a man with a black mask came out of your house. The animals were trying to stop him so I had enough time to get my gun."

"Did it ever occur to you that you might have hit the shysters or Baskerville or Mrs. Bleaty?" Granny scolded. "They would have got him if you wouldn't have scared them with your fabulous Annie Oakley routine."

"Catch that crook! Catch that crook!" Radish shrieked, flying out of the house from the door that had been left open by Silas in his haste. Baskerville, Little White Poodle, Tank and Mrs. Bleaty exited the woods and headed toward the shrieking bird. Radish saw Mrs. Bleaty and flew to her head. "Gotcha, Gotcha, Gotcha."

At that moment, Thor drove up in a Fuchsia Police cruiser. Seeing the group in the driveway of Mavis's house, he and an officer jumped out of the car and joined them. "We had reports of a gunshot."

"It's fine; Annie Oakley here tried to hunt her Christmas tree on the top of her house and she bagged George," Granny explained.

"Crazy people!" Silas shook his head and answered Thor, "Someone broke into your mom's house, the animals chased them, but the crazy guy had a snowmobile hidden in the woods. We haven't checked the house yet."

"You all stay here while we check out the damage," Thor advised.

"Check out my cats too. They seem to have disappeared. They didn't follow the others into the woods. On second thought, I'll check." Granny started across the street.

Silas grabbed Granny's arm and held her back, "I've got this, Thor. You check out the house; I'll keep your mom in check."

"George, Mavis, I'll want to talk to you after I've scoped out the house. You're the only witnesses, besides Mom's menagerie—and I don't think they'll talk," Thor said, and proceeded across the street along with the policeman who had accompanied him to the scene. They both drew their guns before entering the house.

"Why would someone break into my house? Maybe I didn't lock the back and basement doors. What do I know Silas that I don't know?"

Soon, Thor waved the all clear and gestured to all of them that it was safe to enter Granny's house.

"Did you find my cats?" Granny questioned as she entered the house, only to stop and view the scene before her. "I guess my question is answered," Granny remarked as she saw Fish and Furball lapping up a broken carton of milk that had spattered all over her kitchen floor. Looking further, Granny saw that all her drawers had been ransacked and her chairs turned over. Walking into her bedroom, the scene was the same.

"Don't bother to go any farther, the family room and exercise room in the basement look the same. Second floor wasn't touched. Your back door lock was broken. That's how they got in," Thor explained. "Do you have any idea what they might be looking for? Have you been doing anything that I don't know about?"

Granny looked at Silas. Silas gently, in a tiny movement, shook his head no, "Haven't even been locked in the cemetery lately," Granny said innocently, shaking her head *no*.

"I'll get the crime scene guys to go over this. You have to stay somewhere else tonight, Mom," said Thor. "Mavis and George, I'll follow you back to your house and take your statement."

The door opened and Franklin strode into the room and scooped Granny up in a big hug. "Hermiony, are you all right? Ephraim called me and thought you might need me. Thor, he said to tell you he'll catch you back at the station. He didn't find anything new after visiting with the former caretaker of the cemetery."

"She can't stay here tonight, Franklin," Thor informed Granny's fiancé, pointing at the destruction all around.

"Maybe she can stay with Silas," Mavis piped up, "since they're friends now and Granny visits him. That way she'll be close to home if the investigators need her."

Granny stomped the umbrella that had been sitting by the door down on the floor right next to Mavis foot. Mavis jumped as Silas said, "You misunderstood, Mavis, Granny was apprising me of my rights if I so much as touch her animals again. I was just ready to call the police when we heard the shot. I didn't see anything. It's been nice—as nice as crazy gets." With a shake of his head, Silas closed the door that Franklin had left open, but not before turning back to have the final word once he was safely on Granny's front porch. "She needs taking care of. I'd advise the Wrinkle Farm or the Hoosegow."

Franklin started toward the door after Silas, "I warned him …." but Thor cut him off he got too far.

"Mom," Thor said, "do you want to stay with me or Franklin for the night?"

"She's staying with me. After all, we're almost married, and we have to plan our Christmas celebration. It will be a good time to get both our families together right before the wedding and attend church together on Christmas Eve."

Granny had been silent through all of this planning. "Yes, I'll stay with Franklin. Mavis, can you see if Mrs. Bleaty can stay with Mr. Supercilious? I have a feeling she won't leave that darn bird. The rest of the animals will come with us. I need to find out if Franklin snores before the wedding. If I can hear him down the hall in the guestroom, it could be a wedding breaker." With a smug smile on her face, she turned, winked at Thor so Franklin couldn't see, and walked into her bedroom to pack a bag.

CHAPTER TWENTY-FOUR

When Granny woke up the next morning in Franklin's new house, the sun was shining into her eyes through a window above her bed. There were no shades on the window. Franklin had explained the night before that since the window was high up on the wall there was no need for shades. Granny wondered as she blocked the sun from her eyes whether Franklin had ever slept in his guest room.

Hearing no sounds coming from the rest of the house, Granny deduced that Franklin was still snug in his bed. Granny pulled on her street clothes and folded her night clothes, putting them in the suitcase. She had settled on her winter red velour pajamas with the fur trim to bring with her for the night. They seemed appropriate to wear in case the house caught fire in the middle of the night, and she and Franklin would have to meet somewhere in the smoke as they were fleeing the fire. Since no such emergency had ever happened, Franklin had not seen her middle-of-the-road nightclothes.

Granny wandered down the halls to the kitchen in search of coffee. Looking around the kitchen, she didn't see a space occupied by a coffee pot. There was a tea kettle on the stove. Granny opened the cupboard and started sifting through the ingredients, looking for a coffee pot and coffee. All she could find was tea. Why was it she didn't know that about Franklin? He always had coffee when he was at the Pink Percolator.

Granny had nothing against tea. She even sipped a cup here and there but it was coffee that revved her engines in the morning and got her sparkling personality quippy and sharp. Hearing the sound of soft snoring coming through the door of Franklin's bedroom, Granny turned and walked into the mudroom between the house and garage. There were the keys to the cars hanging on the hook. Quietly, Granny grabbed her coat from the closet where Franklin had put it the night before. Stepping out of her furry slippers and into her snow boots sitting by the door, Granny found the keys to her '57 Chevy Corvette Convertible. Slowly, and with great care so as not to disturb Franklin's sleep, she edged her body through the door into the garage. Her face lit into a huge smile when she spotted her car.

"I have missed you," Granny declared to the ghosts of the garage. Granny stopped first at Franklin's black '57 Chevy Corvette convertible, opened the door, and grabbed the garage door opener off the visor at the driver's side of the car. Quietly closing the door, she proceeded to her car.

Granny lovingly ran her fingers over the hood of her '57 Corvette. Settling herself in the driver's seat, she put the key in the ignition and held her other hand on the garage door opener wanting to make a quick exit in case Franklin heard the garage door opening and tried to stop her. Granny counted to three under her breath and hit the ignition switch and the garage door opener at the same time. The car started and Granny hit the foot feed, making sure the car was in reverse first, and the car glided smoothly out of the garage.

Turning into the street, Granny saw that it was a warm Minnesota winter day and the snow on the streets had melted. Feeling the warmth of the sun through her front window, Granny decided to breathe some cool, crisp air, stopping down the block to take the top down on her convertible. As she got back into her car, Granny glanced back at Franklin's house. There was no sign that Franklin had heard her exit. Driving away, feeling the frosty air on her cheeks, Granny let out a yell to the empty streets, "This is living!"

Pulling up in front of the Pink Percolator, Granny took the time to raise the top on her car and note where she had parked it. There were some days that Granny forgot where she parked her car or even if she had driven her car downtown. Since her car had been locked up at Franklin's, her garage having burned down, she might have forgotten how she got here.

Delight had seen Granny drive up and had her coffee and donut waiting for her. "You have your car back."

Granny took a sip of coffee before answering. "I do, hijacked it out of Franklin's garage this morning. Do you know he doesn't have a coffee pot?"

"You stayed at Franklin's last night?" Delight asked, ignoring the coffee pot question in lieu of finding out about Granny's overnight stay with her fiancé.

"It's not what you think. Someone broke into my house last night and Thor wouldn't let me stay there, something about processing the crime scene. So I stayed with Franklin. Get your mind out of the gutter, Delight." Granny gave her a piercing look.

Delight giggled, "The gutter is a great place to be sometimes; it's steamier."

The Pink Percolator was busy this morning and the door bells chimed as customers came in to partake of the delicious, delightful, delectable part of the coffee and confections of the Pink Percolator. Granny glanced at the door each time it opened, expecting Franklin to have found her.

"Why would someone break into your house? What were they looking for?" Delight questioned.

"Probably something I forgot that I know."

"I remembered something I forgot." Delight gave Granny a sneaky smile. Granny leaned closer to hear what more Delight had to say. "Before leaving on his last business trip, Delbert gave me a key with the instructions that should something happen to him I would be taken care of. He bought me a crypt in the mausoleum and the key belonged to the crypt. I completely forgot about it when he died. After he left, I threw the key in a basket but it must have fallen behind the dresser. I wasn't too happy at the time, thinking that if he died, he wanted me to commit 'hari-kari' and end up in that crypt, dead, too."

Granny leaned back with a thoughtful look on her face. "What were his exact words, Delight?"

Delight took a few minutes to think back to the last few moments she had seen her husband, "His exact words were, 'This is the key to the rest of your life. I took care of you.' Since it was a key to the crypt and he used the words the rest of my life and I took care of you, I thought perhaps he wanted my life to end soon after his did."

Granny frowned, "You never told me that. You've been carrying this burden around with you ever since Delbert died?"

"No, I blocked it out. I didn't want to think about being in that crypt. I had Ella to raise."

The door to the Pink Percolator opened and a couple of young women dressed in pink flamingo costumes danced in the door, interrupting their conversation. Delight and Granny watched as they danced around the room, throwing pink feathers and candy canes at the customers. They chirped, "Parade at five, the Flamingos are alive" and broke into the song *Jingle Bells* pulling bells out of their costumes and shaking them to the tune.

"Oh, I so love the Christmas Flamingo Parade!" Delight stood up and started dancing with the flamingo-costumed girls. Granny took the square cover off her shovel and started tapping it on the floor to the tune. Soon the rest of the customers were clapping and singing *Jingle Bells* along with the girls.

When the Pink Flamingo girls exited the store and Delight sat back down, Granny voiced the question that had been running through her mind, "Have you ever visited your crypt to see if there's anything inside?"

Delight gave Granny a funny look. "No, I just found the key again yesterday and I'm not there so it must be empty."

"Maybe Delbert meant something else. Maybe Delbert was involved in something you didn't know about and it's connected to all the grave shenanigans. Ferdinand was in Delbert's grave, two million dollars was in Ferdinand's grave and they exchanged clothes after they were dead. That has to mean something."

"Have you found out who bought your crypt at the same time Ferdinand died?"

Granny shook her head. "They think I did; it looks like my signature. I would forget now but back then I was sharp as a tack. Someone must have pulled the wool over my eyes when I was signing something."

Granny looked up to see Franklin eyeing her car parked out front. "Delight, meet me at the lift in the underground streets at 5:00. We're going to see what's in your crypt. I'll bring Mavis as a lookout. I don't have the code for the lift anymore; they made Gravy change it, so you have to call Gravy and get the code. Tell him you want a few moments of peace by your crypt to plan your passing some day."

"You want to visit the mausoleum? In the dark? While the parade is going on? I love the parade," Delight rambled in fear.

"Delight, get a grip. Franklin's coming and he can't know. It'll be fine. We need to talk the cemetery association into putting lights in the mausoleum. But until then, we'll be fine." Granny stood up as Franklin approached, turning back to whisper to Delight, "Remember to call Gravy and get that code." With a smile, she turned to Franklin, "You don't have a coffee pot."

"You could have woke me up and I would have driven you to the Pink Percolator."

"Oh, but your snoring was so sweet. I couldn't bring myself to stop it." Granny stood on her tiptoes and, uncharacteristic of Granny, gave Franklin a kiss on the cheek to throw him off.

Franklin eyed Granny suspiciously. "What are you up to besides taking your convertible out in the winter?"

"I always took my convertible out in the winter until my garage burned down and you held it hostage in your garage. The Pink Flamingo dancers were just here and they reminded me of the joy of Christmas and the weddings that are going to take place in a couple of days." Granny smiled sweetly at Franklin.

"Speaking of Christmas, I talked to our kids and we are going to have one big celebration. Both our families will go to church on Christmas Eve. *We Save You* has announced for once ahead of time of Christmas Eve that Pastor Snicks will be preaching that night. Since I now own the Mayor's house and he left it furnished, it's big enough for all our families that do not live in Fuchsia to spend the night there. We can celebrate the holiday as one big happy family." Franklin grinned broadly at the plans he'd made.

"I don't recall us deciding that last night," Granny reminded him with a frown. "I thought we decided this year that we would let our families have their respective

Christmases on Christmas Eve, and then we will all get together on Christmas Day."

"This will give you a great chance to see what it would be like having a house big enough for the entire family to visit during the holidays. And...we'll be moving in soon after our wedding."

Granny's eyes became little slivers as she looked at Franklin. Deciding she had other things on her mind at the moment, she let Christmas go. Maybe it would be fun. "I'll drive back to your house and we can put my car in the garage. Can you drive me back home? I have to see if Mavis can take me shopping in Brilliant today while the weather is good. I need to go to Red Hot Momma's Boutique and do some Christmas shopping."

Franklin raised his eyebrows and a wide smile lit up his face when Granny mentioned Red Hot Momma's Boutique. "Sure, we can do that. It's important to shop for our wedding night." He took Granny's arm and led her to the door.

Delight had been silent listening to the exchange between Franklin and Granny, expecting Granny's crotchety ways to erupt at hearing Franklin's plans for Christmas. However, the wink Granny gave her as they left the Pink Percolator reminded her that the plans she and Granny had for the evening were taking precedence over Christmas.

CHAPTER TWENTY-FIVE

Franklin dropped Granny off at her house after leaving her car safely back in his garage, having made plans to meet with her after the Christmas Flamingo parade. Granny mentioned that she had promised to help Delight during the busy time of the parade and she didn't want to let her down. Of course, Granny told herself, she had promised to help Delight; they just wouldn't be attending the parade.

The shysters and Baskerville didn't seem to be around. Mrs. Bleaty was soundly snoring snuggled in Granny's soft bed, back from spending the night at Silas's house. Granny thought it was a good thing Mrs. Bleaty was a small goat and that she liked to take baths or Granny would have to clip a clothespin on her own nose to sleep.

Granny pulled out her cell phone, "Mavis!" Granny barked into the phone.

"Yes, Granny; we're in the middle of taping, 'George's Gorgeous Boxer Short Designs.' Can you make it quick?"

"Don't let on what I'm saying to George."

"A recipe? What recipe is that, Granny?"

"We have a new mission. Zero hour is 5:00 p.m."

"You would like me to deliver it?"

"Meet me here at 4:55 and we'll take the underground street."

"Do you need any ingredients for the recipe?"

"Bring a flashlight, dress warm and bring your courage. No screaming."

"Recipe, ingredients, and wine; got it. See you then." Mavis hung up the phone and turned to George. "I have to help Granny at 5:00. She's working on a tough recipe and she needs my help."

Now that she had Mavis on board, Granny looked at the time on her cell phone. She had a little over five hours before they started their investigation. Granny looked at the mess the intruder had made of her house. She was about to start cleaning up the mess when the doorbell rang *Santa Got Run Over by a Reindeer*. She was going to have to change that ring. Angel might get upset.

Starshine and Penelope were on the other side of the door when she opened it. Their arms were full of grocery bags.

"It's not Christmas. I didn't order any food. Why are you here?" Granny asked, thinking about her plans for later in the day.

"We're going to clean up this mess for you," Penelope stated, moving past Granny into the house, "I called Starshine so she drove over to help. It will be fun. Your wedding's almost here and…we can learn more about Starshine's fiancé."

Starshine followed Penelope into the house. "I'm in love, I'm in love, I'm in love, I'm in love with a wonderful boy!" Starshine sang out of tune as she put her groceries down and twirled around the room.

"We have yet to meet this boy," Granny reminded her.

"You'll meet him at Christmas, since we're all spending it together." Starshine twirled and kissed her mother on the cheek.

Penelope was already straightening drawers and cushions. "Starshine, why don't you dust? Mom, you sit down and rest. I'm so glad you have Franklin now so we don't have to worry about you living alone."

"How's the hardware business, Penelope?"

"Fine, just fine," Penelope said briskly, changing the subject, "We thought once Thor took you away from your secret sleuthing you'd be safe."

"I'll go upstairs and get the bedrooms ready for Christmas and the wedding company." Starshine headed for the never-used upstairs bedrooms.

"Don't bother," Penelope informed Starshine, "Everyone's staying at Mom's and Franklin's new house."

"I don't have a new house. And I haven't been upstairs since last Christmas so it probably does need a little spiffing up," Granny retorted. "In fact, Penelope, why don't you take Starshine downtown and show her your hardware store, and I'll take care of cleaning up here."

Penelope quit arranging drawers and pointed to the grocery bags on the counter. "We brought lunch. Sit down and we can talk about Christmas."

Granny moved to the table, looking into the grocery bags. Lifting one of the packages out of the bag she held it out in front of her. "This is rabbit food and I don't have rabbits."

Starshine took the Greek Salad out of Granny's hands, took the cover off and set it down on the table. Taking out the rest of the salads, yogurt, and juice, she held up the last item in the bag and with a statement of triumph, she announced, "And for dessert, tofu sundaes!"

At the word *tofu*, both Penelope and Granny gave a sigh. Granny sat down resigned to eating rabbit food for dinner. "Tell us why we haven't met your fiancé. What's his name again?"

"Lars, and you haven't met him yet because he's shy. He's such a gentle soul and he's very nervous about meeting you, Mom." The look Starshine gave Granny was one of warning.

"Me? Why would he possibly be nervous about meeting me?"

"Possibly because the first time you met Butch, he ended up in the Brilliant County Jail because you reported that he'd stolen your daughter. They put out a warrant for his arrest because they thought he kidnapped me. They wouldn't believe me when I told them I was with him because I wanted to be," Penelope reminded her.

"I can't help it if they mixed up *stole* and *kidnap*. I maybe forgot to add stole *your heart* when I was reporting it. Oh, well, all's well that ends well." Granny dug into her salad. "Speaking of Butch, he seems to be avoiding me."

Penelope averted her eyes. "He avoids what he knows he needs others to know so others know what he knows," Penelope exclaimed.

Starshine looked confused for a moment and then she let out a delightful Starshine laugh, "Oh, Penelope, you're turning into Mom!"

"I'll warn your kids," Granny said with relish and a chuckle.

"I thought you were going shopping? I ran into Franklin and he said you and Mavis had plans. That's why we came over. We thought we'd have lunch and then you and Mavis could shop and we'd clean." Penelope got up from the table taking the dishes to the sink.

Granny's cell phone chimed with a message. Looking at the message, Granny answered, "We're going to spend a little while at Mavis's house making um …name cards…for…um…the wedding! I'll just toodle along and let you clean. How long do you think you'll be here?"

"We have to be downtown by 4:00. I'm in the parade and Starshine is going to help Butch during the parade handing out cute, red miniature hammers."

"Fine, fine, got to go. Don't mess with the fridge. I'll clean it later. In fact, I'll put a sign on it. After all, I can't have you doing everything for me." Granny grabbed a piece of paper and tape and stuck a sign on the refrigerator door. *Stay out. I'll know, and Santa's watching.* Maybe the sign would make her daughters leave her donuts, ice cream and chocolate and other goodies alone so she wouldn't have to replace them again. Every time her children cleaned, they replaced Granny's goodies with salads and tofu and other things they deemed healthy.

Grabbing her coat and stuffing her feet into her boots and putting on her bomber hat to keep warm, Granny grabbed her shovel cane, turned, winked at her daughters, and turned to exit the house. Stopping quickly she said, "Oh, and if the shysters and Baskerville bring a loud-mouthed bird into the house, it's not mine. Call the Tall Guy." She moved through the door, slamming the door behind her.

"Didn't she always tell us not to slam doors?" Starshine laughed as she caught the picture that fell from the wall from the vibration of the slammed door.

CHAPTER TWENTY-SIX

Granny looked back over her shoulder to see if her girls were watching out the window. Granny could see no sign of eyes peering or noses stuck to the glass, so she thought the coast was clear. Just to be sure, Granny made a beeline straight across the street in a path to Mavis's house. At the last minute, she made a turn and headed to Silas Crickett's door. He was waiting and opened it when she walked up the steps.

"What kind of a message was that? Come quick; I have a stick?"

Silas made a gesture and nodded toward his living room, all the while trying to hide the gleam of amusement twinkling in his eyes. "Well, I didn't think you'd come if I said I was sick. You might think I was playing a trick."

Granny sputtered, "You better leave the rhyming to me; you're not very good at it. What do you want?"

"Did your husband know Delbert Delight?"

"I don't think so. Why are you asking? You're not on the case, your son is. You couldn't ask me that over the phone?"

"I thought you might need rescuing from your daughters and I need information. Silas moved to the new wine rack he had installed in his kitchen, opened a bottle of wine, poured Granny a glass, and then waited for her answer. She'd been strangely silent for the past few minutes.

"About?" Granny asked cautiously, eyeing the wine glass in her hand suspiciously.

"I just told you, your husband."

"Look, Supercilious, I'm not telling you anything until you tell me why you want to know and why you're being so nice all of a sudden. Is that your tactic?, Kill me with kindness? Well, it won't work and I don't need a glass of wine right now; I have work to do later." Granny set the wine glass down on the coffee table.

"If you won't tell me about your husband, then tell me why you turn white every time I mention the Amelia Corporation. And why you don't want to talk about the fact that you have a twin sister? And there's also the fact that the private investigator who was following you for whatever reason that none of us seem to be able to find out, ended up dead on your husband's grave that just happened to have two million dollars stashed inside his coffin."

Granny's face again turned white at the mention of a twin sister. "Are you done with your diatribe you ornery coot? Fine, I'll tell you about my husband, but first, tell me how any of this has to do with you.! Granny settled herself down on the couch, fingering the wine glass sitting on the coffee table.

"It doesn't, but would that stop you? My son doesn't know the real reason I came here but I'm over what happened in Alaska, and I decided to work this case undercover. And if you tell them that, I'll tell them about your sister because for some reason you don't want them to know and … for some reason they have not been able to find out who's behind the Amelia Corporation. It's taken a back seat to the happenings in the Fuchsia Cemetery, even with your son."

Granny finally picked up her glass of wine, took a sip and started talking. "I met Ferdinand when I was young. I was a little headstrong; can you imagine that? Anyway when I married Ferdinand and had children, I knew I had to be the proper wife. I didn't get out much. I stayed on the farm and raised my kids until Ferdinand died and I had to move into town. We had lived on the farm next to the home place. My kids were young when Ferdinand died. Penelope was just entering her teens. I knew I had to raise them up in the way they should go; I promised Ferdinand that on his deathbed. He was most worried about Thor but he turned out okay. Thor, I think, has a little of me in him." Granny took another sip of wine as she continued talking, almost forgetting Silas was in the room. "I worried the most about Penelope when she met Butch, because he was 17 and she was 13. They didn't date until she was 17 but I always worried about them. I guess that turned out okay too. Ferdinand was a good provider. He bought the groceries and took care of the farm. I took care of the kids and stayed home most of the time. We didn't go out much except to church on Sundays. He was the decision maker. What more is there to tell? Do you think he had something to do with the two million dollars?"

Silas took the glass of wine out of Granny's hand. "No, but I had to know what your husband was like. Why in the world do you want to marry Franklin? He seems to me to be a bit like your husband and wants to take care of you his own way."

Granny stood up and stomped her foot on the floor. "Silas Crickett, you are despicable, ornery and old and ...deceitful. You lured me over here under false pretenses and then... and then... tried to get me loose tongued by giving me wine and then ... insulting my fiancé! Wait till I tell Franklin; he's dangerous, you know. I can't believe I fell for your poor detective story when what you really wanted to do was to take advantage of a poor defenseless old woman." Granny was ready to carry on the rant when Radish flew up out of the basement and knocked Granny off balance sending her forward into Silas's arms. "Kiss her! kiss her!" the gray parrot screeched.

Silas was about to oblige when they heard a knock on the door and the door opening. "Dad?" the Tall Guy called as he entered the house. Seeing Granny in Silas's arms, he stopped short.

Granny pushed Silas away and walked by the Tall Guy heading for the door. "Arrest this man for luring me here under false pretenses. I'll be down later to sign the papers and press charges," Granny instructed, giving Silas a withering look before leaving.

Silas chuckled as he watched Granny stomp out of the house, "I think she meant it," he informed his son while grinning from ear to ear.

Granny stomped across the street and entered her house. She looked at the time. She'd been at Silas's house for two hours. Her daughters were gone and the house was spick and span. Opening her refrigerator, she saw that her daughters had left it alone. She grabbed a donut and sat down in her easy chair still steaming from her visit with Silas.

Her girls had left the Christmas tree lit. Granny admired the ornaments that Angel had hung on the tree. Next Christmas she would be a married woman with a new granddaughter. Her other two grandchildren, Penelope and Butch's kids, were coming for Christmas and the wedding. Franklin's younger daughter and her husband would be arriving, too. Franklin had told her not to worry about anything, he would take care of the arrangements for Christmas Eve supper and Christmas dinner. Granny suspected it was because her kids had told Franklin about other Christmas dinners that Granny had made. Could she help it if she'd never learned to cook a turkey properly? Ferdinand's mother had always taken care of the meal when she was alive and wouldn't let her daughter-in-law help. Granny had always been better at hunting wild turkeys than cooking them, but as she got older, she was told proper girls cooked and men hunted.

Hearing the patter of the shysters' feet and Baskerville's howl trying to get in the house, Granny checked the time before getting up and feeding her menagerie when they entered. Mavis, for some reason, tried slipping in Baskerville's big door right behind Baskerville, never mind that she had to turn sideways to use the door.

"Granny, help, I'm stuck!" Mavis cried in alarm.

"Mavis, why are you using that door? It's not a people door. It's too small and slim for you."

"I wanted to slip in before anyone saw me. Get me out of this."

Granny quickly turned off the outside lights that had come on now that darkness was approaching. The only lights inside were the Christmas tree lights. Mavis could not be seen from the street.

"Now what?" Mavis asked trying to unstick herself.

"Hold still. I have to think. I could spray you with oil so you could slip through."

Mavis shrieked at the thought.

Granny took her flashlight so she could see better and aimed it at Mavis's body. "Ah, I see what the problem is, your stomach is stuck. Hold in your stomach."

"I am holding in my stomach."

"Wait a minute; I have an idea." Granny sprinted to her bedroom. Mavis heard doors opening and closing and soon Granny was back with a long wide belt.

Mavis looked at the belt and in a whisper asked, "What are you going to do with that?"

"I'm going to slide it over your head and down your body. See if we can get it in between your stomach and the door and then…I'm going to pull the belt tight and see if we can pull in your tummy and pull you through."

"Is this going to hurt?"

"Mavis, there's no time to worry about your comfort now; we're going to be late," Granny admonished as she slipped the belt over Mavis's head and Mavis maneuvered it down over her belly, barely able to get it between her belly and the door. Granny pulled in and the belt pulled Mavis. They both came tumbling out of the door landing on the floor by the shysters.

Little White Poodle licked Granny's face as Tank licked Mavis's face. Fish and Furball nudged their fingers, wanting to be petted. Baskerville sighed and marched downstairs to lie on the rug in front of the fireplace. Granny and Mavis giggled and then burst into loud laughter.

"We should try this for a taping of our reality show. We could call it 'Belted Window Exercise'." Mavis kept on giggling.

Granny picked up Little White Poodle and moved him away so she could get up. "Mavis, we have to go. We're meeting Delight. We're going to be late."

"Oh, are we going to the Flamingo Christmas Parade together?"

"Something like that," Granny assured Mavis before heading for the basement and the underground street door. "You're going to love it. I promise. Follow me."

176 Granny Snows a Sneak

CHAPTER TWENTY-SEVEN

"What are we doing here? The only thing down here at this dead end is the lift to the mausoleum." Mavis gave Granny a questioning look.

"Ah, here's Delight now." Granny ignored Mavis's question and spoke to Delight. "Did you get the code?"

"Yes, Gravy felt sorry for me and understood when I told him I needed some time alone by my crypt to contemplate my future passing."

"We're not going to the parade?" asked Mavis.

"No, Mavis, we're not going to the parade." Granny moved onto the lift, pulling Mavis on with her. Delight punched in the code and the lift moved up into the mausoleum.

"You remembered to bring your key, right, Delight?" They all giggled that again Granny had made a rhyme. She couldn't seem to help herself.

"Key? Why do we need a key?" Mavis looked pointedly at both of them when asking the question.

The lift stopped and the darkness from the mausoleum surrounded them. Mavis jumped closer to Granny and grabbed her arm.

"Flashlights," Granny instructed.

Delight and Granny flicked on their flashlights at the exact same moment, shining them over the interior of the mausoleum. Mavis fumbled in her coat, pulled out her flashlight and melded her beam with the others.

"Looks safe to me; let's move." Granny pulled Mavis with her off the lift and toward one wall of the mausoleum.

"It's over here," Delight informed them as she took the lead.

"It's right next to mine!" Granny proclaimed in surprise.

"Why are we here?" Mavis asked in a timid voice.

"We don't know, or at least I don't know. Granny knows," Delight answered.

"I don't know either," Granny exclaimed in a loud whisper.

"Well, if you don't know and Delight doesn't know, I'm leaving and going to the parade," said Mavis.

"Mavis!" Delight and Granny exclaimed at the same time. "You have to stay; you're our lookout."

"Oh. What am I looking out for?"

"Mavis," Granny said in a testy voice. "Make sure no one sees us and let us know if anyone is coming."

Mavis carefully moved back over to the lift using her flashlight to guide the way.

Delight pulled out her key while Granny shone her flashlight on the lock of Delight's crypt. Delight put the key in the lock and gently turned the key.

I wonder where the key to my so-called crypt is. No one has it, Granny wondered as she waited for Delight to open the large crypt door.

Grabbing the round handle, Delight pulled. There was no coffin in the crypt, but it wasn't empty. Delight looked at Granny in astonishment. "There's something in there!"

"See what it is." Granny nudged Delight.

"There's something in the crypt?" Mavis chimed in from across the room, fear in her voice.

"I can't reach in there." Delight moved back from the door. "What if it's something dead?"

"If it's something dead, then it was stuffed with paper because that looks like what it is—lots of paper and documents," Granny said, shoving Delight aside and reaching into the crypt.

Delight watched as Granny pulled out rolled bundles of paper. Shining the flashlight on the paper, she half unrolled one. "It looks like plans for a building," Delight guessed.

Mavis, hearing it was not anything dead, shuffled through the darkness following her light beam, joining the other two women. "Lay them over the base of Phineas Fuchsia's statue so we can see them better."

"Good idea, Mavis," Granny complimented, as she unrolled the plans on the base of the tall statue. "They look like plans to different banks and jewelry stores. Check out the names," Granny surmised in puzzlement.

"Why would plans to banks and jewelry stores be in a crypt and why would it be my crypt and why would Delbert have told me it is my future?" Delight shook her head not believing what she was seeing.

Granny didn't have the heart at that moment to tell her that perhaps Delbert had something to do with all that was going on in the cemetery lately.

"He was a crook!" Mavis declared in triumph.

Granny jabbed Mavis in the side while Delight declared, "He wasn't. He was my dear sweet delectable Delbert."

"Delectable?" The other two women asked at the same time.

Granny picked up a smaller folded paper and opened it. All that was on the paper were three large XXXs with a circle around them. "I've seen that somewhere before."

"Do you remember where?" Mavis quizzed.

Granny lifted her head into the air, sniffing. "Smell that? The last time I smelled something similar to that I had found the kidnapped girls in the underground room at Gram Gramstead's."

Granny no more than had the words out when she slipped to the floor and was out like a light. Mavis and Delight tried to grab Granny as she fell, but they, too, slipped to the floor and lay unconscious.

CHAPTER TWENTY-EIGHT

The sound of sirens brought Granny out of her vision of donuts dancing in her head, or maybe it was the feeling of someone tapping her cheeks. Groggily, she opened her eyes to see Silas leaning close. "Breathe, Hermiony, breathe."

She pushed his hand away from her cheek and sat up on her elbows. "I am breathing. What are you doing in my house?"

The sirens seemed to be getting closer. "Is my garage on fire again?" Granny asked in confusion.

"Hermiony, you're in the mausoleum. You were passed out on the floor when I found you." He helped her to her feet as she looked around.

"Where are Delight and Mavis?" she asked, now, remembering what had happened. "Did the perfume get them too?"

"George has them outside, getting some air."

"Silas? Why are you here? How did you find us?"

"George asked if I wanted to go and watch the Flamingo Christmas Parade with him. He said Mavis was helping you with a recipe. I ran into Franklin earlier and he was going to the Flamingo Parade with Heather and Angel because you were going to help Delight. I stopped in at the Pink Percolator and Ella said Delight wasn't working tonight. Now, George and Franklin might have believed all of you, but I know with you what you say isn't always what we get. You need a lot of watching and so I watched. I watched Mavis squeeze through Mrs. Bleaty's door. I saw the lights go out and I figured you would get yourself in trouble again and I didn't want your lights to go out for good. Who would irritate me then? Somehow I guessed the mausoleum figured into your plans."

"How did you get in here?"

"Your son-in-law. I know what he's been hiding and I threatened to tell before he did if he didn't give us the code."

"Did you call the police? I thought I heard sirens when I woke up," Granny asked, still groggy from the fumes that had been in the air, but no longer seemed to be there.

"You did. They had gone to Franklin's house."

"Franklin? Is he hurt?" Alarm bells of concern were clanging in Granny's head.

"No, apparently someone broke into his garage and tried stealing your red '57 Chevy Corvette. They tripped the alarm when the garage door opened."

At that moment, George, Mavis and Delight reentered the Mausoleum. "We just got an update on my cell phone," said George. "The thief had put the top down on your convertible and Baskerville, Little White Poodle and Tank happened to be at Franklin's at the time. The animals jumped into the convertible as it was backing out of the garage and bit the perpetrator, and stole the keys out of the ignition so the car stopped dead." George laughed as he was telling the story. "The thief got away but not before spilling a little blood on the ground next to the car door he left open as he was making his retreat."

Granny looked around at the Phineas Fuchsia statue. "They're gone."

Mavis and Delight shone their flashlights searching the ground.

"What are you looking for?" Silas asked as he watched the three women checking around.

"Plans, floor plans for the layout for banks and jewelry stores; they were locked in Delight's crypt. That's why we came here. We wanted to know what was in her crypt, but we didn't want to tell Thor and the Tall Guy until we found out," Granny explained.

"They took everything but this piece of paper with these three XXXs and a circle on it." Delight handed Silas the piece of paper.

"I've seen that somewhere before." Granny shook her head again trying to remember. She sniffed the air.

"I know! It's Gram Gramstead! She's at it again. Why, that old, old, impersonator!" Granny shook her hand in the air.

Silas knew he would regret it, but he had to ask, "Who is Gram Gramstead?"

Mavis, Delight, and George all started chattering at the same time.

"Why do you think it's her?"

"She's in jail. Isn't she?"

"You think she robbed the banks and killed Delbert?"

"The smell that knocked us out was the same smell that knocked me out during the Gram Gramstead kidnappings. And now someone tried to steal my car. You know, she had a thing for that car," Granny's voice started to get more agitated and louder as she continued, "It's her! I know it's her! She's trying to ruin my life again. She wants Franklin! Over my dead body!"

Silas laughed as he heard Granny's last statement. "Apparently, that's been tried and you haven't felt like complying yet. We need to get out of here before they come looking for you."

"You won't tell Franklin or the Tall Guy until we figure this out?" demanded Granny.

Delight's eyes went wide with worry at the thought that she might be in trouble.

George and Silas looked at one another and sighed. George said, "We'll keep your secret this once until we figure out where those plans went and what they are."

Silas closed the outside door to the mausoleum and locked it. Shining their flashlights around the mausoleum and looking in the nooks and crannies and also in Delight's crypt one more time without success, they moved to the lift to go back down to the street.

As the lift moved downward, Granny remembered something Silas had said. "What secret is Butch keeping?"

"It's not my story to tell but he assured me he'll tell it soon," answered Silas.

When they got off the lift and moved closer to Granny's underground door, they could hear the sounds of the Flamingo Christmas Parade and the revelry now being carried down to the underground streets.

"I should see if Ella needs help." Delight turned to the others. "What's next?"

"We help you at the Pink Percolator since that's what we're supposed to be doing." Granny grabbed Mavis and started walking.

"Wait, I don't need to go. George knows what I was doing," said Mavis.

"Help us keep our cover, Mavis. George can go with Mr. Supercilious since that's what they had planned in the first place," Granny reminded her.

"Come on, George." Silas grabbed George's arm, "Let's go to Rack's and have a little Festive Fuchsia Ale and you can tell me what it's been like living across from Mrs. Cranky all these years."

Granny glared at Silas. Silas winked at Granny as he and George moved towards the underground entrance for Rack's Restaurant.

Watching the men disappear, the ladies kept walking toward the outside entrance next to The Dog Wash.

"Do you think it really is Gram again, Granny?" Delight asked.

"But Gram didn't live here when Delbert and Ferdinand died," Mavis pointed out. "You two didn't even know each other then."

"And her sonny boy was too young to have robbed a bank or anything else at that time," Granny agreed.

"Did you notice the names of the banks and jewelry stores that were laid out in those plans? None of them were in Fuchsia. They were in Fish, Allure, and Brilliant, and some other towns up north," Mavis recalled.

Granny turned to Delight. "Was Delbert in any of those towns?"

"I don't know. He was always gone. He traveled so much with his job," replied Delight.

Reaching their destination, they climbed the steps to the outside. The night was lit up with pink flashing flamingo dancers. The Christmas snowmen and reindeer were climbing up and down the poles and moving from pole to pole and the Christmas trees on tops of the buildings were taking turns playing their music. A light fluffy snow had started to fall. The manger scene in the Town Square was lit up and people were milling all around singing carols and greeting each other.

The three woman linked arms as they navigated through the crowds to get to the Pink Percolator. As they entered the coffee house, Delight noticed a young man behind the counter helping Ella. Next to Ella was Starshine, offering customers more whipped cream on top of coffee and holiday drinks.

Granny spied Penelope and Butch at a table off to the side of the room. "Looks like Starshine and that strange long-haired young man are helping out. I don't see Franklin. I'm going over to see what Butch is hiding."

"Well, you better hurry," Mavis warned her, "Franklin's just walking in the door and it looks like he's looking for something, and I'd guess it's you."

"Stall him, Mavis," Granny ordered.

"Me? Stall him? How?"

"Kiss him."

"Kiss him?"

"Tell him he's standing under the mistlctoe and kiss him. That'll throw him for a loop and then tell him you kissed him because he's in your new reality show. That'll give me a few minutes. I'll give you the all clear."

"But….but…but," Mavis sputtered.

"No buts, just get to it." Granny moved away and pushed Mavis in Franklin's direction.

Granny squeezed through the crowd to where Penelope and Butch were sitting. Glancing back, Granny could see that Franklin had not seen her yet, but he was almost to Mavis. Penelope and Butch looked up when Granny reached their table. Butch quickly stood up, muttered something under his breath, quickly walked away and exited through the door to the donut patio. Raising her eyebrows at his quick exit, Granny asked "Something I said? What's he hiding?"

As Granny asked the question, a loud voice erupted over the crowd. It was George. He had just seen Mavis kissing Franklin. Granny decided it was a good time to follow Butch.

CHAPTER TWENTY-NINE

Granny saw Butch dart into his hardware store. Reaching the front of the store, she pounded on the door. He didn't answer. She put her face to the glass of the door and looked in. Maybe he went upstairs to the apartment they were living in above the hardware store until Thor and Heather's wedding when they would move into Thor's house. She made a step to move to the door on the side of the building when she saw a tiny movement behind a rack in the store. She started pounding again.

"Butch, let me in! You can't hide anymore. I know your secret!" Granny yelled, bluffing.

Granny saw Butch slowly move to the front of the store and unlock the door to let Granny in.

"You forgive me?"

"Forgive you for what? I have no idea what I need to forgive you for or what you're hiding, but it's time to fess up."

"You tricked me," Butch accused, moving in the direction of the back door.

"Stop!" Granny commanded.

Butch stopped and turned around to face Granny. "I didn't mean for it to happen."

"What to happen? What did you do?" Granny jumped back in alarm, wishing she had her shovel but she had left it by her back door in the underground street. "Did you murder Delbert? But you were so young!" gasped Granny.

"No, no, I didn't murder anyone. I worked at the funeral home when I was 17. Mr. Delure and your husband came in around the same time. They were about the same build. Anyway, Mr. Graves always had me dress the bodies and he had tags on them. I didn't know them or what they looked like. I brought both bodies out, side by side. I took the tags off the bodies so I could dress them. But, then, I couldn't remember who was who. I looked at the instructions and it said there would be no viewing. Mr. Graves had told me to put them in their caskets and seal them up because they were not going to be opened. So I looked at the clothes and put the clothes on the guy I thought fit the style. Then I put them in their caskets. I was young and I didn't think it mattered who had which casket since no one would ever see them again." Butch hung his head.

Granny had a twinkle in her eye when she addressed Butch. "Never did like that bow tie on Ferdinand. Glad it went to Delbert. Maybe he was more the bow tie type," Granny chuckled.

Butch looked up in amazement, "You're not mad? I told Penelope because she noticed how jumpy I was after the bodies were tampered with. She told me I had to tell the authorities, but I don't know what Mr. Graves will say."

"That explains the clothes, but it doesn't explain how I came to have a crypt and how Delbert got into my crypt and Ferdinand ended up in Delbert's grave or the money. Can you shed some light on that?"

"No, I put slips of paper on top of the caskets so Mr. Graves would know which caskets to put the epitaphs on, but that's about it. Mr. Graves took care of the rest."

"There was a third casket?"

"I remember there was another casket sitting there, but I didn't open it. It was in between Mr. Delure's and Mr. Fiddlestadt's coffins."

We need to call Thor and the Tall Guy. They need to know this. The door opened and Penelope and Franklin made their entrance.

Penelope noticed the look on her husband's face and moved to give him a hug. Franklin stood in front of Granny.

"Franklin, you have lipstick all over your face. Have you been kissing another woman?" Granny put an innocent look on her face.

"Crazy women, first Mavis kisses me and George walks in and sees it and starts yelling. Before George could get to us, Delight pushed Mavis away and gave me the biggest pucker. I didn't know Delight had it in her. Something about mistletoe, only I didn't see any mistletoe." Franklin, befuddled at trying to explain the kiss, shook his head in confusion.

"Delight kissed you? Delight!" Granny questioned in a loud tone, forgetting why she was in Nail's Hardware Store.

While Franklin and Granny were having their kissing conversation, Penelope had called Thor. "You can settle this later; we're supposed to meet Thor and Ephraim at the police station."

"It's getting late, you can handle this," said Granny. "Franklin and I have some last-minute Christmas items to take care of for Christmas Eve tomorrow night."

"We do?" asked Franklin.

"Sorry, Mom," said Penelope, "they told us to bring you along. Apparently something happened in the mausoleum tonight that you neglected to tell us about."

Franklin gave Granny a shrewd look. "I thought you were helping Delight during the parade?"

"I was, poor dear; she needed some time in the mausoleum and asked me to be with her. Something about the dark and the cold. She didn't want to be alone. And speaking of Delight, I need to talk to her about that pucker."

"You can," Penelope informed her. "Delight has been summoned to the station too, along with Mavis."

"What about Silas?" Granny asked.

"What about Silas?" Franklin asked with a suspicious voice, "What has he got to do with this?"

"That's what I want to know. I have a feeling Mr. Supercilious is a nark, an informer, a tattletale and I'm going to take care of him."

Granny left the hardware store, turning in the direction of the police station before the others could say another word.

CHAPTER THIRTY

This time Granny, along with Butch, Penelope and Franklin, were led to the interrogation room in the police station. The Tall Guy, Thor, Silas, Mavis, Delight and George were already in the room. Granny noticed that Franklin's face turned a shade of pink when he saw Delight.

"Are you having a party?" Granny quipped, taking a chair next to Thor.

"It's late, and now that we are all here we can get started." Thor indicated that the Tall Guy should begin.

"Let's start with tonight and the mausoleum. It's been a busy night in Fuchsia and I'm not talking about the Christmas Flamingo Parade. Mrs. Fiddlestadt, what were you and Mrs. Delure and Ms.—ah," looking down at his sheet, "Mavis, ah—I'm sorry I can't read the writing on your last name." He looked at Mavis for her to give him that information.

"Just Mavis is fine. Just call me Mavis."

"What were you all doing in the mausoleum?"

"How did you know that?" Granny demanded an answer.

"I told him." Silas announced, not in an apologetic tone.

"You said you'd keep our secret."

"I said I'd keep it until we could figure out where the plans were. We now know where they are."

Thor turned and pulled out the plans from a box that was on top of the table.

Granny immediately touched the plans. "Where did you find them? Did you find Gram Gramstead?"

"Gram Gramstead? What has this to do with Gram Gramstead?" Thor asked his upset mother.

"She's back, and she's out to get me and steal Franklin again." Granny pounded her hand on the table to make her point.

"What plans?" Franklin turned to Granny, "Hermiony, you need to explain yourself. What do these plans have to do with you and the mausoleum and why would you think Gram Gramstead is back?"

"Gram Gramstead attacked us with perfume that made us pass out in the mausoleum and stole the plans that were hidden in Delight's crypt. Then she went over to Franklin's and stole my car, only the shysters interrupted her. Check the blood you found, you'll see." Granny took a breath. "I need to find her before she does any more damage."

Thor spread one of the plans out on the table for everyone to see. "This is the floor plan for the bank in Fish. It was robbed the same day that Delbert Delight was stabbed, pushed off a curb and ended up in a tree. The other plans are floor plans for other banks and jewelry stores in communities that were robbed. The money from the banks was never recovered and neither was the jewelry. What do any of you know about this? Let's start with you Delight. Can you explain why these plans were in your crypt?"

Delight gave a sniffle before answering. Granny moved to one side of her and Mavis to the other. They both put an arm around her shoulder.

"I don't know," Delight sobbed, "Delbert left me the key and told me it was the key to the rest of my life and he had taken care of me. Granny encouraged me to check out the crypt to see if we could figure out what it meant."

At the mention of her name, Granny pulled her arm away from Delight. "Leave the poor woman alone. She doesn't know anything. You need to find Gram Gramstead."

Franklin moved to Granny's side. Granny looked up to see Silas staring at her with a strange glint in his eye.

Franklin took Granny's hand and looked into her eyes. "Hermiony, it couldn't have been Gram, she's still locked away."

"Did you check?"

"We're checking on it now," the Tall Guy informed her.

Franklin continued, "Why do you think Gram Gramstead is behind all this?"

"It's the perfume. That smell that knocked Mavis, Delight and me out is what Gram and her son used to knock me out when I found the kidnapped girls. And someone stole my car. Gram always wanted my car."

Granny looked at Thor. "Where did you find the plans?"

"In the trunk of my black '57 Chevy parked next to your car," said Franklin. "When they investigated the theft of your car, they went through everything in my garage and found the plans." Franklin admitted this with a shake of his head.

Granny pulled her hand out of his and stood up, "You—you—you are behind all this. Why haven't you arrested him? You're trying to drive me crazy and let my kids put me in the wrinkle farm. You knocked us out and stole the plans. Of course, why didn't we see it?" Granny started pacing. "You come to town, knowing that the money is in the mausoleum. You make me love you and you use me to find your money and then you make me think Gram Gramstead is back. You've planned this all year, you—you, mister. trusted citizen detective, seducer of all women. Why I bet you even enjoyed that kiss by Delight." Granny turned just in time to see Delight blush.

Silas Crickett burst out laughing.

Granny skewered him with a look before marching over to him. "And you're a sneak, a tattletale and a nark. What are you laughing at?" Granny poked her finger at his chest.

"Let's just say you make life interesting."

Franklin's jaw was still hanging open at all that Granny had accused him of. "You think I would do that?"

Delight decided to intervene and patted Franklin on his shoulder, "Of course, she doesn't; she's upset about the events of the evening. It's getting late and she isn't thinking straight; are you, Granny?" Delight raised her eyebrows as she addressed the last question at Granny.

"Everyone sit down." The Tall Guy issued the order in a loud voice. "Franklin had nothing to do with this, but we do think that this latest development and all the findings in the graves are tied together. Franklin was in plain sight with Heather and Angel the entire evening."

Thor moved in front of where Butch was sitting. "Silas seems to think that you could shed some light on this subject."

Butch shuffled his feet and his hands tapped the table.

"It's okay, Butch, I won't let them harm you," Granny promised in a stubborn voice.

Penelope, who was sitting next to Butch, took his hand, "It's okay; tell them your story—the one you had to be most frightened of was my mother and she already knows."

Granny gave Penelope an unbelieving look, "You would think a daughter would have shared the secret with her mother earlier to soften the blow."

"Go on, Butch, what do you have to say?"

Butch told the group the same story he'd told Granny earlier in the evening.

"Did you place the epitaph plaques on the caskets?" the Tall Guy quizzed.

"No, Mr. Graves always did that. I left notes on top of the caskets telling him who was who."

"But you didn't know who was who, you just guessed," Thor pointed out. "The third casket that we found that had the money in it, had the epitaph for my father. If you put the notes on the casket, then how did the casket with the money get buried in my dad's grave? There should not have been a note on that casket."

"I might have mixed up the clothes. I know I put the notes on the caskets that had the bodies in them."

"Is there anything else you aren't telling us?" the Tall Guy asked, looking pointedly at Granny.

Granny looked pointedly at Silas, Mavis, Delight and George, before innocently looking back at the Tall Guy. "I think that's it."

Mavis started to mumble something, but Delight nudged her and gave her a look to silence her.

"That's it then for tonight," Thor informed the group. To his mother he said, "No more graveyard visits, do you understand? We will check on Gram Gramstead and continue to investigate. If any of you think of anything more, please let us know."

"See you tomorrow night at church and then my new house afterward," Franklin reminded Thor. It's going to be a great Christmas Eve and Christmas Day and then––our weddings."

Thor turned to Silas and the Tall Guy. "You're welcome to join us for our family Christmas celebration. The more the merrier!"

Franklin and Granny gave Thor a glaring look.

Silas answered for him and his son, "Thanks for the invite but we're going to spend Christmas over at the prison with Cornelius. We'll be back the day of your wedding."

"So what's next?" Granny interrupted the conversation about the holidays.

"We're going to interview Mr. Graves," Thor answered before the Tall Guy could say anything.

The Tall Guy interjected, "And you," he gave Granny a stern look, "will leave that to us. The next time I expect to see you will be at your wedding."

Before Granny could answer, Silas piped in, "Wed or dead, what more can be said?"

CHAPTER THIRTY-ONE

The first thing Granny did when she woke up the next morning was to call Thor. "Have you interviewed Gravy yet?"

"It's only 7:00 a.m. Go back to sleep and let us handle this."

"It's Christmas Eve day. You don't want him to skip town with the excuse that he's visiting relatives for the holidays."

Granny heard the click as Thor hung up his phone without answering.

Granny shook her head wondering why they hadn't grabbed Gravy for questioning last night. Maybe they were planning on a sting. After all, Gravy was the only one Granny could think of who had access to the coffins all those years ago. Maybe his way with wine and spirits had caused him to have a lapse and turn into a bank and jewelry store robber.

The lights were twinkling on Granny's tree that Angel and Heather had decorated. Taking a few moments to admire the tree, Granny leaned over to look closely at the tags on the presents. The gifts piled under the tree had appeared out of nowhere one night. It looked by the tags on the presents that Angel had been busy making sure everyone in the family had presents––even the shysters, Baskerville and Mrs. Bleaty. Picking up a colorfully wrapped box with her name on it, Granny gave it a shake. As old as she was, she loved Christmas and giving. It was always a mystery to unravel when a present appeared under her tree.

Since Christmas Eve would be at Franklin's new house this year, Granny supposed someone would have to pack up the presents and move them to the house that Franklin said they were going to occupy after their wedding.

Sinking down on her footstool and basking in the peace of the early morning and the twinkling of the lights on her tree, Granny pondered the happenings of the past few weeks, trying to put it all together. The dead body in her yard, the dead detective who apparently had been following her, the bodies with the wrong clothes and in the wrong coffins, someone breaking into her house, and Gram Gramstead trying to snuff them out with perfume. How did it all fit together?

The loud pounding on the front door shook Granny out of her reverie. Looking down to first check her bedtime attire, she grabbed her winter coat and threw it on over her *Sexy Granny and I Know It* PJs.

"Good, you're ready to go."

"Go, where?"

"To interview Mr. Graves," Silas Crickett informed her, while moving past her into the house.

"Thor told us to stay out of it," Granny answered demurely .

"And you're going to listen? What happened to you, woman? Did Franklin finally turn you into a mellow woman?"

Granny bristled at Silas's words. "No...but I have Christmas and a wedding to get ready for and no time for snooping. Let the police handle this. Go home, Silas."

Silas gave Granny a shrewd look. "You really do mean that. I hope you're happy, turning back into the woman you used to be." Silas opened the door and gave

Granny one last look before walking out and across to his house

Granny peered through the curtain in her window to make sure Silas had actually left. Then, she quickly threw off her coat, traveled down the hallway to her bedroom, and rummaged in her closet for some polyester clothes and her hose. Donning her old sleuthing garb, she plopped on her bomber hat, put her coat back on, pulled on her boots and grabbed her shovel, cell phone and pocketbook. With a sly grin on her face, she made her way down to the basement, over to the fireplace, out the hidden door, through the room to the underground streets, and over to the lift to Graves' Mortuary.

"Gravy," Granny shouted as she came up the lift.

"Granny, I thought we changed the code for the lift." Nervously eyeing Granny's shovel, Giles Graves helped Granny off the lift. "It wasn't my idea to change the code; it was under duress by the police."

"Relax, Gravy, I've got the code now, that's all that matters. Have the police been here to question you?" Granny patted him on the chest with her hand.

"Me, no. Why?" He started pacing the floor.

"Suppose you tell me how Delbert Delure ended up in my so-called crypt and Franklin ended up in Delbert's grave and money ended up in Franklin's grave. I'd also be interested to know how I came to be the proud owner of a burial crypt in my name." Granny nudged her shovel in front of the funeral director to stop his pacing.

"You've got to understand, I wasn't myself back then. I didn't do it on purpose. That's why I didn't tell the police when they found the bodies. I could lose my license. Please don't tell anyone. I'll never change my code again on you," Giles Graves begged.

Granny lifted her shovel and brought it back down on the ground with a clank. It was enough to silence Giles Graves. "We know Butch got the clothes mixed up, but how did you get the graves mixed up?"

Giles Graves sank down on the nearest chair wringing his hands. "I was drinking back then, all of the time. When I got down to put the epitaphs on the caskets, I took the notes off of them and then I couldn't tell which note went where and then I moved the caskets around to make room for more that were going to come in the next day. I attached the epitaphs to the ones I thought were the right caskets."

"Didn't you look inside to make sure?"

"No. I don't know. I can't remember. I didn't even remember putting the epitaphs on the caskets. I had too much smoosy boozy that night," the funeral director explained

Granny shook her head in exasperation. "Didn't you think to look the next day? How did the casket get in the crypt in the mausoleum?"

"I don't know! When I came in the next day to accept the shipment of new caskets, there were only two caskets in the room—Delbert Delure's and your husband's. I didn't remember there was a third casket so how could I know it had disappeared? You won't tell anyone. Please?" the funeral director pleaded.

"I won't, but you will. I'm going back home. You won't tell anyone I was here or I'll tell your wife you've been playing kissy face with someone else and you know if your wife finds out, telling the police will seem like a walk in the park. Do you understand?" Granny lifted the shovel and pointed it at his chest before turning around, pushing the code for the lift, and taking it back down to the underground street.

Granny was so busy straightening her clothes as the lift reached the street that she failed to see Silas Crickett waiting for the lift.

"I can't believe I actually thought you were letting the police handle this matter. I can't believe you snowed me. Me!" Silas barked at Granny.

"Take a lesson from the master, what you see isn't all that you get, Mr. Supercilious." Haughtily Granny pushed him aside with her shovel cane. "In case you haven't noticed, I work alone—unless I invite you. And you weren't invited!"

Silas went to punch the code on the lift.

"You're wasting your time. Gravy doesn't know anything," Granny informed the cranky Silas.

"Where are you going now?" Silas queried, getting on the lift, deciding to question the funeral director anyway.

"It's Christmas Eve day. I'm going home to get ready for Santa and my wedding." Smiling sweetly, Granny blew Silas a kiss.

"You're blowing me a kiss?" Silas asked in confusion.

"No, I'm sending you a kiss off."

CHAPTER THIRTY-TWO

As Granny unlocked the door of her house, a fleeting memory floated through her brain. It was a vision of three Xs with a circle around them. What did it mean? Pulling her cell phone out of her pocket, she barked into the phone: "Silas." She heard the phone dialing.

"Didn't you just blow me the 'kiss off'?" Silas answered, seeing Granny's name on his caller id.

"Well, at least it wasn't the kiss of death. Do you want me to help you solve this crime or not?"

"You help me?"

"Of course, I will," Granny tempered her answer so it sounded like a purr from a contented cat.

"I don't need you to help me. You're the one who needs help," Silas blurted crabbily

"Silas, I would be happy to help you. I understand you are temper challenged, but that will not help you solve this crime. I will be waiting." Smiling and with a chuckle, Granny hung up her cell phone and sat down to wait for Silas.

She heard the downstairs unlocked door slam and the thump of feet on her steps before she heard the muttering coming out of Mr. Supercilious's mouth. "I'm here." Silas stopped a few feet away from Granny.

"Do you still have that paper that the thieves didn't get when they stole the plans for the banks and jewelry stores?"

Silas dug in his pocket, took out the slip of paper and handed it to Granny. "You called me over here for three

Xs with a circle around it? The police had just arrived to question Giles Graves."

Granny studied the paper. "I knew I'd seen these symbols before. These same symbols were on a tag of an old key I found on the street by Nail's Hardware the day Mr. Nail was murdered."

Silas took the paper back from Granny to study it. "Where's the key now?"

"I forgot about it. I threw it in my purse. It's in my summer purse!" Granny jumped up and held out her hands to ward Silas away. "Stay here, don't move. I'll get it." Granny sprinted down the hallway to her bedroom making sure Silas wasn't following. She didn't want him to find out about her secret door in the closet. The thought crossed Granny's mind that if she moved to the big house with Franklin, she wouldn't have her secret door or her secrets anymore. Franklin would want to know everything.

Closing her bedroom door behind her, she turned the lock to make sure Silas didn't follow. She opened the secret door in the back of her closet and dug around for her summer purse. She tossed out her chocolates, five pairs of flip-flops, her risqué books and still no purse. *Where was that purse?*

Silas banged on her bedroom door. "Hermiony, what's taking you so long? Heather, Angel and Franklin just pulled into the driveway."

Granny stopped rummaging in her closet, tossed everything back in, and closed the door, straightening her clothes so that they covered the secret door. Opening her bedroom door, she almost toppled over when Silas, who'd been leaning against the door, fell into her arms.

At that moment, Franklin, Heather and Angel tapped on the front door and, since it was unlocked, opened it and came into the house. Franklin looked down the hallway just in time to see Silas in Granny's arms.

Franklin's thundering voice rose over the clamor of the shysters who followed him into the house. "What's going on here?"

"Unhand her! Unhand her!" Radish chanted as he came into the house on Mrs. Bleaty's head. Baskerville followed on Mrs. Bleaty's heels, carrying a purse and dropping it at Granny's feet as she was trying to get her balance and stand back up, extricating herself from Silas Crickett's arms.

"Silas, are you and Granny playing Twister?" asked Angel.

Silas patted Angel on the head. "Something like that."

Franklin was glaring at Granny and Silas waiting for an answer.

Granny stood up straight, walked over to Franklin and in a *don't-mess-with-me* tone said, "I was stuck in my room. I called Silas to find the key. He couldn't find the key so he leaned on the door. It opened. He fell in, I fell out. End of story."

Silas raised his eyebrows at Granny's explanation as he leaned down to pick up the purse that Baskerville had left at Granny's feet.

Still addressing Franklin, Granny reminded him, "Remember, you're the person I'm always falling for," referring to the first time they'd met where she had fallen into his arms.

"Is this what you're looking for?" Silas held out the purse, handing it to Granny.

"Yes, it is. How did Baskerville get it?"

"I gived it to him. He liked it the other day so I gived it to him when I was playing with it," Angel informed the group.

"Where did you get it Angel?"

204 Granny Snows a Sneak

"You gived it to me to play with, don't you remember, Granny? Baskerville dug a hole in the snow and buried it. He just dug it out now. We seed him." Angel looked at Granny with innocent blue eyes.

"I must be going," said Silas. "Have a Merry Christmas and don't get stuck anymore, Hermiony, or you might be stuck for life." He nodded toward Franklin as he gave the warning.

Granny, catching his meaning, answered with a blazing glare of fire in her eyes.

Turning toward her visitors, she asked, "What are you all doing here? I thought you would be getting ready for our big get-together?"

"We came over to transport the presents under your tree. I'll pick you up at 7:00 for Christmas Eve service. Plans are that we will all meet there and head to our new house afterward," Franklin reported, satisfied that his plans for the evening were taking shape.

"It's snowing, Granny. Will you make a snow angel with me tonight?" Angel twirled around the room demonstrating her snow angel move.

"What a beautiful angel you're going to be in the Christmas program tonight. I look forward to being an angel with you." Granny touched Angel's cheek before turning to address her mom and Grandpa, "We'll see you later. I've got a lot to do before the wedding and this is my last chance. Go on now, but don't get stuck in that new snow."

Franklin gave Granny a kiss on the cheek, "Hermiony, stay out of trouble until after our wedding."

Granny gave Franklin a smile and a hug before giving him a gentle push out the door. "I'll remember what you said."

Listening to Franklin's car drive away, she locked her front door. She jiggled the purse, still in her hand. Nothing moved. She had thought she'd emptied it out before putting it away for the winter. Plunging her hand into the recesses of the purse, she came out with an empty hand. Where had that key gone?

Grabbing her cellphone, she spoke softly into the microphone, "Heather."

Heather picked up the phone. "Did we forget something, Mother Hermiony?"

Granny held the phone in front of her and put it on speaker as she asked: "Mother Hermiony?"

Heather laughed, "Well, you are going to be my mother."

"Ask Angel if there was anything in the purse." said Granny.

Angel, hearing the question as Heather had also put her phone on speaker, answered in the background, "There was a key. I was playing fetch with Baskerville and he hided it in the snow by where he buried the purse."

"Thank you, Angel. Santa will be here soon. I will tell him you are a good girl. Bye."

Granny hung up the phone before Heather could say anything more. Granny checked the time on her cell phone before picking it up one more time and bleating into the phone, "Delight."

"The Pink Percolator. Delicious, delightful and delectable coffee and confections," Delight's voice rang out in singsong fashion as she answered the phone.

"Can we meet?"

"Where?" Delight's voice held a wary tone.

"My house. I need help."

"Granny it's Christmas Eve."

"You'll be back in time for the service. It's about Delbert." Granny hung up the phone before Delight had a chance to protest some more.

Granny threw on her bomber hat, coat and boots. Digging in her pockets for her gloves, she came across a hard object. She pulled out the object. It was the crystal from the watch that she'd found by the tree in the cemetery. Who did it belong to? She'd forgotten all about this clue. Looking at it carefully, turning it over in her hands, she decided to put it away for later investigation. Opening the bag of coffee beans on her kitchen counter, she stuck the crystal inside. No one would see it there.

It was still light outside, but the neighborhood appeared to be empty. Granny grabbed her shovel cane from its place by the front door and took off the cover. Delight pulled up in the driveway just as Granny reached the spot in the yard where Baskerville had dug up the purse.

"What am I doing here Granny?"

"The key. The key with the tag on it that matches the piece of paper in your crypt is buried under the snow. I forgot I found it last fall when Mr. Nail was murdered. Baskerville buried it in the snow. We've got to find it." Granny stuck the shovel into the snow and began digging.

Delight got down on her knees and burrowed her hands into the snow, feeling around for something solid. "What if someone sees us and asks what we're doing?"

"We'll tell them Santa buried our presents and we're trying to find them," Granny answered sarcastically. "No one is going to see us. You worry too much, Delight."

"I've got something." Delight pushed aside the snow with her hands and grabbed something solid, holding it up in triumph. "I found it!"

"You found Baskerville's bone. He must have buried that, too."

Delight looked at the object she was holding up. "It could have been the key."

Granny took a shovelful of snow and flung it aside. Something silver landed halfway across the yard. Delight and Granny watched as it landed on Granny's snowmobile. "Bull's Eye!" Granny yelled, trudging through the snow to the snowmobile.

Granny held up the silver object. It was an old key, similar to a skeleton key with a tag that had three Xs with a circle around them. "This is it."

"Now can I go home? It's cold out here."

"This must be why someone broke into my house. How did they know I had it and what is it for?" Granny put the key closer to her eyes to see if she was missing something on the key.

"It looks like a big version of my key to the crypt," said Delight. "Now can I go home?"

"That's it! Let's go."

"You're coming home with me?"

"No, we're going to the cemetery."

"The cemetery?" Delight's voice quivered as she asked the question. Do you remember what happened the last time we were at the cemetery?"

"Yes, but it's daylight and we're not going to the mausoleum. We're going to Delbert's grave."

"Why? He's not there; they haven't reburied him yet. Is that what they call it reburied?"

Granny shook her head. "Delight, we have a duty to solve this before Christmas and before my wedding and Thor's wedding. Then, we can all rest in peace."

"I don't want to rest in peace. That's what they say at funerals," Delight commented in alarm.

"Get on."

"Get on what?"

Granny pointed to the snowmobile.

Delight shrieked, "Snowmobile! I've never been on a snowmobile!"

"Well, let's live dangerously before you get to take a nap in the crypt," Granny suggested as she pulled Delight onto the snowmobile after her.

Granny turned the key and revved the engine. "Hold on," Granny advised, as she took off heading for the ramp in her backyard.

CHAPTER THIRTY-THREE

Delight still had her eyes closed when Granny pulled up by Delbert's grave. "We're here. You can get off now and open your eyes."

Slowly, Delight got off the machine. "What are we looking for here? There's no place for a key."

"Look at the tag. It looks like it could be a Roman numeral or something. Everything seems to happen out here these days and we haven't been out here during the daytime. Maybe we missed something."

Delight shuffled her feet in the snow. "Maybe it's in the mausoleum."

"We know it doesn't belong to any of the crypts. It's too big for that unless it's an old key to the mausoleum door. Let's check that out."

"You go ahead; I'll just sit here and talk to Delbert even though he's not here." Delight sighed and patted the little mound of dirt where Delbert should have been buried but now was left open until the police were done with the bodies.

Granny took a step in the direction of the mausoleum when Delight said, "I used to write love notes to Delbert and I signed them with three X's. He would always put a circle around them and said it was his hug. I guess someone else did the same thing."

"Delbert wrote this?" Granny stuck the key and tag in front of Delight's face.

"No, that's not his handwriting or the way we made our X's." Delight pointed to the tombstone in front of her. His writing looked more like this."

Granny quickly knelt down and grabbed Delight's shoulders. "Delight, that's it. Why didn't you tell me? You knew all along!"

Delight gave Granny a puzzled look. "I didn't. I just saw that now on his tombstone. See, it's almost hidden in the seam of the base and the stone."

"You didn't have it put on when you ordered his tombstone?"

"I didn't order his tombstone, he did."

"He ordered a tombstone when he was dead? Didn't you think that was a little odd?" Granny quipped.

"Well, he was a tombstone salesman. That's why he traveled so much. When we got married, he said his motto was 'better wed than dead,'" Delight giggled, "I thought that was so romantic."

Granny raised her eyebrows at Delights statement, "Did he have a big ego that he needed such a big and tall tombstone? It's almost as big as Phineas Fuchsia's statue in the mausoleum."

Delight stood up and walked around the large tombstone. "He said he wanted a tombstone that had a tall stature to represent the person he wanted to be."

"I suppose he picked out this saying on this large metal plaque on the back too. *Jewels and money are in the past, just like marriages they don't last.* Don't you find that kind of strange?"

Delight brushed a hand over the metal on the tombstone. "Well, he was married before and it didn't last and he's dead so I guess our marriage didn't last either."

"You didn't tell me he was married before, and what about the jewels and money thing?"

"He didn't like to talk about his first wife— something about her being a little crotchety and there was something about her taking him to the cleaners. He bought the tombstone before he married me and we had

Ella. I didn't think he'd need it for a long time." Delight put her hands on the metal plaque and sobbed, pressing her head against her hands.

Granny, not usually being moved by tears, moved over to Delight to comfort her, putting her hands on Delight's shoulders to move her away from the tombstone and turn her around to embrace her. Delight brushed her hands hard on the metal one last time before turning to Granny. Granny happened to be looking over Delight's shoulder. "Delight, you did it!"

"Did what?"

"You found the lock for the key."

"I did? Where?"

Granny turned the still sniffling Delight around to face the large tombstone. The metal with the saying had popped open to reveal a metal door. Granny moved Delight aside, pulled out the key, and stuck it in the lock. Looking around to make sure no one was watching them in the dwindling light, Granny turned the key. The door popped open.

Delight gave a gasp.

"You must have triggered something when you put your weight on the metal and moved away," Granny concluded, reaching into the large cavern of the tombstone. She felt her hand hit something soft. It felt like a bag. Pulling the bag out of the tombstone, she saw that it was a medium-sized velvet pouch.

"Granny, we're going to be late for church," Delight whimpered in fear, "Don't open it."

"Don't you want to know what your husband was up to?"

"He was a good man," Delight stated vehemently.

Opening the bag, Granny stuck her hand in and came out with a couple of what looked like diamond and ruby necklaces. "A good man with a stash of jewelry."

Delight stared at the jewelry in Granny's hand with an open mouth, having a hard time getting the words out that she finally uttered. "He told me we had to live on love because tombstone salesmen didn't make much money. What else is in there?" It was Delight's turn to push Granny aside and dig into the large opening of the tombstone. When she did, she came out with handfuls of money. Looking at Granny with an astonished look, she held out the money for Granny to touch.

Granny took a few of the bills out of her hands. "First, two million dollars in Franklin's casket and now this. Apparently jewels and money aren't in the past."

We have to go, we have to tell the police." Delight took the jewels out of Granny's hands and tossed them back in the tombstone, then she grabbed the money out of Granny's hands and tossed the money back in the tombstone.

Granny slammed the door shut and put the metal plaque back in place. "Delight, we're going to go. We're going to church and we're going to celebrate Christmas and I'm going to get married and then—we will tell the police."

"But...but...but..." Delight muttered in protest.

"Get on the snowmobile. We need time to figure this out. Someone had the key; someone knew I had the key and someone murdered your husband. That same someone knocked us out in the mausoleum to keep us from learning the truth. They stole the plans. That means your husband had an accomplice and he, or she, big emphasis on SHE, is still out there."

"You really think Gram Gramstead is back?" Delight asked, climbing on the snowmobile behind Granny.

"She liked her jewels and she liked to make her own rules. I put her away, I thought she was there to stay, but it looks like she's back and she isn't here for a snack."

"Oh, Granny," Delight giggled, "you should write a book of poetry. I bet it would be a best seller."

Granny revved the engine and took off over the ramp into her yard, parking by the shed in the back.

"There's just one thing I haven't figured out," Granny said to Delight when the snowmobile was silent. "Gram Gramstead didn't live here when your husband and my husband were alive."

"Are you sure we shouldn't tell the police?"

"And ruin Christmas and the wedding? The Tall Guy and Supercilious are leaving this afternoon for the holiday and I don't want to ruin Thor's wedding to Heather and—Franklin forbade me to get involved. What do you think? It's Fuchsia; nothing happens over the holidays in Fuchsia except holiday cheer."

As Delight headed for her car, Granny called out after her, "Mums the word, do you understand?"

CHAPTER THIRTY-FOUR

Granny kicked off her snow boots as she entered her house but kept her coat and hat on. Opening the hall closet door, she dug out an empty box that had been stashed on the overhead shelf and picked up the Christmas wrapping paper sitting in the corner of the hall closet.

Putting the box and paper along with the key on the kitchen table, she rummaged in her junk drawer and pulled out some tape, a piece of paper and a pen. Granny then tossed the key in the box and wrapped the Christmas paper around the box. She wrote a little note on the paper and stuffed it in an envelope writing *Do Not Open Until the Day After Christmas* on the front.

Stepping back into her boots, she opened the front door and trudged across the street through the snow to Silas Crickett's house. Granny rang the doorbell.

"What do you want?" Silas queried when he saw who was on the other side of the door.

"I brought you a Christmas present. Do not open it until after my wedding! Promise."

Granny walked back down the steps before giving Silas a chance to reply.

Silas called out to Granny, "Good thing you caught me. I was just leaving town. Remember, once you're wed, you may dread, waking up and feeling stuck."

Calling back over her shoulder, Granny yelled, "You never were any good at rhyming, Mr. Supercilious."

Granny made it to her porch and into her house before Silas could counter with an answer. Granny checked her watch. She had just enough time to change and pack a bag before Franklin picked her up. They were all staying at Franklin's place for Christmas Eve since he now had an enormous Victorian house. She would come back home Christmas night so she could prepare to become Mrs. Franklin Jester Gatsby the next day.

The overnight bag and Granny were waiting by the door when Franklin pressed the bell to let Granny know he had arrived. "Remind me to change the music on that doorbell, Franklin. Angel might get upset that Santa may get run over by a reindeer."

Franklin chuckled as he took the bag from Granny's hand. "She's too excited to get upset. She can hardly wait to have a new Grandma. Both our families have arrived and are meeting us at church."

"I haven't seen the shysters, Baskerville, or Mrs. Bleaty," Granny remarked, turning back to lock the door.

"They are all at my place frolicking in the big house. Mrs. Bleaty is enamored with the deer head on the wall in the study." Franklin held open the car door for Granny.

"You have a deer head on the wall? You didn't have that in your old house."

"Didn't have room to put them up. I also have an elk head and a fox mounted on the wall now."

"I don't like dead bambis hanging on my walls. I like live bambis peeking through my window. Mrs. Bleaty is probably scared that she'll be next."

Franklin pulled into We Save You Christian Church's parking lot and left Granny off at the door so he could find a place to park. Thor was waiting and opened the church door for her while Starshine and Penelope were huddled to the side whispering.

"What are you two plotting?" Granny asked before noticing Penelope and Butch's children talking to Angel. Without waiting for an answer, Granny moved to her grandchildren and gave them both a big hug.

Tweaking her grandson Bernard's cheek, she asked, "How's college? I see you've become your own man and have let your hair grow out."

Turning to Penny, her granddaughter, she joked, "Penny for your thoughts?"

"Granny, that was cute when I was little, but I'm graduating from college this year with my Bachelor's Degree in Psychology. I have to be professional."

"Well, Penny Ann, is that better?"

"Granny, did I tell you I am going to study you for my thesis."

"Your whatsis?"

"My thesis. I told my professors I had this forgetful Granny who didn't know she was old and thought she was an undercover detective. I'm going to study you to see what happens in your brain when you leave reality and live in fantasy."

Bernard, seeing his grandmother start to make funny faces to answer his sister, quickly interrupted, "It's time to go in; everyone's here. Have you met Franklin's other daughter Miranda?" Taking Granny's arm, he led her over to Franklin. Franklin took Granny's arm, led her down the aisle and whispered, "The next time we walk down the aisle like this it will be our wedding."

"No, the next time we walk down the aisle like this it will be for Thor and Heather's wedding; don't get ahead of yourself," Granny reminded him.

The church became quiet as Pastor Snicks stepped up to the pulpit. Granny took a second to catch Angel's eye as Angel stood in front of the church in her angel costume as part of the manger scene.

Pastor Snicks cleared his throat. "I would like to welcome all of you to this special time, the time we celebrate the birth of Jesus. As you listen to my sermon later on in the service, take yourself back in time and imagine you were present in that tiny manger the night our Savior was born. Close your eyes tonight, listen to the music and the words of Mary and Joseph and the Wise Men. It truly is a holy night."

Franklin reached over and took Granny's hand. Granny looked around at her family, feeling very blessed to share this night with those she loved. She sat back to enjoy the service, noting that she did miss Tricky Travis Trawler, especially on Christmas Eve. It was the one night he didn't try and pilfer from the collection plate. He, too, was in awe of that which took place so many years ago.

At the end of the service, Angel sang *Silent Night*, and the entire church joined her on the last verse, candles lit and church lights out. Granny hadn't known what a beautiful voice her new granddaughter had. A little tear uncharacteristically dropped from her eye. Hearing Angel's pure voice brought memories of Christmas past with her own family and sharing that song in a solo with her twin sister. The lights switched back on, bringing Granny out of her memories.

Pastor Snicks stopped Franklin and Granny as they were exiting the church. "Are you ready for the big day? Any more instructions for me?"

"Nope, we've got it covered. Are you sure we can only use the music from *Wedding Bell Blues* and not the words?" Granny asked hopefully.

"Just the music Granny and don't try to slip them in either," Pastor Snicks warned, "Remember this is a church."

"Fine, fine. I won't remember anyway what with staying at Franklin's tonight with the entire family. I'll probably be too tired for my own wedding," complained Granny.

"What are your plans for tonight, Pastor Snicks? Do you want to join us?" Franklin threw out the invitation generously, "I invited Delight and her daughter, too." Turning to Granny he added, "I hope you don't mind."

Pastor Snicks interjected, "I have plans of my own, but thank you for asking. Sometimes being a pastor can get lonely. We'll see you, day after tomorrow. And Granny ....we'll leave the hay from the manger scene for your goat. I assume she'll be attending the wedding, too, along with the other furry creatures you call family."

Granny was about to reply when Pastor Snicks turned quickly and left.

With a loud laugh, Franklin commented, "He made a quick getaway."

Turning to his family, he indicated it was time for all of them to leave to begin to celebrate their holiday.

CHAPTER THIRTY-FIVE

It was a good thing Franklin's new house was so big. Between the people and the animals, it was chaos. Little White Poodle, Tank, Angel and Baskerville were examining the presents under the tree. Fish and Furball were trying to climb on the kitchen cupboards to get a taste of the turkey before it was carved. Butch and Penelope were engaged in a loud conversation with their children on the merits of living in a dorm versus an apartment, and Miranda, Thor and Heather were plinking on the grand piano in the corner of the parlor.

Granny wandered through the house, checking out the decorations and the furnishings. All were tastefully done. On a scale of 1–10, when it came to high end, Granny would give it a 10. But could she live here in all this finery?

Wandering into the dining room, she saw that the table was set for a sit-down meal with the finest china and silverware correctly placed around the table.

Franklin hadn't wanted any help with the meal. It reminded her of Ferdinand's mother. Granny had thought she left those days behind. If they were at Granny's house for Christmas, it would have been paper plates and cafeteria-style serving.

Granny fingered the lace tablecloth before deciding to find Franklin in the kitchen to offer her help again. When she found Franklin, Delight was by his side and they were putting the finishing touches on the carved turkey. Delight was spooning the gravy into the bowls.

"We're just about ready, Hermiony. Will you get everyone seated?" Franklin asked.

"Delight, I knew you were coming to dinner; I didn't know you were making it."

Delight blushed. "When Franklin asked us to join your family, it was the least I could do to help Franklin. We worked well together; my weaknesses in the kitchen are his strengths."

"Where's Ella? I didn't see her with the others?"

Delight frowned. "She has a new boyfriend and she's spending Christmas with his family. I haven't met him yet and I'm suspicious. She doesn't want me to meet him."

"I thought he was the long-haired kid who was helping Ella the night of the Christmas Flamingo Parade."

Delight shook her head and gave Granny a funny look, "No, that was Starshine's fiancé, Lars. I thought you knew."

"No...I haven't met him yet either; in fact, he was supposed to be here tonight but I haven't seen him." Granny turned to leave the kitchen, "I'll get everyone seated."

Starshine was already standing in the dining room when Granny called the others in. "I thought we were going to get to meet Lars tonight," Granny said as she indicated where Starshine should sit.

"He went home for the holidays with his family. He's supposed to be back tomorrow. I couldn't go because I didn't want to miss your wedding. I might get some ideas for my own." Starshine gave Granny a big smile before turning to talk to Miranda.

When everyone was seated, Franklin said a prayer of thanks before making a toast to his new family. "In with the old, in with the new, I'm so lucky to have all of you!" Franklin leaned forward and kissed Granny on the cheek. "I learned to rhyme from the best of them, Hermiony Vidalia Criony Fiddlestadt, soon to be Hermiony Vidalia Criony Fiddlestadt Gatsby."

Granny took one look at Franklin, raised her glass and her fork and said, "Dig in!"

The meal continued with jovial conversation until Franklin asked, "Delight, I imagine you miss your husband Delbert. So sad that all that has happened recently must bring up some sad memories for you."

Delight picked up her wine glass and held it in front of her for a moment before answering, "You have no idea." Taking a sip, she was about to continue when Granny interrupted.

"No sad talk tonight, no mad talk tonight, just glad talk on this Eve night." Granny threw down her cloth napkin and stood up from the table before Delight could continue. "Time to open presents."

Mayhem ensued as Angel handed out presents and the family teased one another about their gifts. Wrapping paper flew left and right giving the shysters something to chase while Mrs. Bleaty tried to eat the paper. Baskerville plunked down in front of the fireplace and went to sleep.

No one noticed when Granny took Delight aside to remind her of their secret.

"What did you do with the key?" Delight whispered, making sure no one was around to hear.

"It's taken care of. We're going to forget about this until after the wedding. I don't want anything to ruin Thor's wedding."

"But Granny, that could be dangerous. Did you tell Mavis and George?"

"No, they had already left for George's kids down in Iowa. Besides, the fewer who know, the better it will go." Granny hugged Delight as she left for the evening.

Franklin came over to join Granny and they both watched as their children melded together in conversation as one big happy family.

"See how great it is having this house?" He clapped his hands to get everyone's attention. "I need your help. I want to get Hermiony moved before we go on our honeymoon so we are delaying our trip one day to move and since you will all be here for the wedding, I thought you could help us the next day."

"But, but—I haven't agreed to move!" said Granny.

"Hermiony, we'll be married! We want to start fresh. This way I don't have to sell my house, because Miranda wants to move to Fuchsia to be closer to me and Heather, so I told her she could have my house."

Starshine, hearing the conversation, joined them. "And, Mom, I didn't tell you this yet, but Lars and I are moving to Fuchsia, too. He has a new job at the Pink Percolator. I'm going to become a writer so I can write from home. We were going to move in with you until we found a place, but this is perfect, we can rent your house, Mom!"

Granny stared at Starshine. She glared at Franklin and she couldn't think of a thing to say about the matter. *Must have been the wine,* she thought. "I ah, think it's time for me to turn in. This old woman needs her rest and Angel should go to bed, too. She'll be up bright and early to see if Santa left her anything."

Kissing Franklin on the cheek, Granny moved person to person, hugging each good night and walking down the hallway to her room, feeling all eyes upon her. Plopping down on the big comfy bed in what would soon be hers and Franklin's bedroom, she wondered if she could find a place to build a secret closet. Laying back and closing her eyes, the last thought that went through her head was a picture of Silas Crickett holding her gift in his hand.

A strange noise woke Granny from her deep sleep. Sitting up on the bed, she realized she'd fallen asleep in her clothes. Listening closely, she heard someone talking in the hallway outside of her room. Granny glanced at the clock on her cell phone. She hadn't been asleep as long as she thought. It was 1:00 a.m. Moving to the door, she put her ear against it to see who was outside her room.

"What do you mean you can't get back for Christmas? Lars, you promised me you'd be back tomorrow. Snowed in? Snowed in? Since when do they have snow in California? No, I didn't hear you wrong; you said snowed in, not blowed in. You were talking about a sand storm? I thought you said snow! Where are you?"

Granny stepped back from the door. Starshine was clearly talking to her fiancé, not realizing her mother was on the other side of the door. She guessed when she finally met Lars she would have to keep an eye on him for her daughter.

The bathroom in the master suite beckoned and Granny decided to try the newfangled whirlpool tub. Maybe she could get some sleep then. She ran the water and turned on the jets. Watching the water bounce about in the tub was making her sleepy. She turned off the water and decided to shower in the morning. She donned her sedate pajamas that she had brought along so she knew wouldn't shock her kids. Granny turned back the covers and crawled in and again fell into a deep sleep.

Franklin was about to put the wedding ring on her finger in her dream when she heard her name being called. She never seemed to marry Franklin in her dreams.

"Granny, Granny, come see what I got from Santa," Angel's excited voice penetrated the door. Granny grabbed her robe, slipped on her suede slippers and padded to the door. Angel was accompanied by all of Granny's and Franklin's array of furry creatures. They, too, were jumping and howling, meowing and bleating.

"See, see!" Angel pointed to a picture in her hand. "It's a pony. I'm getting a pony!"

Granny took the picture and held it in front of her. "Why I guess it is. Who did you get that from?"

"*Santa*, it says *Santa*. I also got a new bike, see?"

Granny saw that the others also were coming out of their respective rooms from upstairs and downstairs. They gathered around the picture.

Thor frowned. "Santa brought you a pony?"

Heather looked at her dad. "Santa brought her a pony?"

Franklin shrugged his shoulders and looked at Hermiony, "Santa brought her a pony?"

Confused by everyone asking questions, Angel piped in, "He did, he did, he did! His name is Paint and he will be delivered in the spring. When's spring, Granny?"

Granny's eyes misted over and a sudden catch in her throat prevented her from answering.

Thor, seeing that his mother's eyes were tearing up, put an arm around her shoulder. "Are you ok?"

Granny cleared her throat and looked at Franklin. "Yes, ah, um, how did you, ah, I mean, Santa know that I also had a pony by the name of Paint?" Kneeling down to get to Angel's height, she took the little girl in her arms. "This will be a very special pony. Mine was. I loved him with all my heart. He was my best friend and this pony of yours with the same name, will be your best friend too."

Granny stood back up, the tears escaping from her eyes. She looked at Franklin and mouthed the words,

"Thank you." Moving closer, so Angel couldn't see, she asked Franklin, "How did you know?"

Before Franklin could answer, the doorbell rang and they could hear carolers outside.

The group opened the door so they could enjoy the music from the We Save You Christian Church Carolers. It was a Christmas tradition that those who could, spent Christmas morning wishing the citizens of Fuchsia a Merry Christmas with their gift of song.

Pastor Snicks hollered out from the back row of the group, "Get your snowmobile ready, Granny, we're supposed to get heavy snow tomorrow. Your guests might have to be escorted to the church on snowmobiles or they might get stuck there all night."

The Fiddlestadt and Gatsby group chimed back singing, "Let It Snow, Let It Snow, Let It Snow!"

Bidding the carolers farewell, the families settled down to spend Christmas eating goodies, watching football and playing games.

Watching her family enjoying themselves, Granny moved to Franklin's side. "It's almost four o'clock, Franklin; I think I want to go home and spend my last evening as a single woman quietly and by myself. Will you drive me?"

Hearing that her mom was about to leave, Penelope stood up and walked over to Franklin's bar. She passed out a glass of wine to all the legal drinkers in the room. "I want to make a toast to Mom and Franklin. Franklin, since you have come into my mother's life, you have changed it for the better. She no longer seems to have as much of a memory problem."

Starshine lifted her glass, "She doesn't need a cane anymore, only occasionally; you have put a spring in her step."

Thor stepped forward, a twinkle in his eyes. "Yes, Franklin, her memory is better, her step is quicker and remember, the key to knowing my mother is to look at what shoes she has on in the morning and what she holds in her hand." He raised his glass.

Starshine and Penelope said at the same time, "What?"

"Time to go," Granny said quickly, "I'll toast and roast you tomorrow, Thor and Heather."

Watching Franklin and Granny leave, Thor commented, "Granny has left the building."

CHAPTER THIRTY-SIX

Franklin walked Granny to her door, carrying her bag for her. As Granny was about to unlock her door, she looked closely at it in the darkening light. "Franklin, I have hole in my door."

Franklin moved closer. "That's not a hole, that's a gunshot. Someone shot at your house! I better call it in."

"Franklin, Granny," George hollered at them from across the street.

"I thought you were gone?" Granny yelled back.

Mavis came out of the house and she and George came across the street.

"We came back for your wedding, and it's good we did." Mavis nodded toward the door as she spoke.

"You know something about this?" Franklin asked, "I was just going to call it in."

George hung his head. "I shot the door."

"George I warned you, you could hurt someone." Granny pounded a finger into his chest.

"I was shooting at the guy who was trying to get into your house. It was the same one as before."

"Are you sure it was a guy and did you hit him?"

"No, Granny, I couldn't tell if it was a guy or a gal, but I didn't hit him, I hit your door. He didn't get in. I scared him first. All the lights were off in the neighborhood so he must have thought we were all gone and it was safe."

"All of you, stay here, I'm going to check the house." Franklin waved them away from the door as he searched the outside of the house. When he returned he said, "It's all clear! George is right; it doesn't look like he made it in. But, Granny, you can't stay here tonight."

Granny picked up her shovel cane that was sitting outside on the porch and stomped it down. "It's my last night as a free woman and I'm staying here." Granny announced giving them a *don't-mess-with-me* look.

"We'll watch out for her, and Thor is across the street. Let him know what happened," George advised Franklin.

Reluctantly, Franklin agreed. Bending down to kiss Granny, he advised, "Lock your doors and keep your phone by your bed. Call Thor if anything happens."

"I've got my shovel cane, my knitting needle cane and my umbrella. What more do I need? Oh, and Franklin, that was a very nice thing that you did getting a pony for Angel. How did you know that Paint was special to me?"

Franklin looked uncomfortable; he shuffled his feet, and looked up at Granny with a sheepish look. "I didn't. I have no idea where the pony came from. I didn't know that you had a pony named Paint that was special to you."

Granny thought about what to say. "Franklin, you are a good man—pony or not—and if any of you tell anyone you ever heard me say that, I will haunt you after I'm in that crypt that's supposed to be mine. I loved the necklace with the umbrella on it that you gave me today. Good night. See you tomorrow."

Granny watched as Mavis and George exited the house. Granny issued an order before Franklin could follow them. "Stop, Franklin."

Franklin stopped and turned. Granny issued her second order, "But not before the wedding; it's bad luck you know."

Issuing her third order in typical Granny style, "You can go now." She shut the door after him, walked to her footstool and pulled out her bottle of wine, walked to the cupboard and pulled out her chocolate donut, opened the refrigerator and pulled out her ice cream and arranged them all on a tray.

Making sure all the doors were locked, since the shysters, Baskerville, and Mrs. Bleaty were staying at Franklin's, she carried the tray to her bedroom and set it down on the bed. She opened her hidden closet door and grabbed her flip-flops and put them by the bed. Digging some more, she pulled out one of her risqué books and set it on the bed. Remembering she had forgotten her chocolates, she dug around in her closet to find a box. Setting them on the bed, she pulled out her summer hot pink shortie nightie with the red hearts on it and put it on. Having everything she needed, she climbed into bed and was ready for a final single night binge when she remembered she needed to call Thor first. She didn't want to have to think about the grave shenanigans on her wedding day.

Thor answered immediately, "Are you ok? I can come right over. Franklin let me know what happened."

"I'm fine. I just wanted to know if you checked on Gram Gramstead."

"I did; she's safely locked away. I thought someone told you that."

"Um, maybe—I don't remember. And what about that private detective who ended up a stiff on your dad's grave? Did you find out why he was investigating me?"

"The theory is that you apparently applied for disability income a few years back before you retired and you're still receiving that income. The insurance company got a call that you weren't disabled and he was investigating and happened to be in the wrong place at the wrong time."

"I did? I'm disabled? They're sending me money?"

"We haven't had time with all the stuff going on to check it out. Our main concern was his death which happened to be wrong place, wrong time. Mom, get some rest, we're all getting married tomorrow. Forget about all this, we'll take care of it."

Granny hung up the phone and grabbed her wine and chocolate donut. She nodded her head. *Well, wine and a donut—there was a first time for everything,* she thought as she started sipping and eating.

CHAPTER THIRTY- SEVEN

When Granny opened her eyes the day of her wedding, it was late. She knew because she could see the sunlight through the cracks in her shades. She wallowed in the warmth of her bed. She stuck her big toe out of the blanket to determine the weather. Her toe barometer was very blue. She had known since it was winter that it was not a flip-flop day, but it was her last day as a single woman, and flip-flops seemed the order of the day—inside at least.

Granny sat up and moved her feet over the side of the bed to slip into the flip-flops. She took a moment to steady herself; her head was pounding from her freedom binge last night. Grabbing the post of the bed for support, she stood up. She shivered in the cold having forgotten that she had on her summer PJs. She picked up her warm, red chenille robe decorated with red hearts and put it in on, tying the robe tightly around her.

Since she'd been engaged to Franklin, she didn't have to worry anymore that she would be surprised to find her kids already here cleaning her house as they had in the past. No more did she have to listen when she got out of bed to make sure no one else was in the house as she had had to do in the past. They had turned their *watching Mom duty* over to Franklin.

Flip flopping down the hallway, her eyes half open, her mind counted off everything that was going to happen today. Yawning, she was about to flip the switch on her coffee pot when she heard giggling.

"Surprise!"

Granny jumped and tripped over the cat and dog bowls at her feet, putting one flip-flopped foot in Baskerville's large water bowl.

"Surprise, surprise!" Mavis and Delight jumped up and down with glee.

"It certainly is," Granny remarked, shaking one flip-flopped foot in the air to dry it off. "What are you doing here and how did you get in?" Granny asked, pulling the belt on her robe tighter so she wouldn't reveal what was underneath.

"We are whisking you away to the new Dotty's Glam and Dram Shop to get ready for your wedding. Franklin let us in. We'll all have our hair done, makeup, pedicure, and sip a little bubbly. It'll be fun and then the car will pick us up and take us to the church for your wedding. Heather and Angel will be glammed, too, although there's no bubbly for Angel except for Ginger Ale." Mavis's smile gave away her excitement. "You're getting married, you're getting married!"

"Ladies, this is a nice idea, but I thought I'd do my own hair and I have to give the shysters a bath so they are all cute and ruffly for the wedding."

"They are going to the Meow and Bark shop to get glamorous themselves. Come on, Granny, let's go!" Mavis grabbed Granny by the shoulders and moved her toward the door.

"I can't go out in the snow in my flip-flops. Did you see my blue toe?"

Delight gave Granny a slight push toward her bedroom. "Get dressed, we'll be waiting."

Back in her bedroom, Granny threw on some clothes, made sure everything she'd dug out from the night before had been put back in her secret closet, and rejoined her friends. "Do you think I should dye my hair red for the wedding?" Granny teased, laughing at the thought.

Mavis and Delight gave each other a knowing look before Mavis answered, "That's the spirit!"

Driving to the Glam and Dram shop, Granny noticed small snowflakes starting to fall. "It looks like Pastor Snicks may have been right about the snow. Delight, do you have that special bouquet made and is everything set up for the reception?"

"Bouquet is ready and at the church. Rack's and I have the reception all together. It was so nice of you and Franklin to compromise and have dinner at Rack's with dessert and the dance at the Pink Percolator. Once everyone has had their dessert, we will clear the tables for the dance. Relax, we've got it all covered!"

Dotty, Heather and Angel were waiting for them at Dotty's.

"This is the first time I've been in here," Granny remarked, walking around the shop, noticing the large wine selection on the inside wall. Granny felt a tight squeeze around her legs.

"Hi, my very own Granny! Look!" Angel twirled around. "See the rings in my hair? They're not the kind of rings like you put on your fingers, but I can put my finger through the rings in my hair!"

Dotty handed Granny, Mavis and Delight each a glass of white wine, handing a glass of ginger ale to Angel.

"I haven't had breakfast yet. Do you have any coffee?" Granny started to set the wine glass down. "On second thought, it's my wedding day, one glass of wine for breakfast going down."

"Can you spike my hair?" Mavis asked Dotty.

"Why don't you add a little pink to it, too?" Granny suggested, with a sly smile on her face. "That should boost ratings for your pretend reality show."

"Sit here, Granny; I'm all ready for you." Dotty moved the chair around so Granny could sit down. "We'll do your hair and then your makeup."

Granny frowned. "Not much to do, just wind it up on top of my head."

"I have instructions, just relax."

"Instructions from who?"

"Mavis and Delight."

"And what might those instructions be?" Granny asked, as she looked at Mavis and Delight suspiciously.

Heather interjected, "Relax and enjoy the spa experience. I'll be in having a massage. Let them surprise you; they wouldn't do anything that would make you look bad on your wedding day. Would you ladies?" Heather gave them a warning look.

"This is kind of like one of those shows on television where they surprise you with what you look like. So you can't have a mirror. You're in Dotty's hands," Delight explained, covering the mirror in front of Granny's chair.

"And I get to watch," Angel said in excitement. "But I can't tell you what you look like."

"Great, Granny said sarcastically. "Ok, I'll live dangerously. Let's do it."

Headphones were put on Granny's ears and Mavis set Granny's glasses on the side table. Mavis indicated they would be in another room getting themselves glammed up, too. Granny leaned back and listened to the rock and roll music shaking through her headphones.

When Dotty returned Granny's glasses, took off her headphones, and turned the chair around, Angel beamed. "Granny you look beautiful!"

"Now, for the makeup, less is more." Dotty began work on Granny's face. "Now, I know you usually don't bother with makeup, you really don't need much."

Granny stretched her lips and felt the pull of her eyelids as Dotty touched here and there on her face with different brushes.

Mavis, Delight and Heather came back into the room and all three gasped as they got a look at Granny.

"That bad?" Granny barked in alarm.

"No, that good," Mavis answered.

Granny raised an eyebrow, puzzled and suspicious. "How can a little makeup, a hair trim and a hair wash make you gasp like that?"

"My Grandpa gave them the idea and he said you would be beautiful. I love you, Granny." said Angel.

"Do I get to see myself? You have all the mirrors covered," said Granny.

"It's time to get dressed; our car will be here soon. Dotty has a couple of bride rooms in the back. Let's go," Heather chimed in, taking Granny's arm and walking with her, talking in a whisper, "You do look beautiful. I wasn't sure about this but you can always change it later if you don't like it. My dad made a few suggestions to your friends. Just go with the flow and remember it's the love that counts." With a squeeze, she went into one room while Delight and Mavis led Granny to the other dressing room where her dress and shoes were waiting for her.

Granny got dressed in the red satin and velvet sequined skirt, jacket and blouse she had chosen. She slipped on her shoes. There no mirror in the dressing room. Granny was sure that was on purpose since her friends seemed to want to do a reveal.

The first person Granny saw when exiting her dressing room was Heather. Taking Heather's hands, she remarked with a tear in her eye, "Heather, you are beautiful and I'm so very lucky that you will be my new daughter." She gave Heather a hug.

Turning to Mavis and Delight, she noticed the gleeful expressions on their faces. "Is it time for the reveal? I want to know what all of you have been gasping about."

Dotty led Granny over to the large mirror while Mavis and Delight tore the paper off the mirror. Granny stood in front of the mirror and was speechless.

Angel was dancing up and down and clapping her hands, enjoying the surprise on Granny's face.

"Who is that?" Granny's speech finally coming back, "I have red hair! I look like Gram Gramstead did. Whose idea was this? It's my wedding day and I have red hair!"

Frowning, Mavis moved forward, "Granny, what's happened to you? Shake out if it. You like the new, you like the adventure, you like change! What did you do with you?"

"I would have liked it to be my idea. What is Franklin going to say? Who's going to hire an undercover red-haired old lady?" Granny asked in alarm.

"It was Franklin's idea," Delight informed Granny. "He thought you liked Gram's red hair and he thought it might give you a little more polished look for your wedding."

"Polished? I'll polish him later."

Heather moved forward. "He loves you, Mom Fiddlestadt. You really look nice and it's your wedding day."

Granny turned away from the mirror. "You're right; it's only hair and I always wanted to try red hair. Why not on my wedding day?"

Angel had been watching out the window. "Your car is here, Granny! Your car is here to pick us up."

Granny moved forward to the window. Sitting outside was her red '57 Chevy Corvette driven by George. Behind the red Corvette, was Franklin's black '57 Corvette with Butch driving. Mavis moved to open the door of the salon for Granny. "Franklin thought it might make you happy for you to ride to the church in your Corvette on your wedding day. Heather will follow in Franklin's car and we'll be right behind you with Angel.

Granny moved through the door with a smile on her face. "I guess at least my hair matches my dress and my car. I am so color coordinated. Did anyone wrap my shovel cane in red?"

CHAPTER THIRTY-EIGHT

The parking lot was filling with cars when George dropped Granny off at We Save You Christian Church. While the women had been at Dotty's Glam and Dram shop, the snow had accumulated on the streets and was falling fast. The wind was swirling and blowing, making drifts look like waves on the streets.

"Perfect day for a blizzard," Granny remarked to her grandson, Bernard, as he opened the door of the car to escort Granny into the church.

"You have red hair!" Bernard proclaimed when he saw his grandmother.

Ignoring her grandson, she moved out of the snow and into the church.

"Look at all the people here, Granny! They made it through the snow," Heather gushed, realizing that she, too, was going to be married in a manner of minutes.

"It's Fuchsia; we aren't scared of weather."

Starshine and Penelope, seeing their mother, pulled her into the corner. "Your hair is red!" Penelope screeched.

"You should have added a little pink or purple strip," Starshine suggested, admiring the color.

"What made you do this, Mother?" Penelope asked in an exasperated tone. "It's your wedding day, you can't have red hair!"

Bristling at Penelope's tone, Granny answered haughtily, "Angel thinks I look beautiful. Excuse me. I need to talk to Heather. Her wedding is about to start."

Granny moved to where Heather was waiting and handed her a necklace. "This is something old. It was given to me by my grandmother."

"Don't you want to keep that for Starshine or Penelope?" Heather asked with tears in her eyes at Granny's sentimental gesture.

"I have something special for each of them, but this necklace seems to fit you. She was a gentle soul and showed everyone love, especially her children and grandchildren. I didn't inherit that gentle attitude. No matter what she went through, she kept that gentleness of spirit. She gave me this necklace and told me when life got too much for me to wear it and feel her spirit. I would know she was with me. The necklace has a dove engraved on it. The symbol of peace and love, and I feel she would want you to have it because you are so much like her."

Heather reached out and hugged Granny tightly.

Granny gave her a quick squeeze and moved out of the hug, taking Heather's cheeks in her hands, "'Nough said; let's get you and my son married." Granny turned toward the organist and yelled, "Hit it!"

With Granny as Matron of Honor, and Franklin as Best Man, along with Angel as Flower Girl, Pastor Snicks pronounced Heather and Thor man and wife. The entire congregation stood and clapped as Heather and Thor and the wedding party exited the main sanctuary of the church.

Pastor Snicks indicated the congregation should sit back down. "We will have a few moments of Christmas music performed by the Cranberrys while we are waiting for Franklin and Hermiony to come back down the aisle so I can perform their ceremony. I want to thank you all for coming on this beautiful snowy winter day. The Fuchsia Highway Department asked me to announce that they are working on the roads and they hope to have them plowed by the end of the wedding so you will be able to travel to Rack's for the reception. For those of you who live in the country, they suggest you make alternative arrangements for staying in town. Now let the music begin!

In the back of the church, Granny paced left and right, telling herself to breathe deeply.

"Mom, are you okay?" Starshine asked, trying to keep up with her mother's pacing.

"I'm getting married, I'm getting married, I'm getting married."

"Of course you are," Starshine replied, confused by Granny's pacing and muttering.

"We're almost ready to go in," Penelope announced, stopping Granny in her pacing track.

"Granny, do you like the dress you helped me pick out for your wedding?" Angel pirouetted in front of Granny.

Granny looked down at Angel and a lump formed in her throat. "You are my Angel. Are you ready?"

Wedding Bell Blues floated through the air. Franklin and Thor took their positions at the front of the church. Pastor Snicks joined them. The congregation, hearing the music, stood. Granny could see Mavis, George and Delight beaming. She could see Giles Graves, Ditty Belle and all the other owners of the businesses in Fuchsia smiling, waiting for her to walk down the aisle. Bernard and Penny were sitting at the front of the church with Butch.

Penelope handed her mother the bouquet of flowers. "Delight said to tell you it's arranged exactly as you wanted, whatever that means."

The patter of furry feet approached them along with the click of Mrs. Bleaty's hooves. "They're ready, too, Granny, they're going to be flower girls with me."

Dotty from the salon was with Granny's furry family. "I was keeping them occupied until it was time for your wedding. I hope you don't mind, but they've already had their ice cream and cake when I stopped to check on the dessert at the Pink Percolator. I helped Ella with some of the details before we came here.

Granny took the time to lean down to hug Fish, Little White Poodle, Furball and Tank, then admired the ribbons in Furball's and Little White Poodle's hair. Fish and Tank sported bow ties around their necks. Mrs. Bleaty nudged Granny's arm with the flower that was pinned to her head.

"Where's Baskerville?" Dotty nodded toward the front. "He's with Franklin and Thor." Sure enough, when Granny looked, the three were side by side. Granny's eyes misted over a little at the sight of her furry menagerie taking part in their special day.

Heather, being the first attendant, started walking slowly down the aisle, followed by Penelope, Starshine and Miranda. Angel, along with the furry ones, moved into place after them. Angel then began dropping petals of roses in her path and Mrs. Bleaty followed, eating them up on the way down to the front of the church.

Granny took a big breath, a big step, and looked over the crowd that was waiting. She was about to take another step when her eyes settled on someone staring right at her with a thoughtful expression on his face. Silas Crickett was at her wedding. She faltered on the next step, took another deep breath, and walked down the aisle to join Franklin at the front of the church.

Franklin reached for her hand, leaned over, and whispered, "You look beautiful. I love your hair. I knew you would be a bombshell in red, Hermiony."

Granny closed her eyes a moment before turning to Franklin to listen to what Pastor Snicks was saying.

When it came time for the vows, Franklin turned to Granny.

Please repeat after me said Pastor Snicks, "I, Franklin Jester Gatsby, take thee, Hermiony Vidalia Criony Fiddlestadt, to be my loving wife."

"I, Franklin Jester Gatsby, take thee, Hermiony Vidalia Criony Fiddlestadt, to be my loving wife." Franklin leaned over and whispered to Pastor Snicks, "I can take it from here, I have it memorized. To have and to hold from this day forward, for better or worse, for richer for poorer, in sickness and in heath, to love and to cherish till death do us part, according to God's holy ordinance and therefore I plight thee my troth."

Pastor Snicks turned to Granny, "Do you Hermiony, Vidalia, Criony Fiddlestadt…"

Granny leaned over and whispered to Pastor Snicks, "I got this; I just heard it a few minutes ago. I, Hermiony Vidalia Criony Fiddlestadt, take thee, Franklin Jester Gatsby, to be my loving husband, to have and to hold from this day forward, for better or worse, for richer for poorer, in sickness and in health, to love cherish and uh, and uh," Granny happened to look up at Pastor Snicks as she was trying to get the word *obey* out of her mouth when her eye caught the face of his watch. Her mind switched to the day in the cemetery when she was watching the workers exhume Delbert Delure's grave.

Granny dropped Franklin's hand, jumped back, and faced Pastor Snicks. "It's you, and you're the murderer and the grave robber!" She held her bouquet in front of her pointing it at Pastor Snicks. Your watch. It's missing its crystal; you were there that day. You tried to murder me, too!"

Pastor Snicks dropped his wedding book and moved behind the pulpit. Franklin stared wide-eyed at

Hermiony. Whispers mingled in the church at Granny's outburst.

Pastor Snicks reached for something on the pulpit shelf then brought out a gun as Granny was moving toward him just as Franklin was trying to stop Granny. Pastor Snicks fired his gun. Granny heard a yelp and turned to see Franklin hit the floor. People moved for cover. The shysters were ready to attack, but were held back by Granny's daughters who were afraid the animals would be shot.

Baskerville and Mrs. Bleaty, too, were down on the floor caught between Franklin and Thor.

At the same time, Pastor Snicks moved forward, grabbing Granny, moving her backwards with an arm around her neck, pointing the gun at her, while informing those in the congregation, "Don't move or she'll be dead, not wed." With Granny in tow, he moved toward the room off the sanctuary and the side door leading to the outside. Still holding the gun on Granny, he made his way out of the church, making sure no one was following. There was only barking and bleating at the closed door.

Granny, still holding her bouquet, protested, "I don't have boots! It's cold! We need coats; we'll freeze!" trying to get her captor to loosen his grip. "You'll never get away with this. Franklin and Thor will come after you."

"Franklin's down for the count; someone shot him," Pastor Snicks said in a snide tone, "and Thor, well, I guess you couldn't see but he had a small accident as he tried to follow us."

"What did you do to my son?" Granny struggled in his arms but then she felt the gun in her side.

Pastor Snicks led Granny through the falling snow to the parking lot. Seeing Granny's Corvette parked near the church, he led her over to the car. Keeping one arm

244 *Granny Snows a Sneak*

still around Granny, he opened the car door. "How convenient; they left the keys in the car. Fuchsia residents are so trusting." Granny could hear the sneer in his voice before he thrust her into the driver's seat and, still holding a gun on her through the windshield, got in next to her in the passenger side.

"Now drive."

"Me? You want me to drive in this weather?"

"Don't argue, drive," he commanded, throwing the keys in her lap and pressing the gun to her neck.

"Where?"

"To your house to get the key and don't get stuck."

"This car doesn't have four-wheel drive or even front-wheel drive and here's a little more information— it doesn't have snow tires. We're gonna get stuck."

Glancing back at the church, he nudged her with the gun. "Faster. Go through the cemetery. We'll park there and go over the fence on the ramp. You can give me the key and I'll make use of your snowmobile. In between, I'll deposit you in your crypt and by the time they find you, I'll be long gone."

Granny slowly made her way to the outside of Fuchsia and the street leading to the cemetery.

"I like you, Granny. I wish I didn't have to do this but you got in the way."

"How did you know I had the key and how did you know about the key?" Granny asked, trying to distract him so he'd take the gun away from her throat. "I saw Angel playing with the purse and the key when they were at your house decorating. I stopped by to talk about the wedding."

"Let me go; I'll help you get the money."

"You'll help me, no doubt about that, but then I think the crypt will be all yours. It might be warmer than the weather outside with you having no coat and boots."

"Pastor...your title somehow doesn't fit with a life of crime."

"Faster," he nudged her with the gun.

"If I go any faster, I'll be going slower, such as in stop, we'll be stuck. How did you get into this?"

"Fell in love. I was living and working in Fish in a jewelry store when this tombstone dude, Delbert Delure and his wife, were casing the joint for a robbery. Of course, I didn't know that they were casing the joint for a robbery. She batted her eyes at me and I was hooked. Told me her husband was a traveling salesman and she was lonely. I started seeing her undercover when he was out of town. She convinced me we could be rich so I teamed up with her and her husband and we made some pretty good heists. He had no idea I was in love with his wife. Come to find out, this Delbert Delure fellow had two wives. The other one lived in Fuchsia."

"Delbert Delure had two wives at the same time?" Granny's shock at the revelation made her put her foot on the brake. The car fishtailed just as it reached the entrance to the Fuchsia cemetery, gently hitting the metal building that housed the caretaker's equipment.

Granny felt the gun against at her neck. "Can't you drive? Now you've done it, we're stuck. Get out!"

"In this snow, with no boots and no coat?" Granny feigned alarm, "How far do you think we'll get?"

Pastor Snicks looked around, trying to come up with an idea.

The snow was coming down and blowing so hard it was impossible to see even the entrance to the cemetery.

"Finish the story; at least I'll know why I became a stiff." Granny wiped a pretend tear from her eye.

"It's not going to help to cry. Delbert stashed his money and the jewels in his huge tombstone every time he came home to see his wife in Fuchsia until he ran out of room. Then he hid the rest in the base of the large sign for We Save You Christian Church—his tombstone company had also erected that large sign. Delbert made sure a hole was dug in the ground and a false bottom was put in the base with a hidden door. He stashed the rest of our money there. If we didn't spend it right away no one would know. We were patient; we could wait for our money but then—Delbert told his wife who lived in Fish that he had a wife in Fuchsia. He had told his Fish wife he was stashing the money in a storage vault on the edge of Fish but he wasn't because he didn't trust her. Only I knew about the tombstone stash. We had just hit another bank and made a big haul. Delbert took it back to Fuchsia, hid it, and came back to Fish. By this time, I was over my big love for his wife. She wasn't to be trusted, but I loved the money and I knew where the key was."

Granny shivered from the cold seeping into the warm car, and looked over her shoulder beyond the gun pointed at her to see if anyone was coming to help her. "Did you kill Delbert?"

"No; once his Fish wife found out about his Fuchsia wife, she offed him. Knifed him and knocked him right into that motorcycle. She thought she'd get all the money. I saw her do it and decided it was time for me to scram so I came to Fuchsia as a pastor."

Granny couldn't see anyone in the blowing snow. She was on her own. She had to rescue herself. The police cars were probably stuck, too, and who would know they were here. Pastor Snicks, having the chance to finally unburden himself, couldn't seem to quit talking.

"I could be patient for all that money and that jewelry. I was already a pastor. That's all my parents had ever talked about—me becoming pastor and so I had gone to seminary to please them. Worked in the jewelry store after seminary because I wasn't sure the holy life was for me, but after seeing Delbert die, I changed my mind. I wanted to put the past behind me and do something good for a change. I could have my money and still help people. So I became your pastor and since pastors don't make a lot of money, I used the key that Delbert gave me to help myself to a little extra cash from time to time, saving the big money for retirement. And then I lost the key!"

"And I found the key! I know this part, but how did the money get into my husband's grave? Don't you think you could put that gun down? Us being friends and all," Granny suggested.

The gun fixed firmly on Granny as Pastor Snicks continued, "As you may recall, Delbert and your husband weren't buried right away after they died."

"I do remember. I wanted to get it over with, but Ferdinand's brothers had to be here and so we waited a week."

And Delbert's body wasn't brought to Fuchsia for a week due to the time the paperwork involved," Pastor Snicks added. "I was interviewing. I hightailed it straight to Fuchsia when Delbert died and saw there was an opening for a pastor. During my interview, they brought me over to meet Giles Graves and he gave me a tour of the funeral home. I was in town when they brought the bodies back. Giles brought me back into the room where they kept the caskets and I got the bright idea of putting the money in a casket and putting it into a crypt where I could get to it when I decided to retire."

"Why did you pick me?" Granny sat up straight in her seat, forgetting there was a gun pointed at her.

"Ferdinand's papers happened to be lying in Graves's office when we were visiting and I got the idea. I asked him how one bought a crypt and he brought out the papers to show me, since he was on the council at the church, as it was pretty certain I was going to be a pastor with the other clergy at the church. When he wasn't looking, I slipped them into your papers and when you finalized the papers for your husband, you signed them and bought yourself a crypt."

He looked around in a worried manner. "That's enough talk, we need to get out of here." He waved the gun in her face.

"Wait, you haven't told me yet how the money ended up in Ferdinand's grave."

"I guess you'll never know; we've wasted enough time. We have to go before they find us."

Granny tried to buy more time. "They put my shovel cane in the trunk when we went to the church. We forgot to take it out. You can shovel our way out."

Pointing the gun back at Granny, he instructed, "Pull the latch for the trunk. Don't try anything funny." Granny reached down and popped the latch to the trunk. When the trunk popped open, Pastor Snicks motioned with the gun for Granny to get out of the car, at the same time getting out himself, keeping the gun trained on Granny. He motioned her toward the back of the car. Granny held on to her flowers as she moved slowly toward the trunk.

"Hold on to those flowers, Granny; they'll look nice on your grave." Still keeping the gun on Granny, he took the shovel cane out of the trunk and set it on the side of the car. He motioned for Granny to get in.

"You're going to lock me in the trunk? I'll freeze, but I guarantee it'll be warm where you're going to end up when it's time for your epitaph." Granny spit the words out as she skewered him with a warning look.

Granny moved to comply with his command, keeping an eye on his gun. As she was ready to climb into the trunk, she pretended to slip in the snow, catching the crooked reverend off guard. As she went down, her bouquet went up and the pointed knitting needle in the middle of the flowers hit the reverend's hand that held the gun, puncturing a hole in the skin. He lost his grip and the gun went tumbling to the ground.

Granny scrambled for her shovel, then heard the roar of a snowmobile. Pastor Snicks had recovered and was moving toward Granny as Granny was moving toward the shelter of the shed. A shadow moved closer through the blowing snow. Pastor Snicks turned to see a snowmobile coming straight at him. He turned, and plowed through the snow, slipping and sliding for the shelter of the shed. The snowmobile advanced. Granny picked up her shovel and moved aside for the snowmobile, which came to rest near the metal building ready to make Pastor Snicks a shiny decoration. .

Granny caught up to the snowmobile and Pastor Snicks, lifted her shovel, and tapped hard on the metal roof of the shed. "No!" Pastor Snicks exclaimed while staring at the snowmobile that was keeping him immovable. Hearing the rumble, he looked up to see—a large wall of snow sliding off the roof, over the side. It hit with softness and heaviness, encompassing his entire body, knocking him to the ground, leaving his body covered as the snowmobile moved away now that he was trapped by the snow.

Granny looked up from her catch to see the twinkling eyes of Silas Crickett through the falling snow. "Hi there, Red!"

With an answering gleam in her eyes, she asked, "What took you so long?"

CHAPTER THIRTY-NINE

When Granny made it back to We Save You Christian Church, after catching a ride with the Fuchsia snow plow, the first thing she did was find Franklin. "I knew they couldn't keep a good man down," Granny said gruffly.

"It's just a flesh wound. Thank God, you're okay!" Franklin stood up and grabbed Granny in a big bear hug.

"Where's Thor? Pastor Snicks said he had an accident," Granny asked.

"He's fine," Penelope assured her. "When Pastor Snicks shot Franklin, Franklin toppled on top of Thor before he could catch Franklin and Thor went down, too, and broke his ankle. He's at the hospital." Penelope burst into tears and hugged her mother. "I thought you were dead."

"Well, I'm not dead and I'm not wed, thanks to Pastor Snicks."

"We had to call the street department to help the police department. We all got stuck coming after you."

Chuckling, Granny remembered the scene. "They got there right after Silas called. Imagine Snickers' surprise to see policemen jumping out of snow plows and arresting him."

Loud barking and screeching erupted from the back of the church. Mavis and Delight, having just heard that Granny was back, came running down the aisle with the shysters, Baskerville and Mrs. Bleaty following. They both grabbed Granny at the same time and were talking so fast Granny couldn't understand a word they were saying. Little White Poodle and Tank got into the act, jumping on Granny while Fish and Furball jumped on Franklin's lap and licked his face. Mrs. Bleaty nudged Granny's hand and gave it a good lick. Baskerville plunked himself down beside her and howled until she turned and gave him a hug.

"One at a time," Granny yelled as she held up her hands trying to get her friends to calm down.

"Did you get him?" Mavis asked.

"How did you figure out it was him?" George questioned.

"I can't believe Pastor Snicks wanted you for himself so much that he kidnapped you from your wedding. Who knew he was in love with you!" Delight shook her head.

"He wasn't in love with Granny, Delight," said a voice from the back of the church. "He was the one who was digging up the graves." Silas gave Granny a look before he continued.

"Maybe you should sit down, Delight." Granny took her over to sit next to Franklin, whispering to Franklin, "We have to help her through this."

"Why am I sitting?"

Silas continued, "Delight, your husband not only sold grave stones, but he was a bank robber and a jewel thief." Silas paused as he looked to Granny. "And he didn't have a former wife, he had *another* wife at the same time he was married to you."

Granny looked at Delight to see how she was taking the news.

Calmly, Delight nodded, "Go on."

Thor or my son, Ephraim," said Silas, "would fill you all in on this if they were here, but Thor is getting his ankle taken care of. He's given me permission to fill you in as has my son, who is snowed in up by the prison. He's been kept up to date on the investigation. Delbert hid the money here in Fuchsia."

Delight bravely looked Silas straight in the eye, waiting for him to finish. Franklin moved over a little, putting his arm around Delight as if to shield her from more bad news.

"Did he tell you how the money got to be in Ferdinand's grave? Was Ferdinand a part of this?" Granny stood up taller waiting for the answer.

"No, that was a fluke. After visiting the funeral home that day, he waited until dark and retrieved the money from underneath the sign by the church. Apparently, Giles Graves was a little tipsy and so Pastor Snicks was able to steal an extra key and get back into the funeral home, and put the money in the extra casket sitting between Ferdinand and Delbert. He sealed it. He had stashed his van outside and was going to move the casket to the mausoleum–he also stole that key—when he got interrupted by Mr. Graves who'd come down to put the epitaphs on the caskets. If you remember, that's when things got switched."

Franklin interjected, "I see where you're going here. Graves put the epitaphs on the wrong caskets because he moved the notes that had been taped to the top. Ferdinand's epitaph got put on the casket with the money, Delbert's epitaph got put on Ferdinand's casket and the casket that didn't have the epitaph but mistakenly had Delbert's body in it got put in Granny's crypt."

"You got it," Silas chimed in. "That was his retirement money but he panicked when he lost the key to Delbert's tombstone and couldn't get his money out of the tombstone so he decided to get the money out of Granny's crypt."

Mavis piped in, "It's a good thing Granny didn't die and need her crypt."

That statement earned a glare from Granny.

"When he broke into the crypt because he couldn't find the key, he found Delbert's body and you know the rest."

Delight, still sitting quietly, looked up at Granny. "Who was Delbert's other wife?"

Frowning, Silas looked at Granny. "Maybe you better sit down, Red."

Granny glared at Silas at the name he'd called her, but sat down on the other side of Franklin anyway.

"Delbert's other wife was none other than Gram Gramstead, otherwise known as …."

Granny broke in, "I know, I know; we all know her real name but we don't have to say it. We'll just leave her as Gram. Delbert was married to Gram! Then she *is* the one tormenting me."

Silas shook his head. "No, that's what Pastor Snicks wanted you to think. He learned his tricks from her: the perfume, the car. He knew all her little tricks because while she was in town, he was secretly seeing her."

Franklin put his other arm around Granny, saying nothing as he was still trying to process the news.

Delight stood up, moving Franklin's arm away from her shoulders. "I have an announcement to make."

All eyes turned to listen to Delight. "If Delbert weren't dead, I'd murder him." Quietly she sat back down, picked up Franklin's arm, and put it back over her shoulder.

"How did you find me?" Granny looked to Silas for the answer.

Sheepishly, he admitted, "I opened your Christmas present early, before I was going to leave. I read your note about the key and where it belonged. I borrowed your snowmobile to get to church. Since I was in town I thought I might as well attend your wedding to see if you really would marry him. I figured he'd want the key and so I checked your house and, when you weren't there, I figured the only other way to the cemetery was the road."

Franklin looked at Granny, "Christmas present? You gave Silas a Christmas present? I thought you didn't like him. You're always complaining about him. You've tried to have him arrested and you gave him a Christmas present? What more don't I know?"

"Hello, Hermiony Vidalia."

Granny raised her eyes from Franklin's to the voice at the back of the church. With all eyes now on her, Granny's friends and family watched as Granny's skin turned as white as the snow swirling outside the church. The last thing Granny remembered before falling to the floor like an apple falls from a tree in what some might call a dead faint, was Delight's giggly voice stating: "Franklin, Granny's falling for you again!"

THE END

ABOUT THE AUTHOR

Julie Seedorf believes that if you believe it, you can do it. Julie retired from her computer business in 2014 to journey into writing full time. Putting her creativity to work, she is the author of the fictional Fuchsia, Minnesota Mystery series. Her first book *Granny Hooks A Crook* weaves a story about a fictional town in Minnesota that doesn't conform to the conventional rules and regulations of the communities that we live in today. Granny herself is unconventional and many say unbelievable. Perhaps she is only unbelievable because we have stereotypes of the way older people are supposed to age. Julie's books in the Fuchsia, Minnesota series (in addition to *Granny Hooks a Crook* and *Granny Snows a Sneak*, there is also *Granny Skewers a Scoundrel*) are meant to poke fun at those ideas.

Adding to her career as an author, Julie also writes freelance human interest stories for Minnesota area newspapers, the *Albert Lea Tribune* and the *Courier Sentinel.* She hopes to expand her freelance career in the future. Seven years ago Julie started her career as a columnist. Her column *Something About Nothing* can be found in the *Albert Lea Tribune, the Courier Sentinel* and online at her blog http://www.sprinklednotes.com.

Having lived in small communities all her life Julie knows the richness that a small community can have in bringing up a family. Julie raised her children in small communities and takes the time to make sure her grandchildren learn the importance of the saying, it takes a village to raise a child.

The experiences of grandchildren learning who a grandparent was when they were young, is the subject of the *Granny's In Trouble* series that Julie writes with her grandchildren. The first book in the *Granny's in Trouble* series, "Whatchamacallit? Thingamajig?" was published in 2012. The next book in the series will be out soon.

You can find Julie on Facebook at http://www.facebook.com/julie.seedorf.author on her blog sprinklednotes, on twitter at @julieseedorf or on her website at julieseedorf.com. Her books are available on Amazon, Createspace, Barnes and Noble and other independent bookstores.

CPSIA information can be obtained at www.ICGtesting.com
Printed in the USA
LVOW11s0609231214

420068LV00001B/95/P